Word's End Press, LLC
Sandy, Utah, USA 84092
dsplatt1@gmail.com

Printed and Distributed by
Ingram Spark
www.ingramspark.com

Printed in the United States of America

I

DEDICATED

to the people of England
with gratitude for your unconditional acceptance.

BELONGING

A NOVEL
BY

DORIS S. PLATT

To Ruth,

I hope you enjoy reading this book.

Copyright 2015 by Doris S. Platt
All rights reserved

Sincerely,

Doris S. Platt

IV

OTHER BOOKS BY THE AUTHOR

Friendship - Bread for the Journey
Sentinels Along the Way
Whisper My Name To The Grass

ACKNOWLEDGEMENTS

Family, old friends, new friends and thoughtful strangers.
Your insight and practical assistance allowed this work to
exceed my abilities. Your encouragement humbles me.
My profound thanks to each one of you.

Ilse Battaglia, David Brake, Nicole Castroman,
Andrea Christiansen, Pamela Dosch,
Elisabeth Kohler-Embacher, Robert and Penny Gray,
Ruth Hassler, Jane Hedges, Bob and Karen Hills,
Kirsten Major, Eliza Naumowicz, Linda Newman,
James S. Platt, Lorin and Judy Pugh, Lynnea Washburn,
Sir Andrew Lloyd-Webber and
Penelope Wilton

BELONGING

CONTENTS

PROLOGUE

The house stood isolated at the end of a tree-lined drive. Its windows were shuttered and no sign of life could be detected by anyone curious enough to investigate. Everything had taken on a gloomy, neglected look. The lawn was ragged, uncut. Deeply rooted, determined grass moved its silent, tenacious fingers and gained a stronger hold between the widening cracks of the road. Before long it would be victorious in its battle against time, and the men who could have stopped it from doing so were fighting for their lives on a different front.

Inside the house a battle of yet another kind was taking place. Two women, one of them tall, young, the mistress of the house; the other one short and gray-haired, were facing each other with equal determination.

"You simply can't go now. Not alone," Martha appealed. "It's too dangerous, especially for someone in your condition."

Blue eyes bored into the lined face of the older woman. It

was enough to discourage any further comment she might have wanted to make.

"My decision is final," came the stony answer. "I don't recall any housekeeper of mine getting paid to tell me what to do. Someone needs to stay with my son and you are the only one available."

The young woman took a coat from its hanger in an empty closet, and without saying another word she walked to the door, shutting it behind her with a defiant ring of authority.

Once outside, and not quite so sure anymore since the need to put on an act no longer existed, she paused for a moment then directed tired steps toward the more populated section of town.

Her thick-soled shoes echoed in the silence of the deserted streets. Buildings were barely recognizable in the damp November fog. Three days ago she had traded her warmer coat for some potatoes, hoping the cold weather might hold off a little longer. Perhaps that had been premature, because she noticed the lack of it now. The coat was gone and so were the potatoes but it could not be helped. The situation in which she found herself dictated desperate actions; her walk at this hour was just one more struggle on a long list.

She had last eaten yesterday, and she felt slightly light-headed from lack of food. When a sudden, searing pain moved across her abdomen she gasped, and steadied herself by holding onto the rough bark of a nearby tree. Rest, she thought, if only she could rest and forget about all of this, but the pains were coming closer together. Thank goodness the hospital was not too far. If she took a shortcut through a small park, she would get there even sooner. Slowly, she resumed her hampered pace.

For a fleeting moment she thought she heard a distant hum over the sound of her footsteps. When she stopped and strained to hear it again it was gone. I must be imagining things, she told herself; my mind is playing tricks. Everyone's nerves were stretched. Living for weeks in the questionable security of a cellar doubling as bomb shelter had taken its toll on all of them.

There was that sound again. The enemy was getting better at escaping detection but surely they couldn't be this close. And then the sirens told their own chilling story. She, who had braved hunger and cold, trembled when the now unmistakable wail ripped through the night. The deep drone of planes with their deadly cargo followed closely behind and the knowledge of what it meant made the blood run cold in her veins.

She was in the open, without shelter of any kind. In the distance she saw the first faint flicker of light. After a moment another, and then still another, until the sky was lit up in a bright orange fireball.

She tried to walk faster and cursed the weight of her swollen belly which made it impossible to do so. Wave after wave of excruciating pain knifed through her defenseless body, making her reach for air in ragged gaps. When yet another wave engulfed her, she screamed, a long drawn out sound that was lost in the uproar around her. Grasping for support she found a void. For a moment, her hands scrabbled in the air, then she fell into a blackness darker than anything she had ever experienced.

~ ~ ~

Long-fingered searchlights were probing the night sky over the German city of Düsseldorf, the capitol of North Rhine-Westphalia. Cradled on the east side on a bend of the Rhine River, the city had received its first charter in 1288. Since then it had become the financial center of some major industries. This evening not many of its inhabitants slept. Bombers were reducing the once beautiful city to rubble. It was November 1940, and Germany fought a war doomed from the beginning, conceived as it was by leaders out of touch with reality.

~ ~ ~

The young orderly, his face etched with the demands of many a sleepless night, nodded his head in the direction of the form lying motionless on the stretcher.

"We found this one in a ditch about 500 meters from the bomb shelter," he told a nurse. "Looks as if she was heading for the hospital but didn't quit make it. Where do you want me to put her?" Then, almost as if talking to himself, he added, "I have a feeling she might not thank me for saving her. It's not a good time to be bringing another life into this world."

~ ~ ~

"Mrs. Albrecht, can you hear me? Mrs. Albrecht?" The nurse said hesitantly to the woman on the bed in front of her.

There were other, more critically wounded patients needing her attention. Every inch of space had been utilized. Some of the wounded were lying on make shift beds; others sat on the floor, backs slumped against the wall, awaiting their turn for medical care. It was not an ideal situation but it was the best the seriously understaffed hospital could offer. At the beginning of the war, not many soldiers had been brought here. Now members of the armed forces and civilians were admitted in ever increasing numbers, their injuries often so grave that it was a wonder how any human being could endure, let alone survive them. But the nurse had been advised to handle this patient with kid gloves even though it was proving to be difficult.

The woman was conscious and aware of what went on around her yet she refused to communicate with anyone. Admitted two days ago, the young wife of a high ranking military officer had not spoken a word other than giving her name, date of birth, marital status, religion, and place of residence. Her husband was at the Russian front. It would take a week before he could reach the hospital.

"Mrs. Albrecht, it's over. You're doing fine but you still need more care than we are able to give you. Our wards are filled beyond capacity. We thought that since you are Catholic you might not object to being moved to a nearby religious house. We took the liberty of contacting the sisters and were told that you are welcome to stay with them for as long as necessary. You and your baby girl."

The woman on the bed shuddered. A baby. Her baby. And a girl at that. So it had survived. She turned her head to the wall. She could sense what the nurse was thinking. Both of them, the nurse and the doctor who had come to check on her, were puzzled by her lack of interest in the child.

Well, let them wonder. Let them assume the worst and they would probably not be too far from the truth, she thought with sudden anger. She had not wanted this pregnancy but the physician caring for her son, Wolfgang, had advised her to have another child. Wolfgang was dying. Much as she might try, she could not deny that reality. Lack of adequate food and medication had made irreversible damage on her son's health. A miracle was needed even if enough nourishment were suddenly available again. His ability to walk lessened every day. It was only a matter of time before death would claim him. Yet one more innocent victim of circumstances. A son was needed to carry on the family name. And she had given birth to a girl. What good was a girl to her husband? What good was a girl to anyone?

~ ~ ~

The child's father left the ugliness of the war behind him long enough to toast the latest addition to his family with a good bottle of French champagne carefully hoarded for the occasion, named his new daughter Andrea, and returned to the front. Since that time his whereabouts were unknown. It was thought that he had become a prisoner of war but no one could be sure. The communication system did not fulfill its role anymore. During his prolonged absence, his wife, and Martha, their housekeeper, tried their best to keep themselves as well as his two children alive.

CHAPTER 1

THE FENCE

A ccording to my mother, no nurse could look after my brother as well as she did. As a result, I was free of her supervision, and spent most of my waking hours in the company of Martha. It was Martha who taught me the rudiments of childhood; how to eat with knife and fork, tie my shoelaces, and ride a bike.

Not everyone is able to recall their early childhood, but for me fragments stand out with detailed clarity. I turned five in 1945; the conflict of WW II had not yet ended, and my father was a soldier still fighting on the front. This left my mother, brother, Martha and me to fend for ourselves. We were not the only ones; others also struggled without men to help shoulder their burdens.

Children took on responsibilities not normally expected of

them. I well remember the cold and moonlit evening my mother and I joined a group of mothers and their sons and daughters making the tiring walk to a coal mine to replenish our only available source of heat. It was illegal, but we were desperate and had no other choice.

Walking in their company, I felt grown up to be included. Yet at my age it was a tiring trek along crater-pocked roads where bombs had left their marks.

The shoes on my feet had belonged to someone else. They were uncomfortable and made the distance seem twice as far. More than one person suffered from angry looking blisters with nothing at anyone's disposal to relieve the pain. But all of us were thankful just to be alive, there were no complaints.

We reached our destination under cover of darkness. Living on sparse rations we had all become very thin. Children easily crawled under the barbed-wire-topped fence surrounding the perimeter of the mine. Pieces of coal could be found at the bottom of the steep embankment and had to be carried back up. The mothers then put them into burlap sacks and loaded them onto small carts.

Shivering with fear and cold, my stomach hollow with hunger, I slithered down with the other boys and girls. Much had to be accomplished in a short time if we wanted to be warm during the next few weeks. Before the war, my parents had employed a cook, a gardener and a chauffeur. Now, only Wolfgang and Martha counted on relief from the harsh cold that inched under doors, seeped through walls, and penetrated our clothing. I understood what was expected of me and intended to take the obligation seriously.

Come daybreak we must not be found in the area. Guards

on duty did not hesitate to shoot anything that moved. At least that was the story we told each other, though no one had actually ever been killed. At night, two German Shepherds patrolled the mine. Just to be on the safe side, I tried to befriend the thin, underfed-looking dogs by sharing my meager sandwich with them.

Much of the coal had already been picked over, and in the dark, the remaining pieces were chosen by feel and weight. Stones were smoother and heavier than coal. I was not the quickest, but after I had run up and down several times, already exhausted, I stumbled over a large piece of coal and felt that my problems had been solved. If I could manage to carry this one chunk up the hill, many trips with much smaller pieces would be unnecessary.

Working on my own, progress was painfully slow. Nobody offered to help nor would I have asked; this was one of those times when one depended only on oneself.

"Andrea! Andrea!!" I could hear my mother's loud whisper. She only used my name when she was angry. "Look at the other children. They know what they are doing," she went on. I knew what she meant, but I ignored her. In the East, a pale lemon color smudged the horizon. The sun was on its way. Soon it would be time for us to leave. By now my hands were hurting, the skin on my knuckles torn and bleeding. My face streaked with coal dust, and a few tears of frustration at my slow progress, I stubbornly persisted at pushing and dragging the chunk of coal up the incline.

Again and again the other children stumbled past me. I was aware of them but did not give up on my goal and finally managed to get the large chunk to the top. All that remained now was to slide it through the gap in the fence and load it into our cart. But the piece proved too big. We had no tools strong enough to break it up, nor was there time to enlarge the hole. To accomplish that task we needed the dark and daylight was working against us. I felt terrible, but the result of my effort had to be left behind. Empty-handed we had come, and nearly empty-handed my mother and I made the long trip home.

It was hard to find any fuel in the city. Unless some kind-hearted souls shared some of their own meager supply, there would be nothing to warm us during the bitter days and nights ahead. The worst part for me was the knowledge that I had failed my brother. Unable to move and put warmth into his crippled limbs, he would suffer from the freezing temperatures more than anyone.

On that day I made a solemn promise to myself. I would never again leave anything on the wrong side of a fence!

CHAPTER 2

ADAPTATIONS

I had no early memories of my father, but Martha shared hers with me. She told me that shortly after I was born he had come home on leave. I never tired of hearing how proud he was of me, how he had held me in his arms, walking back and forth to soothe me to sleep and had even changed my diapers. The diaper part had really made an impression on Martha.

Growing up with Martha's stories, I learned to love my father before I ever met him. I could see him in my mind. But the tall bearded stranger standing in front of me, his uniform showing signs of prolonged wear, was not at all like the picture I had created. Yet he won my heart when he gave me a semi-melted chocolate bar – pulled out of his pocket just seconds after he walked through the door.

The barely discernible silver writing on the crumpled brown wrapper spelled the word HERSHEY. He said that it had come all the way from America. It was my first taste of chocolate and I ate the pieces carefully, letting the sweet gooey substance slowly dissolve on my tongue.

My father had returned from the war and was trying to re-adjust to civilian life. He did not look as proud now as in the photograph on the piano – one that had been taken years ear-lier. Since then much had happened, and he frequently relived the trauma of the war.

Unable to blunt the images of scenes he had witnessed, at times the screams of his nightmares echoed through the house. Once, when he suffered from a particularly bad dream, I had gone to his room, gently shaking his arm to awaken him. His fist had come up in a quick reflex movement, the swift blow narrowly missing my face. After that, I had put a pillow over my head and left him alone. In the morning he was always him-self again. No explanations were given and I did not ask. It was enough that he was home.

~ ~ ~

My friends and I had looked forward to our first day of school. Tomorrow could not come soon enough. All German kindergartners carried their supplies in a satchel. Mine was made of deep brown leather and I loved the scent of it. My supplies included a lead pencil and a small blackboard on which I would learn to write. There was also a sponge to erase any mistakes.

After Martha had dropped me off at the school, I was on my own, waiting with the other children for the adventure to begin. After we were divided into age groups, we had to follow our teacher, Miss Clara Wortman. She was not very tall and her severe expression matched her hairstyle – gray hair pulled into a bun at the back of her head. A sharp prominent nose and two small warts on her chin gave her a sinister appearance.

I recognized none of the faces in the classroom. Miss Wortman frightened me, and the excitement of the day before gave way to total discouragement.

No one had said that I would be separated from my friends just because I happened to belong to another religion. Lutherans had to attend school in a building away from and much smaller than the larger Catholic one.

Both schools were on the same property but an invisible line divided the playgrounds, and we Lutherans dared not cross that unseen yet noticeable forbidden zone. Even during recess boundaries were strictly enforced by teachers and students of the graduating classes.

The only other time when religion had created a slight barrier between us was when my friends went to First Communion; the girls in white dresses – gloved hands holding a tall candle; the boys self conscious in their dark suits. I had not been invited to their celebrations – had not walked the rose petal or confetti covered path to their front door – and it hurt. Their church was bigger and more beautiful; it did have not the severe austerity of the Lutheran buildings.

Once, when I said I wanted to become Catholic, my mother had told me to wait until I was older. That's how it was with most of the things I wanted to do. Some grownup would invariably tell me to wait.

The Catholic school didn't seem all that welcoming, but I

still wanted to be there. It was where I belonged. Not in this small room with children I didn't know. And since my friends were not coming to me, I would have to go find them. Twice I had tried to walk slowly towards the classroom door. After several warning looks, Miss Wortman took my ear in a firm grip and led me to the front of the class to scold me.

In spite of that stark introduction, my classmates and I received the traditional cornucopia given on the first day of school. It reached from my shoes to my hip and most of its space had been filled with paper as not much candy was available. But the sweet pieces were not enough to take away my loneliness.

After I had attended school for several months and the routine was more familiar, I made it a point to arrive early, getting to class before the rest of the students. On most days, one teacher would briefly put her hand on my shoulder and say, "You are early again," or "Would you please clean the blackboard for me." I always shrugged off her hand; yet if the teacher had stopped extending her brief moment of kindness, I would have missed her gesture terribly.

CHAPTER 3

WINGED MARVELS

I do not know when I first realized that my brother Wolfgang was my mother's favorite. Martha called him an obedient soul. Even with heavy, cumbersome metal and leather braces on arms and legs, he never complained and I loved him for his patience. Thoughtful and unpretentious, he spoke several languages, and was very good at math. So much so that the teacher allowed him to decide his own grades. When Wolfgang, in modesty, did not place them high enough, the teacher corrected them and gave him better marks.

My Brother spent hours drawing butterflies and shared much of his knowledge with me. Because of the war, good paper was unavailable. Yet the rough pages of his notebooks were filled with lifelike images of these winged marvels, almost as if he wanted to give them an ability he himself did not have. He drew the distinctive Swallow Tail, the Red Spotted Purple and the Adonis

Blue, their iridescent colors intense or delicate. One butterfly was called Question Mark. Wolfgang told me that when I was a little older he would teach me the Latin names of each one.

Sadly, his health continued to deteriorate. One day, my young mind had the idea that if each one of us gave up a functioning limb to him, he would no longer be challenged. It made total sense to me. My mother didn't think so – I could tell.

In her care for Wolfgang, my mother had been flawless. Towards me she was indifferent, keeping me at a distance. I was alive, but lonely – a satellite – just not one in her orbit

When my brother died after a long illness, I could not help hoping that surely now, at last, my mother would have some time for me.

I was to learn otherwise. On the evening of Wolfgang's funeral, my mother had taken me to his room and told me to sleep in his bed. Nearly hysterical, I implored my mother to change her mind but nothing helped. She turned off the light, closed the door and locked it. The cold click of the key echoed loud in the silence. And then I was alone.

Feeling the breath of fear on the back of my neck, I was absolutely sure that some huge, terrible thing would pounce on me as soon as I closed my eyes. I could feel it crouching in the dark corners just biding its time. Sinister shadows created by the moon crept slowly across the floor towards me, increasing my panic.

Not daring to move, I slept fitfully. I was familiar with death that came from nighttime bombing raids; raids that brought fear and destruction. Even though they were frightening, everyone in the bomb shelter knew how to react to these situations.

The type of death that had claimed Wolfgang, quietly and unannounced, worried me more. I did not know the sound or look of it and could only hope that morning would find me still alive.

The shadows left with the first light of dawn. My fears did not.

~ ~ ~

I felt selfish for even thinking such a thing, but with my brother gone I wondered if I would be allowed to play with his electric train. I had always been fascinated by the efficient way the Märklin model moved along the shiny tracks, with guardrails opening and closing and lights flashing at the push of a button.

My favorite was the engine, but I was also intrigued by the stamped black metal of the coal car. Once, when I was alone in the room, I had furtively run my fingertips over the top of its uneven surface. Of all the possessions my brother owned, I loved nothing more than his train. Though generous, he had not entrusted it to a five year old girl. But now, especially if I promised to be really careful, hopefully that could change.

However, without anyone asking me, the whole set had been traded for a doll. She was tall and took up a lot of space. And her rough dark brown hair was so matted, I didn't even want to touch it. When she closed her glassy eyes the noise coming out of her prim little porcelain mouth was not "Mama." To me it sounded more like a sheep bleating. I never played with that doll and after a week someone took her away.

There were other troubling experiences. Every day long hours were spent at my brother's graveside with my mother staring vacantly into the distance. Too afraid to interrupt, I entertained myself by building towers and walls with small stones I found on the walkways.

CHAPTER 4

A PIECE OF LUGGAGE

---

y mother seldom gave anyone advance notice of her
plans. Made in her mind, they were kept there until
she thought it convenient to share them. With
some apprehension and carrying a suitcase Martha had packed
for me, I accompanied my mother to the bombed-out Düsseldorf train station one year after my brother's death. The smell
of coal and smoke was noticeably in the air. Only a few tracks
were usable and the newly painted train I was on contrasted
sharply with the rusted girders reaching their twisted arms into
the sky.

Uneasiness of yet another kind took hold of me. Ever since
my first train ride, I had been fearful of anything involving them.
Memories of that wartime journey still haunted me. Afraid that
the Russians would advance beyond Berlin to my hometown,

my mother, brother and I had fled to the Bavarian town of Passau to stay with relatives.

The war had disrupted rail service. Tickets for space had been limited, and most of those sold for a much higher price on the black market. So, like others, we had used the only means of transportation available: an open cattle car, but considered ourselves fortunate. Some brave men were desperate enough to travel on the roofs of the passenger carriages, clinging to any handhold for their very lives.

Since there was no roof on the cattle car we were exposed to the elements. On the sides, ill-fitting slats were the only protection from the fierce rush of the wind. It had been necessary for the train to stop and hide in forests or tunnels during the day, moving only in the secrecy of the night.

Too sick to sit up for any length of time, my brother was forced to lie in a corner on a meager handful of straw. There were not enough blankets, and the pitiful amount of straw my mother and I had managed to scrape together was insufficient to shield his emaciated body from the bone-jarring effects of the journey.

Now I was on another train – this time by myself. I felt like an ownerless piece of luggage. My name and other identifying information were written on a cardboard sign hanging around my neck. Other than a stern warning not to take off, or lose the sign, my mother's explanations about the trip had been rather sketchy. She had said something about my living for a while with a family in a country called Switzerland. But I had already forgotten most of it.

My mother had put me on the train and then stood there waiting for it to pull out. The odd smile on her face gave the impression that she was glad to see me go.

I saw it and quickly closed my mind against it. It could not be; it was all a mistake. I understood that I was leaving, just not the reason why. Why was I being sent away? What had I done that was so awful?

"Please, let me out," I begged, "I don't want to be in here. Please…"

~ ~ ~

My brother's death, and my departure for Switzerland would always be inseparably linked. Later, I would learn that in the late forties and early fifties, the Swiss Red Cross put out an appeal to its citizens asking them to take hundreds of undernourished children from the war-torn countries of Europe into their homes, there to be restored to physical, mental, and emotional health. I was fortunate to be among those who benefited from the generosity of the Swiss people.

But today, I was a six-and-a-half year old child, alone in the compartment and terrified. Frantically, I beat my fists against the window until they swelled up in red, puffy welts. I must have made enough noise to draw attention, because a woman in a nurse's uniform jerked me away, pushed me down on a seat and left.

Before long the corridor was filled with people carrying battered suitcases, boxes and miscellaneous bundles tied with string. There was scarcely room to move or walk. Seeing me as the only occupant, passengers angrily knocked at the compartment windows, until the conductor pulled down the shades. Then he left, locking the door behind him.

His action solved one problem – but now I had another one. How would I get out if he forgot about me?

Soon the train gathered speed and my home town slid out of sight. I sat totally bewildered and when the nurse brought food, I ate mechanically. Unaware that the upholstered armrests between the seats lifted up, I draped myself over them and slept a troubled sleep.

Long, tense hours passed. Day had changed to evening before I was ordered to leave the compartment and board a bus. After a short ride we stopped in a city at the border between Germany and Switzerland. I was led to a large hall filled with children of different ages and nationalities. The hall served as a kind of collection point. From here the boys and girls would be sent to individual Swiss families for the duration of their stay.

I was immediately swept up in the confusion of the chaotic and noisy place, but the people in charge soon had things organized. Our hair was cut until boys and girls, shorn of identity, closely resembled each other. Segregated once more, and told to take off our meager clothing, we formed two silent lines and then stood there without protest, shivering in the cold and afraid to ask what was going to happen next. I was the first to find out.

A wide-hipped woman wearing a white coat, her front covered by a long black rubber apron, abruptly motioned me towards a tiled enclosure.

"You there, get over here. Come on, hurry up. Come on, come on."

When I just stood there afraid of making a mistake, she gave an annoyed sigh, walked over to me with short angry steps and propelled me towards the shower, almost sending me flying.

Then, in full view of everyone, she started to scrub me with a stiff-bristled brush. At home, Martha used one like it to scrub the kitchen floor. I had never felt such a sense of embarrassment which changed to terror. I was forever tripping over my feet, so I was never without scabs on my knees and now the brush tore them off. The needle-fine, stinging spray of water, mingling with my blood, made me think that I was bleeding to death, but nobody paid attention to my screams. Undaunted, the woman continued with her task.

"You better be quiet. I have some exhausting hours ahead of me and taking extra time with one like you is not a part of it," she threatened.

Once we children had dried ourselves off, disinfectant powder intended to kill lice was sprinkled on us in uncaring liberal doses, making us cough and sneeze. After our clothing was fumigated, we were told to get dressed again. The evening meal was taken cafeteria style in another large hall. Some of the children staggered around sleepily. The more resilient girls and boys had already made friends and were chasing each other up and down the narrow aisles, adding to the noise level.

In the hectic pace created by the necessity of feeding a large crowd, I had not wanted to bother anyone. Afraid to ask, yet longing to know what would happen to me, I had finally gathered enough courage and asked one the nurses. She promised to get back to me later but she had evidently forgotten all about it. Not wanting to trouble her again, I wandered around aimlessly, at last sinking into an exhausted sleep on a frayed canvas cot I shared with another girl.

In the morning, orders blared from an overhead loudspeaker. For me, another train ride was ahead and once again I had a compartment to myself. A brief check by an attendant had shown that no one else shared my destination – the town of Chur, Switzerland.

Discouraged, I tried to decipher the name of every town the train passed through, hoping to find a match to the one written on the sign hanging around my neck. The scenery rushed by too quickly and before long my eyes ached as if they had become too big for their sockets.

When we did stop, I was unable to understand the garbled arrival and departure announcements that might have given me a clue.

At last, with a long screeching sound of the brakes, the train slowed and jolted to a standstill. I heard a loudspeaker announce in German 'ENDSTATION' – end of the line. And the name CHUR matched the one written on my cardboard.

My heart beating faster without knowing why, I went to the window and pulled it down. Some distance away I saw a tan building and next to it a newsstand. There was nothing to hold my attention and I almost went back to my seat.

CHAPTER 5

HERR HASSLER

I will never forget my feeling of relief when a man stopped in front of my open window. He was tall, clean-shaven with fine lines around his eyes, and his thick dark hair had a sprinkling of gray at the temples.

"Hello," he said. "I've been waiting for you. I'm Hans Peter Hassler. The name on your sign tells me that you are Andrea Albrecht. If that is so, you belong to me for a little while. I've come to take you to my home."

He smiled, and the smile was reassuring. I was too tired to think of what to do, but to hear my name again erased some of my misgivings. At the beginning of the trip, I had become a number and I was worried that I might stay one forever.

Bewildered, I nodded. Instinct told me I could trust this

man. What other option did I have? There were few other people at the station, and none of them showed any awareness of me.

I looked at him carefully. He seemed friendly, and I was too exhausted to try and make sense out of the last two days. He certainly appeared to know more than I did.

"Yes, I'm Andrea Albrecht," I answered in a shaky voice. "I think I am lost and I don't know how to get back. I live in Düsseldorf," I added hopefully.

"No, you're not lost," he said. "We'll telephone your mother and let her know that you arrived safely. Now, hand me your suitcase. If we want to get home on time, we need to catch the next bus. I haven't milked the cows yet and they don't like to wait. Maybe tomorrow you can help me with some of the chores. Would you like that? I'm always glad to have an extra pair of hands around feeding time."

I held up my arms and he lifted me and my case through the window. Taking my hand firmly in his we walked out of the station.

My mind was still on the cows. I knew what cows were and what they were for. I had seen herds grazing in some of the pastures the train had passed by, but that was the closest I had ever come to these large animals. What help could I possibly be when I didn't know the first thing about them? Hope, a feeble flame for just a few minutes, had been quickly extinguished.

What would happen to me now? Would Herr Hassler send me somewhere else once he became aware of my ignorance? At the very least, he was sure to be disappointed. His animals were obviously very important to him.

We rode a yellow postal bus up a switchback road through tree-covered hills until we stopped in the small village of Malix. A steep mountain range walled off the valley's east side. I had never seen such high peaks before.

Some houses were set back behind well-tended gardens, others stood close to the road, but they all had vivid-colored geraniums tumbling from balconies or wooden windowsills. A church stood at one end of the village; its black spire stark against a blue sky.

"That is where we live," Herr Hassler said. I looked up the hill at a large solitary house. It was brown and white, with a balcony running the length of the building.

The border in front of the house was bright with red, pink and orange Zinnias. Yellow and copper-colored roses draped over a brown picket fence. Immediately below was a herb and vegetable garden and an orchard with pear, plum and apple trees and red currant bushes.

Herr Hassler opened the door into a hallway and I heard the reassuring ticking of a clock. To the left, a steep staircase led up to the bedrooms and Herr Hassler's office. He told me this was where he wrote letters, paid bills or did his thinking.

We walked straight ahead to a bright and roomy kitchen. On one side was the cook stove; across from that a sink, a table, and an L-shaped bench. A large window gave an uninterrupted view of the valley below.

"If you stand right here by the window, you can see me as soon as my work is finished," Herr Hassler said. "I'll be in that gray and white barn. It's where the cows and goats are. Come here, I'll show you."

I followed the direction of his finger as he pointed down the hill.

"Do you know which one I mean?" Sensing my concern, he added, "Don't worry. You'll be fine until I get back. I won't be long."

With those words Herr Hassler took a milk can from a shelf in the cupboard and left the kitchen. Uschi, a sturdy woman with gray hair and a face cross-hatched with lines, remained behind with me. Uschi was the Swiss German name for Ursula. I had learned that she was Herr Hassler's wife, and I knew that I liked Herr Hassler much better. Only at this moment he was not here.

Uncertain of what was expected of me, but trying to make myself useful, I set the table. Then I followed Uschi to the cool cellar to get a wedge of cheese and some butter kept there in a glass container on a wide cement ledge.

Uschi wiped her hands against her apron. "Would you like something to eat or drink?" she asked. "Surely you must be hungry. You look as if you could use it."

She talked incessantly about anything and everything. Much of it didn't make sense to me, and what was worse, her talking kept me away from the window where I really wanted to be. Herr Hassler could not come back soon enough.

Uschi's suggestion of food created another problem. Not having eaten since early morning, I was very hungry. If Herr Hassler took much longer I didn't see how I could wait. Uschi's urging only reinforced my need, but surely it was impolite to start without him.

I could feel the water pooling in my mouth. I looked at the

bread, cheese and sausage on the table and fought a quick battle within myself. During the war starvation had created its own etiquette. With the courtesy of the hungry, at home only people insensitive to the plight of others accepted an invitation to a meal when the invitation was first given.

Once, when extreme hunger had made me do so, I was harshly reprimanded by my mother. She had told me in no uncertain terms that one politely refused at least three times. If the invitation to share was extended a fourth time, it was all right to accept.

In food-starved Germany that had seldom happened, but maybe the people here could afford to do so. They didn't look as if they were hungry. In the end I ate a little of everything. I especially liked a cheese with a nutty flavor; "Roesti", a fried potato dish, and polenta with melted browned butter drizzled on top.

True to his word, Herr Hassler had come back from the stable and joined us in eating the tasty meal. He and his wife spoke a language unfamiliar to me. Hearing only voices, not words, I could not understand a single sentence. But I was sure they were talking about me, and that made me feel even more uneasy.

"How about another helping of polenta?" Herr Hassler asked in German.

I didn't ask what polenta was. I didn't question anything. I just nodded and ate. The milk in my cup had been heated in a pan and then poured into a white pitcher decorated with a sprig of red poppies and daisies. I was not used to the taste or temperature of the warm milk, but I drank it dutifully. It had also made me very tired, and Herr Hassler was the first to notice.

"Don't worry, you will feel better in the morning. What you need now is rest. Uschi will take you upstairs to your room."

Uschi motioned for me to follow her. "The bathroom is here," she said. Opening another door she stood to the side and let me enter. "And this is where you'll be at night."

The good-sized room was furnished with a bed, nightstand and a wardrobe. Left on my own, I took a bath and went to sleep.

CHAPTER 6

A HOUSE ON THE HILL

I awakened to sunlight coming through the windows; momentarily disoriented until I remembered where I was. Though beyond the reach of fear and hunger, it was hard for me to believe that I didn't have to sleep night after night fully dressed in a crowded, dimly lit bomb shelter. Nor would there be the probing beams of searchlights and the sound of sirens making my heart race with fear during the ever-present air raids. It had been terrifying not knowing which target would be hit next.

There had been many things to be afraid of — all at the same time. Grown-ups talked, thinking that we children did not listen or understand. They tried not to frighten us more than we already were and had failed at both tasks. Not blind or deaf to details, we soon interpreted the sudden silences that punctuated seemingly benign conversations. We had become adults before we were adults.

For the first few weeks after my arrival in the Hassler home I tried to make sense of unfamiliar sounds; branches creaking against each other as they did on windy nights, or the soothing gurgle of the nearby stream.

Windows were left open and lacy curtains fluttered gently in the breeze. There were no sinister-looking black-out drapes that puddled to the floor like liquid gloom to stop light from escaping and drawing the attention of an alert enemy pilot. And the light bulbs were white, not blue like those to which I had been accustomed.

Everything in the Hassler house was different. Floors, walls and doors in each room were made from the same amber colored wood. Only the Salon, the seldom used more formal living room had wall paper, chintz covered chairs, and a sofa upholstered in a big floral print.

There was also a wind-up gramophone that played big black disks. I would have liked to know how it worked, but I didn't want to ask.

Although Herr Hassler was not my father, Uschi had told me to call him Papa, so that is what I did. After an awkward day or two it became very comfortable and I couldn't imagine ever calling him by another name.

At bedtime, he and Uschi tucked me in sheets that smelled of sunshine. It had become a ritual I liked, a recognition of the day turning into evening. I was supposed to settle down, but who could sleep when there was so much to explore. I loved to sink my toes deep into the soft sheepskin rug by my bed, and I did it again and again just for the feel of it. The fluffy feather comforter on my bed almost seemed to drown me. Once, a piece of delicious chocolate had been put on my pillow, and after I had eaten it, no one insisted that I brush my teeth again.

Understanding my fear of the dark without having been told, the Hasslers left a small light burning in the hallway. Everything was quiet and peaceful, with only the occasional sound of a car going past. On nights when the rumble of thunder frightened me, Papa carried me into the big bedroom and let me sleep between him and Uschi in secure surroundings.

The big house overlooking the valley became my home. At first everything had been new and overwhelming, although that didn't last long. Free from the gnawing dread of what tomorrow might bring, I learned to relax and the past began to recede like a bad dream.

Yet I also knew there had to be a day of departure. So there would be no painful discoveries later, Papa had told me at the beginning that my stay was to be for only three months. But whenever that awareness nibbled at the edges of my mind, I pushed it into the background. I would deal with it once the need arose. Returning to Germany was something in the future. For now this was my refuge.

Every morning I waited for the day to come alive and soon immersed myself in the easy pattern of the household. Uschi was responsible for the running of the home and the needs of the small livestock: six chickens and a pig, in their own section of a small barn. Nothing was wasted, everything was neat and within its own boundaries.

My duties consisted of helping her weed the vegetable garden, taking split logs from the woodpile to the shed, stacking the rows as straight as soldiers marching in a parade, and making sure the kitchen wood box was filled.

Uschi had a brusque personality and like the other women in the village she usually wore an apron – dark and serviceable during the week, a light colored one on Sundays. She made sure I took baths and always had something clean to wear. A good cook of comforting food, she worried that I ate too little, yet I never felt any warmth from her.

Nothing made me happier than when I was allowed to go with Papa to the barn. The lower section housed the animals, the upper part held feed and old machinery in need of repair. Large, heavy-hinged doors were wide enough for a loaded, horse-drawn wagon to enter. I helped Papa water the livestock, and forked straw and hay from the barn into the stalls below.

He had a routine. Normally, he would take a string attached to a low beam and wind it around the end of the cow's tail, preventing it from inadvertently connecting with his face; leaving him free to concentrate on the milking. But now and then, he gave me the job of holding each animal's tail in turn, making me feel as if this was a most important responsibility. Once, when I was not paying attention, the tail had come loose in my hand and splashed into Papa's face. But he had not scolded me – not even then.

In addition to teaching school and taking care of his three cows, he kept a dozen beehives, two goats and a large draft horse called Norma. When deerflies, big ugly things, buzzed annoyingly around her, I did my best to shoo them away. Once in a while Papa lifted me up on her broad back and my legs would stick out horizontally like those of a ballerina. Norma had the reputation of being somewhat unpredictable – loud noises made her jumpy – but with me she was always calm and gentle.

The single-minded productive bees occupied quite a bit of Papa's time. When he spun honey out of the dripping golden combs, he let me eat all the sweet nectar I wanted. I quickly learned that there could be too much of a good thing.

A tall man, Papa's complexion was the brown color of hazelnuts. He was seldom without an unlit pipe. A thin gold wedding band hung loose on the ring finger of his left hand.

He was used to children's behavior and answered my questions with inexhaustible patience. Nothing was considered unimportant and he never sighed the way some grown-ups do, but explained until he was sure I understood. There was something reassuring about him. But he was also strict, as in "If you do something, do it right. If you don't know how, ask. It's the only way to get an answer."

To his surprise, Papa became my hero. His kindness drew me like a magnet and I constantly trailed after him. On the day he took me shopping and bought me a smaller version of his brown leather hiking boots with identical markings on the soles, I knew that I was the luckiest child on earth.

Ruth and Helen, the couple's two daughters, were away at school and seldom visited. Their absence made me the fortunate sole recipient of their father's attention. When the girls were home, I tried to make myself invisible. Helen, the oldest at twenty-one years of age, rarely paid attention to my comings and goings. Ruth, younger than her sister by two years, was not very friendly – treating me as though I had taken away something that rightfully belonged to her.

I was fascinated by everything Papa said – especially when he told me about the local history, such as Chur being Switzerland's oldest city. But I especially loved to hear stories about

Malix. I tried to visualize how the valley, slung like a giant hammock between long sharp-edged ridges, had been formed by glaciers.

Since its first mention in a document in the year 1149, Malix had stayed much the same. Even now it had less than five hundred inhabitants. One could walk from one end of this peaceful village to the other in less than half an hour. The sloping streets were not wide enough for two farm wagons to pass each other. Some houses' upper stories leaned out over the street. Papa had said it was so the wagons could turn the corner without damaging the building. No planner had applied his talent to the lay-out. In the center of the village houses stood clustered together; beyond that they were spread out randomly. Built of wood and stone most of the sturdy dwellings were similar in design, yet each house had its own personality.

CHAPTER 7

HEIDI

On most mornings mist clung to the lower slopes until the heat of the day burned it away and the mood of the valley changed. At first, a faint brightening above the jagged lines of the mountains, then sunrise traveled like a shaft of light across the valley.

With it came the crowing of a rooster; fussy with self-importance as if he had to share a warning only he knew something about. Before long his vocal cords sounded unrehearsed, but that never stopped him. Not to be outdone – and feeling they also had something to impart – others of his kind took up the challenge.

The rivalry was all part of the village symphony. Sometimes I liked to lie in bed just listening to this 'fowl' orchestra. Sounds were clustered according to the time of day – beginning when

Rudi, the young goat herder of the village, would blow his horn. Goats and sheep, their bells clanking busily, would gather by Papa's barn and be taken into the hills for the day. During cold winter months the animals stayed in their stalls. In the summer the mountainside was theirs.

Once in a while I accompanied Rudi and his charges. He knew each one of them by name and pointed out their particular characteristics to me.

Papa's twin baby goats were included in the herd. Dark brown with black legs and a black stripe along the back, they seldom were still, jumping straight-legged into the air with uncomplicated joy. Then they stood — as if surprised by their own exuberance — but only for a moment, before they ran across meadows dusted with wildflowers.

A clear blue sky rested easily on the hills. Only the hum of insects and the melodic trill of a bird interrupted the quiet. It was a good place to daydream and I sometimes pretended that I could stay in Malix forever. I wanted to believe it, even if I knew it couldn't be.

Papa had given me the well-known children's book *Heidi* to read. The author, Johanna Spyri, had spent some of her childhood in the town of Chur, a twenty minute drive from Malix. I loved the story and recognized similarities. And although no one called me Heidi, I had been named after my mother's sister Adelheid, making this setting even more meaningful.

Other than Papa and his animals, I really liked the mountains. A few were timber-topped; others held their barren face to the elements. They reminded me of people, some gentle, some a little rough, similar to the man on the Alp who spent his summers taking care of the cows and making butter and heavy wheels of cheese. Although he never smiled, he was not anyone to be afraid of nor was he really all that old. With his face deeply edged with wrinkles, he just seemed that way. Rudi said that was what trolls looked like, the kind who would grant you three wishes if you answered his riddles. I didn't believe it was true even before the man had given me a hand carved little goat which I kept on my bedside table.

In conversation, Papa and Uschi still switched between German and the language spoken in this part of the country. But before long I could follow most of what they were saying. Slowly, people and their names became familiar to me. I had met Uschi's sister Gretchen, her husband Urban, their daughter Irene and son Arno, but Papa remained the center of my world.

I also met Ilse, the daughter and only child of Papa's nearest neighbor. Outgoing, blond and blue-eyed Ilse Battaglia was six months older than I. Her nose crinkled when she laughed. And immune to worry, Ilse laughed often. Sharing secrets and giggles, we became inseparable to the point where we could finish each other's sentences.

Having her so conveniently close was a bonus. Nothing kept us apart for long; individual chores were done in record time. When a day reluctantly tiptoed into evening, we took it as a signal to squeeze in just a little more fun before we had to go home. Neither Ilse nor I cared to play with dolls. I knew my reason – I never asked what hers might be.

Ilse's mother, a hunchback, was from another village and her acceptance by the people of Malix had been slow. To the extreme disappointment of the local village maidens she had married good-looking Paul Battaglia, Ilse's father.

Nothing ever bothered Herr Battaglia. Showing a remarkable tolerance for our escapades, he just shook his head at whatever adventure Ilse and I embarked on.

But he also knew when to be serious. "That is where God tucked her wings," he said, when he saw me observing the noticeable bump on his wife's back. His explanation made perfect sense and I never questioned why the rest of us didn't have such heavenly appendages.

Here, as in my hometown, I observed the comforting rhythm of family life from a distance.

On the rare instance when Ilse stayed overnight with me at Papa's house we waited until after dark, then she and I would step out on the balcony and dance, dressed in our long white nightgowns. We didn't pretend to be anything specific. We were just young and carefree, and for the moment unaware of the occasional splinter getting stuck on the soles of our feet.

In the quiet, we could hear the night wind sing in the trees. Mountains were robed in moonlight, and stars, like specks of silver dust, covered the sky. All of it was like an invitation to an enchanted kingdom.

As school's headmaster Papa had to set an example, so on Sundays we walked to the outskirts of the village and attended services in a white church with a tall, thin black steeple. During the rest of the week Ilse and I were left free to wander – though not quite free from the consequences of our wanderings. Adults permitted some things – but tried to prevent others.

Visually accessible from my bedroom balcony were the remnants of an old castle, built centuries ago by men intent on controlling the area. Narrow vertical windows put in high above the ground made it possible to see unfriendly forces approaching.

With the exception of a square thick-walled tower, little remained of the two-storey structure. The roof had fallen in and left the interior open to the elements. Abandoned centuries ago, it had a dark, secretive feel to it. As there was not much history available, my friend Ilse and I made up our own. We saw the ruin not as something hazardous but a mysterious, romantic place where long ago gallant knights and their beautiful ladies lived.

We had been warned not to go anywhere near the unstable building. However, Ilse and I were a team. Together we visited places we would never investigate alone. And being told not to do something, guaranteed that it was all we would think about. Exploring the tower was not wise, but we did it anyway. Thankfully no one was ever hurt. Yet even without injuries, and no matter how hard we tried to maintain an innocent-until-proven-guilty appearance, grown-ups always learned of our mischief.

Even with carefully crafted excuses and alibis it became important to stretch the time between discovery and explanation. Papa never had to scold me. A simple look was enough to make me suffer pangs of remorse, followed by a fierce resolve not to get into trouble ... again.

Resolutions didn't always last long. Malix was where curiosity taught me the taste of cigarettes.

Acting bored, and superior, some boys showed up in the village one day. They lived somewhere near the sawmill and were not often seen in the area. I didn't know them all that well, but they dared Ilse and me to try smoking.

"Or are you too scared?" they jeered, showing off. "We

knew it! Just don't expect us to wait until you find your courage."

My friend and I really were not that interested, but peer pressure affected us and we changed our minds.

Our new acquaintances had the necessary ingredients ready. The concoction made from straw, hay, twigs and threads of tobacco from cigarette stubs, (previous owners unknown) was rolled up in green leaves and lit. To be safe from accidental discovery we entered a small shed, dark as the inside of a box. When it became too difficult to breathe, we moved back outside.

Although Ilse and I had agreed to this exploration, we knew with the first puff that it was a big mistake. The boys were immune to the effects of the blend. Ilse and I were beginners and it showed. My stomach heaved with the smoke and the smell before I felt a burning in my eyes and then my throat.

"You can't tell anyone about this," the boys had insisted in a threatening tone

There was small chance of that. We choked and coughed, trying frantically to get some air into our lungs. The noxious fumes clung to us so strongly that we knew we could not leave until the smell dispersed.

Even if things couldn't be made better, they certainly could be made worse – and they would be if Uschi became aware of our escapade. Uncannily accurate, she seemed to know everything. There was never a need to enlighten her.

Finally, so ill we wanted to die, Ilse and I staggered home, hoping we wouldn't be too late for dinner. I felt sorry for my friend. She had to go a quarter of a mile farther than I did, and the way there led past Papa's house.

With her hands on her hips, Uschi was standing at the gate as if she had been waiting for us, which of course she had.

Ilse and I had feared that this latest incident would not remain a secret – and it didn't. Perhaps our faces gave us away. Uschi made no comment, but after taking one glance at us she announced she would make my favorite dessert: layers of rhubarb and Zwieback, topped with vanilla sauce.

Just the sweet-smelling preview of her thoughtful gesture was sufficient to make me ill. And what really seemed unbelievable was that Uschi asked Ilse to stay for dinner and spend the night. Since an invitation rarely happened; the offer came as the second surprise in half an hour.

I thought the meal would never end. Ilse and I dared not look at each other, fearful that by doing so our own misery would be mirrored back to us. Seemingly oblivious to our condition, Uschi served both of us a generous helping.

Normally I would have enjoyed the treat but now each bite tasted like sawdust and I had to force myself to swallow every mouthful. All I wanted was to crawl upstairs and bury myself in my bed. My friend and I frequently laughed at things that were not even funny. We didn't laugh about this. Nor would be there be any dancing on the balcony this evening.

Papa must have felt sorry for us, but he said nothing – though he didn't quite succeed in keeping the smile off his face.

He also had not said anything when he learned that Ilse's grandmother caught us in one of her treasured cherry trees. Ilse and I had seen a number of birds enjoying the juicy produce and decided to do the same. We had been sitting on a branch, busily munching away and making up stories as to what had given these specific cherries their hue — a deep yellow with just a blush of red.

I suggested that it was where the sun had gently touched them one early morning. Ilse offered that it had been done by some mischievous wood sprite with a pot full of color.

We hadn't yet decided whose idea was better, when we were rudely interrupted by the sound of someone yelling something in the local dialect, startling us so that we nearly fell off our perch. It was Ilse's grandmother letting us know that those cherries were hers — not the birds' and definitely not ours.

Usually, Ilse and I stood shoulder to shoulder. In this instance she understood that it was better for her to leave the scene and run home. I had stayed, letting the old woman's angry words rain down on me.

CHAPTER 8

THURSDAY
HAD NOTHING TO SAY

A t the beginning of summer in a general exodus, residents of Malix moved to their chalets in the high meadows, taking with them food, household goods, and small livestock. Most of the cattle were sent to the higher alp to graze on aromatic grasses.

I watched as Papa cut the lush grass with rhythmic sweeps of his scythe. Sometimes the hay was put on sturdy canvas squares, fastened at the top, and slid down the steeper parts of the terrain.

When Papa stood on top of a wagon piled high with hay, lines of perspiration streaking the back of his shirt, my heart was in my throat, but I never said anything. He would not have liked for me to show fear. Once the hay had been safely stored in a barn, we moved everything we had brought with us from the village to another chalet, repeating the process.

Not much else happened in the way of change. It was a good place to be a child and I never felt a moment's homesickness. Cocooned in the familiar, I had something steady to look forward to with green hills to roam and cozy sweet-scented haylofts for my friend Ilse and me to sleep in. At night, the last sounds I heard before drifting off to sleep were the deep-toned, randomly clanking cow bells and the more silvery ones of the goats.

Ilse had taught me how to yodel and as her family's chalet was close to Papa's, we yodeled as a means of communication. There were many things to do and explore. We observed the quick, unerring zeal of ants and wondered if a slow-moving snail forgot its intended target along the way. Feeling free, we created our own entertainment, making necklaces and bracelets from yellow buttercups. Ilse told me that the reflection of the flowers held under our chin would show whether we liked butter – and both of us did. We also picked wild strawberries and drank from a stream; its water so cold it made my teeth ache.

But it was not all play. Here also Uschi gave me chores to do. One of them was taking lunch to Papa. Always ready to lend a hand, Papa was helping a neighbor cut the grass in that man's meadow. And the way there led through a tall-treed forest. I was a six and a half year old child of the city, and the thought of going through this darkness was unnerving.

I loved the deep scent of sun-warmed evergreens but not when they stood drenched in long shadowy stretches. The woods appeared hushed and eerily quiet, as if they were listening, waiting. Sounds gave everything a different texture and so did the lack of it. I could almost taste the looming silence. Thick roots bulged under the path – a path that had been there forever or so it seemed. I raised my feet only high enough to clear the ground, the way Papa had taught me.

Although a spongy carpet of needles muffled my steps, I reasoned that if whatever was hiding in the furtive, threatening shadows couldn't hear me, I would not be able to hear it either. Just because I saw no one did not mean that I was alone. A faint whispering could be the wind – or it could be anything. And the towering trees, with their spread-out arms, looked menacing.

Fears flung themselves at me. Though I normally didn't believe in fairy tales, right then I did. Perhaps Uschi was unfamiliar with the story of Red Riding Hood. But I had read it – enough to be scared! When a squirrel chattered a warning call, I ran until I reached the safety of Papa in the meadow.

That experience was not the last of the day's adventures – the next one involved cows.

At the lower alp, at this time of year, a few cows were left free to roam. On the way back to Papa's chalet I saw two of them fighting. In the village they had appeared to be friends – in a cow-like way. I must have been wrong, because now they were in a muscle-straining effort to push each other backwards. With heads lowered and breathing heavily, they were engaged in out and out combat; first one – then the other– gaining advantage.

There was nothing gentle in their action. In fact, it looked rather brutal. The ground was studded with lichen-mottled boulders, young leafy trees, and tangled sapling evergreens. But they had picked this place for a contest, or maybe the moment had picked it for them.

For some seconds, I stood and watched this bizarre performance. Then, not thinking about any potential harm that might come to me and vigorously waving a stick I jumped into the fray, trying to separate the animals while at the same time avoiding their twisting bodies.

I was still struggling to make a difference when I heard Uschi's call. Though she couldn't see me, it was not a good idea to ignore her. I immediately gave up my futile peacemaking efforts and headed home. Only later did I realize that Uschi may have done me a favor. In a time-honored process, the cows had been establishing their dominance when I tried my best to interrupt them. The thoughtless risk I had taken was just one more event I didn't share with anyone.

There were other, less life threatening experiences – such as Uschi showing me how to gather the freshly laid brown eggs from the hens' nests. None of these feathered producers pecked her as she moved them out of the way. Observing me with their beady eyes, the chickens were less eager to afford me the same privilege. I found the way they clucked to each other comforting, but they didn't share my appreciation and I sported more than one nasty mark on my fingers.

Yet it was Papa who educated me to the details of country life. I learned how to tell time by where the sun stood in the sky. He taught me how to find my way in the forest, which mushrooms were safe to eat and which were poisonous; how to distinguish animals by their calls and tracks; plants and trees by their fruits, colors, and shapes.

Now and then he would pose questions. "Do you know what kind of a tree that is? No? Picture an apple or a pear, and you'll have the answer. An apple tree is round. A pear tree is longer and narrower, just like its fruit."

Papa made learning fun and his expectations of me were not unrealistic. Mistakes were allowed but had to be corrected. Of course there were also difficult days. I vaguely understood that this was because I was German, a child of the former enemy, and some people had trouble adjusting to my presence.

Two years earlier during the war, a twelve year old French girl had come to stay in Papa's home for a while. Her father had been one of Papa's university friends and it was thought she could benefit from the same environment I now enjoyed. Tragically, on the way back to Paris her train had been bombed by Germans and she was killed.

I had arrived in Malix against that emotional background and soon picked up a bewildering amount of undercurrents. Although I didn't hear or see them, I sensed them and tried to cope to the best of my ability. There is mercy in ignorance, but for reasons of her own Uschi had told me the French girl's tragic story.

I listened as she spoke of this and other unimaginably hideous things people in my country had done. According to her I was connected with something terrible but I was at a loss as to what she expected me to do about it. Her words had been brutal and my mind struggled against absorbing the pictures they created.

Could anyone really have committed such things? Yet on some level I believed that she told the truth. The weight of the information had crushed me. Everything I had known had fallen apart and when it came together again it was not the same.

From then on, I was uneasy when not in the company of Papa. I did not share my fears but in my mind he was my protector, shielding me from all the things I could not name. If his responsibilities made it impossible for me to be with him, I was restless until he returned.

At times Uschi asserted her authority. Without giving a reason, she would not allow me to accompany Papa when it came time to milk the cows. Waiting at my observation post by the kitchen window, I wondered how he could possibly manage without me. Papa jokingly said that if I kept this up, the pattern in the linoleum would wear off.

But Uschi could also be kind. When I noticed that the other children wore around their necks little drawstring bags filled with cloves of garlic, I had asked her to please make one for me. Garlic was said to ward off colds. Later in the day I also owned one of these small bags. Without saying a word Uschi had hand-sewn it for me.

After being outdoors for much of the day I brought a healthy appetite to the evening meal which consisted of a glass of warm milk, dense chewy bread, different types of cheese and sausage, and once in a while polenta. If there was any polenta left over from lunch, Uschi would fry it to golden brown perfection in a huge pan. Topped with freshly grated Gruyere cheese, I thought it was food fit for a king.

Perhaps as an insurance against reprimands for future wrongdoings, Ilse and I made ourselves useful by picking elderberry blossoms. We took them to Uschi, who dipped the blossoms into a light pancake batter, fried them, and served them as dessert, with a sugar and cinnamon topping.

Papa was an avid reader of professional journals and the newspaper — the last, preferably without interruption. After the chores were done, he and Uschi and I sat around the table in the Stube, the family room. Usually the adults discussed the day's activities. When it was my turn to speak Papa's questions were more detailed. Uschi didn't contribute much to this conversation, but busied herself mending the holes in Papa's socks with a wooden darning egg, its surface slightly pitted from where needles had missed their mark.

Papa invariably asked, "So, what did you learn today?" He would listen thoughtfully, his eyes half-closed but they would snap open when my answers were not to his satisfaction. "That's it? That's it?" he would demand.

"It's all I can think of."

"But that is not enough! I want you to see and feel and think! You should care, because if you learn something on Wednesday and you don't know any more on Friday, it means Thursday had nothing to say."

That was a lot to digest. Perhaps the war years had made children mature faster, but whatever the reason I understood Papa's intent. He was not comfortable expressing his feelings and his compliments were rare, yet when they came, I basked in their warmth.

My three and a half month stay in Malix ended all too soon.

In another burst of kindness, Uschi gave me a dark blue and white knitted cap as a 'going away' present, which also doubled as a Christmas gift. My return to Germany meant that I would not be with Papa for the foreseeable future. Uschi had also handed me a short broom, the kind given to misbehaving children. That, I did not tell anyone.

CHAPTER 9

RED FLAGS

C hristmas in Germany. People were celebrating all the caring, thoughtful magic of that season.

I loved that my parents followed tradition. There was an Advent's Wreath and a glittery Advent's Calendar. Did any child not know how many days it was to Christmas? But it was fun to open each of the small windows and see what surprises they held.

A hand-carved nativity scene which had been in my family for decades occupied a place of prominence. I was put on an honor system; a good deed performed meant that I could put some hay into the manger. The manger had to be filled by Christmas Eve, because that was when my father read from the Bible and the Christ Child would be placed into the manger.

I had helped my father cut down a tree selected weeks ago. After bringing it into the house, we positioned beeswax candles on the tree's evenly spaced branches, and then we decorated this aromatic gift of the forest with jewel-colored ornaments. Martha had been baking for days. Although special ingredients were saved for just such an occasion, a few were difficult to find. But friends and neighbors shared and somehow it all worked out. There was even enough for Martha to make a Stollen.

It was a good time of year. Even my report card had shown better entries than expected.

"You have done well in school, including math," my father told me. "So, your mother and I have decided to give you something really nice for Christmas."

However, anything related to school took a backseat on Christmas Eve, when a yipping protest coming from inside a large wicker basket caught my attention. I stepped closer and there he was, a wiggly black and silver German Shepherd puppy with big paws, floppy ears, and a soft pink tongue. When his fat little tummy momentarily hung up on the rim of the basket his paws scrabbled until he fell into an awkward heap in front of me.

My father laughed. "I was going to put a big red bow on him but I decided that might only embarrass such a fine-looking fellow. Do you have a name picked out?"

"Artos," I said immediately. "His name is Artos."

~ ~ ~

Miracles come in different shapes and sizes. I had lived at

home in Germany and gone to school there for the last five years, but even with Artos to keep me company I missed Malix. Terribly so. And my references to Papa and Ilse were frequent. It had taken considerable effort to wear down my parents until they finally gave permission for me to return to Malix. This time my stay was to be for a year. I would attend classes at the school where Papa taught and I considered myself fortunate.

There were many things to be happy about; inclusion by the village children was the only thing missing to make my life complete.

It had been so during my earlier stay. With the exception of my friend Ilse, I had little contact with those of my age. We regarded each other warily, talking only when necessary. Even though they were aware of my existence I was not invited to join their games, making me feel as if I were standing on the other side of a glass wall.

My childhood had been about survival – trying to stay alive. Games were never a part of my early years. But now, watching, I learned fast. I also realized that I would never be welcomed as a participant. Although there had been no confrontation, I was denied admittance to their charmed circle. And I had no idea how to earn membership.

I had reached out eagerly. But my efforts had a desperate, hungry edge to them, and the children were uncomfortable around me. Once again I was excluded. Only now I was older and this hurt went deeper, worse than anything I could remember.

I had learned the language of the region, but my slight accent was one of the red flags which encouraged the merciless teasing. The other one was the fact that I came from a country which had started and lost yet another war. That reminder and having been labeled and then excluded, set me apart. It had also made me stronger. Nobody would recognize the forlorn newcomer in me now. I wanted more than anything to be accepted. But however much I wanted it, it remained beyond my reach.

Aware of my frustrations, Papa drew me aside one day.

"Belonging is very important to you, isn't it?" He took off his glasses and cleaned them with the corner of a spotless handkerchief. "Much as I would like to give it to you, it's something you have to earn for yourself."

Papa was right and after some thought I had the answer to my problem. I would need to win a confrontation on their ground, beat them at their game. Being victorious in the upcoming ski race was the perfect solution. I just had to stop thinking of it as something overwhelming, something impossible. There was no need to share these thoughts with Ilse. My feelings would only hurt her and since she belonged to a more advanced group, we would not be in competition.

With an eye on my goal, I outlined an ambitious training program for myself. I believed that without natural ability, and any evidence whatsoever, I could win by following the other children's example.

Not wanting to use the equipment my parents had sent, I took an older set which had been stored in Papa's woodshed. No one would be able to accuse me of having an unfair advantage. Since the boots were too big, I wore two pairs of socks to keep my feet from sliding around in them. I had walked long miles in shoes not my size when revenge was not the motivating factor. Surely I could win a race in boots that were too large, when winning all but consumed me.

The skis and poles were also too large but they would have to do. My need for vengeance was strong enough to make me leave my warm bed every morning and return to the slopes after everyone else had gone home. I was there now, trying to stand up on the snow covered slope and regain control of my skis, but more slowly this time. My mind had not counted the many times I had fallen, however, my body knew and it reminded me.

Warily, under half-lowered lashes I glanced at a group of teenagers standing on the slope. I had become an unwilling expert at avoiding them, but today they were watching every move I made. So much for the element of surprise.

"Take a look at the new champion," a rather homely boy, his nose red from the wind, called mockingly. "It's only three more weeks before the race and she thinks she'll beat us at our own sport."

He had shown an immediate dislike towards me and it was too much to hope that he would feel differently now. He said something else, something not intended for my ears, and the others joined his derisive laughter. I dreaded moments like this when I knew myself to be the target of whispered comments yet was unable to do anything about them.

Several hard-packed snowballs were thrown in my direction but did not reach me.

"And your name isn't Heidi. You made that up. That name belongs to people from here," the boy yelled again. "What are you trying to prove anyway? Just because you're old enough to enter doesn't mean you know how to ski. We'll never let a foreigner win. Never! Especially not a German! Why don't you just give up? Do you hear me, Nazi?"

Being called names was nothing new. Back home, my friends occasionally referred to me as Bambi. Since I had long skinny legs perhaps the name applied. And it was never said in a mean way.

This was different. The snowball had missed; the insult found its mark. Shoulders hunched defensively I cringed as if it had struck me. That is what I was to them – a Nazi. It was the label I carried and the main reason why I didn't have a place in their midst. I knew where this was going and didn't respond because I'd heard that hated expression before and it always made me want to coil into a little ball. But at least for now the boy's annoyance seemed to be over.

What else was there left for him to say? Though his words had been meant as a deterrent, little did he know that I took them as an additional challenge. And I needed no encouragement in that regard. I hadn't failed yet, because I hadn't yet stopped trying.

If I could endure their taunting a little while longer, it would work out. It simply had to. Somehow I knew my tormentors said openly what their parents expressed in private. None of the adults were overly friendly. Most ignored me or treated me with distant politeness, without apparent hostility, but cold nonetheless. There was nothing I could do to the parents. I would have to take out my anger on those my own age.

They refused to understand that I had tried to win them over. Wanting to belong, I had tagged after them, trying to do what they did. Only last summer, I had run barefoot through the hard stubble of a wheat field, rather than be left behind. They had waited to see if I would be afraid. Cut and bruised, my soft city feet had hurt for days, but even that effort had not changed anything. You couldn't make people like you if they didn't, but that knowledge didn't take away the sting.

The reasons why I had tolerated their rejection were known only to me. I felt I had to behave because if I didn't, no other German child might then be given the opportunity to come here. Papa could decide that it was not worth the trouble to open the door to a kind of miniature warfare in his village again.

There were more than enough children from other European countries in equal need of help. He had never said anything to that effect but even so the concern was frequently on my mind. And I didn't want to live with guilt as big as that.

However, over time, my resolve to be patient had been replaced. Now, every waking minute was filled with the vision of winning the race. Over and over I pictured myself flashing through the gate as the loudspeaker announced the fastest run of the day. It would be mine! It had to be mine! I was going to be the one receiving the winner's cup filled with delicious chocolates.

CHAPTER 10

ONE HEARTBEAT

O
n the morning of the race the sky was filled with ominous clouds. And something between snow and hail sent chills through spectators and participants alike. I stood at the starting line, the last one to compete. Doing so might be a small thing for those born here and used to these mountains. For me it was a heart-pounding leap of courage.

Competition on the icy slopes had been fierce. Did I really have grounds for the optimism I felt? 'Don't be so sure', a voice in my head whispered insistently. What if I was not as good as I thought? I had practiced for many hours, becoming better in the process, but tension tightened my muscles and I felt a flutter of panic in the region of my stomach. Not quite so sure now, my insecurity bloomed, making me almost sick with worry.

Securely grounded in their talent and experience, the other skiers had good reason for their confidence. I only had determination on my side. But there was another important difference. I wouldn't – couldn't – lose because I had everything to gain.

For a moment I closed my eyes, visualizing the course, emptying my mind of everything except what was happening at this moment. It all came down to timing and I intended to use mine wisely.

The clock in my head counted the seconds. Knees flexed, my hands wrapped tightly around the poles, I waited for the signal to start. When it came I pushed off and immediately gathered speed. My body moved of its own accord, leaning into the curves, pressing close to the gates but not too close; ripping them out would mean disqualification.

I felt light, nearly weightless, as one with the snow and the skis on my feet; unaware of the spectators lining the course and the cold biting my face. I loved the surge of power – the wild rush of air. Exuberant, defiant joy carried me forward as I flew over the last stretch to the finish.

The race was over and it ended exactly the way I had envisioned. Incredibly, or perhaps miraculously, I had won the trophy. I might never accomplish this again, but today victory was mine.

My breath came in ragged bursts and my heartbeat had not yet returned to its regular rhythm. When I tried to yank off my gloves, it felt as if my fingers might come off as well if I pulled too hard.

Time heightened each detail. 'I have won', I repeated to myself as I stepped out of my skis and made my way to the winner's stand. After listening to a few short speeches and mumbling some words in reply, I accepted the cup, too relieved – too elated – to speak coherently. The visible sign of victory was in my hand, making the moment more real. A fierce triumph surged through me. This alone made enduring the taunts and all the many hours of practice worthwhile.

Next, the customary walk past the other competitors. I had beaten my peers at their own game, finally achieving my goal. And then a thought struck me. What was I supposed to do now? I had made no preparation or plans for anything beyond this moment. All of my effort had gone into winning.

My legs were rubbery with fatigue and my boots felt heavy, as if they were embedded in thick tar. Every step dragged and I had only walked past two participants. There had been no shouts of encouragement for me during the race – there was no applause for me now.

The silence was deafening. My breathing and the beating of my heart – the only things discernible to me.

I had won, but now it hardly mattered because it felt as if I'd lost. If this was victory, why did it taste so hollow? And it became worse with each passing second. Was this emptiness what I had worked so long to achieve? Shouldn't revenge feel deeply satisfying? Yet could I really expect the others to understand the reasons for my actions? It was probably asking too much.

A quick straightening of the shoulders, a few steps, and I was back at the start of the line.

Arm extended with the chocolate-filled cup, I invited my longed-for friends to share. There was no caution in my action, in its own way even more daring than attempting the race, because I had left myself no room to recover if I should once again be rejected. My intent was all too recognizable. "Please," I silently begged, "One of you step forward. Just this once don't let me stand alone."

One heartbeat – two – then more. My rib cage was suddenly too tight. No one spoke. No one moved. Everything was still. I stood... waiting... listening... and trying to bring my fears under control. Self-conscious, nervous, I clenched my fist, spread out my fingers and clenched my fist again.

Finally, a girl took a chocolate and smiled her thanks. Then, all together, my opponents closed around me, sharing my prize with laughter and congratulations in the first sign of friendship I had received from them. And it was as if the past had never happened.

When I caught sight of Papa, I saw the approval in his eyes. It was enough. More than enough. I needed nothing more.

In the evening, still bubbling over one minute and silently content the next, I smiled in anticipation. Uschi had outdone herself in preparing my favorite dishes. Glad they had been invited to this specific feast, my taste buds went on high alert. There was polenta; air-dried beef, cut paper thin; and Salsiz, the sausage I liked best. And though I could have eaten anything, never had food tasted so good.

Papa was strangely quiet during the meal. It was he who broke the spell I was under.

"I may as well tell you. Your mother called," he said. "She wants you home." He stood up and abruptly pushed his chair towards the table, an action that was very unusual for him.

An enormous hole opened up in my mind and I could feel the blood leaving my face. Somewhere the day had taken a turn and I had missed it. I concentrated on pulling air into my lungs as anger unlike any I had ever known before engulfed me.

"No! Not that! Not now! She can't do this!" I yelled. I jumped up and my chair hit the floor.

My reaction stunned both Uschi and Papa. Embarrassed, I said more quietly, "Maybe it's all right. You know how she is. Every so often, she thinks I could absorb more culture somewhere else. Thank goodness it always lasts just a little while."

Papa shook his head. "This time it's different. Your mother doesn't think it's good for you to be here any longer, or come back to Switzerland. According to her you are getting too attached to us."

I stared at him, trying to understand the implication of what he had said. I was the same as I had been only moments ago, yet everything else felt different.

"I don't understand. What do you mean?" I asked.

That was not really the question. It just got in the way of what I truly wanted to know.

My throat felt lined with sandpaper and the tears came before I had time to stop them. "Where am I going then?"

"To Germany. To stay," Papa answered, and with those words all the despair in my world gathered in one room. It was as though I had been told of a place where the sun didn't shine and I had to live in it.

And then I heard the rest of the story. After hearing me talk incessantly about Papa and Malix, and the horse and the cows, my friend Ilse and the alp, Rudi and the goats, my mother had reached the limit of her understanding. She demanded that

I leave Malix and had forbidden any further contact with the Hassler family, giving me no choice but to agree.

A separation from Papa, while painful, had been endured in the past. The thought of never returning was more than I could handle, especially when I had at last been accepted by the children of the village. As a young frightened child I had not wanted to come here. But things had changed and now I was desperate to stay.

It wasn't that I didn't want to go back to Germany. I loved my country, and hometown with its wide boulevards, elegant shops and cafés; black swans surveying their watery domain with languid beauty; the flowing sweep of the Rhine River as it curved around the city. But I hardly knew anyone there anymore. And the people I remembered would not remember me. It had been that way in the past.

Visits home had been too brief to make me feel as if I actually belonged there. Because I had attended one school after another in different places, it had been hard for me to make and keep friends. I had no meaningful circle of people ready to welcome me back. In a way I was considered a foreigner in my own country almost as much as here. People thought of me as rich and spoiled, being able to do and have anything I wanted. But it came with a price. What they didn't know was that it had never made me happy.

In spite of some frustrations, Malix held many special moments. And today it had promised to become even better. I wanted to stuff that feeling into my pocket, to keep with me. How could I possibly leave it all behind? The small niche I had carved for myself was the closest thing I had ever come to having a home. And now, because of my mother's whim, I was to leave it behind?

Would Papa allow all my struggling and fighting to be for nothing, when he more than anyone knew what it had cost me? Was he just going to let me go? Although in reality what could he say to make any difference? My mother's timetable was not open to negotiation. Even if my father's decision might be filled with regret, the judgment had been made.

Papa reached out and touched my arm in a brief, wordless assurance and then he left the room. It felt as if I had been saying goodbye to people my whole life. First it had been to my brother, and now to Papa and Malix. Beyond confusion and hope, my thoughts went round and round in my mind until I couldn't catch the tail end of any of them. I had nowhere to turn for answers and asking more questions would not bring what I wanted to hear.

CHAPTER 11

AS IN A DROP OF WATER

For reasons she did not share with me, my mother had put off my departure for a month. The reprieve gave me time to be on the slopes with my new friends. Not exactly friends, yet much closer than we had been. I tried to make each day count against the empty ones to come. But inevitably the moment I dreaded arrived.

I was in the kitchen an hour before I had to leave for the station. Through eyes blurry from lack of sleep, I watched the large black hands of the clock move. They sounded incredibly loud and the seconds were ticking away too fast. One moment I wanted to reach out and stop them, the next to speed them on to get the unavoidable behind me as quickly as possible.

All the goodbyes had been said, except those to Papa. His, the last, would be the most difficult. If only I could disappear without having to go through that specific hurt. Perhaps I could leave and then write him a note mailed from somewhere along the way. But on another level I knew it would only make things worse.

I remembered my first separation from Papa at the age of seven, after a stay of only three months. Not wanting to leave Malix, I had crawled under the table in the front room, now and then peering through the floor length fringes of the cloth hiding me from view. It was like entering a secret place where nothing could reach me. I'd heard Papa and Uschi call my name but I had ignored them. Torn between relief at not having been found and anxiety at the possible consequences of my action, I had stayed there until I was sure that the train returning me to Germany had left the station.

The delay had given me a few more precious hours. Papa had not said much, nor was I punished. He called my mother, made arrangements for me to take a train the following day and had accompanied me as far as Lindau, a town at the Swiss-German border. Longing to remain, I had clung tightly to his hand during the trip there without saying a word. Still silent, I had kissed his cheek through a chain link fence, while emotionally neutral guards studiously ignored the scene.

The moment had come to go through all of it again. Even without the restriction of a fence, this parting would be much harder. The war years had made me grow up fast, but it did not mean I was ready to cope with this separation from everything Malix, because in that village, as in a drop of water – my whole world revolved.

I moved to the window, my back towards the room and Papa. I had stood there on that first day years ago, when I had anxiously awaited his return from the barn.

Now I was not waiting for anyone. I was there for myself, gathering memories of all the little things that made the parting so wrenching. Feeling miserable didn't even begin to describe my emotions.

I had the strange sensation that everything was pulling away, shutting me out once more, even though it was I who was leaving – against my will and against Papa's better judgment – but leaving all the same. A lump rose and refused to dissolve in my throat. Biting my lips to steady them did not help.

My voice choked with tears, I asked, "Papa, would you mind if I went to the station alone? You know how much I dislike farewell scenes. I won't hide, I promise."

Saying anything else would be the beginning of the real goodbye. Aware that I was trying hard not to cry, he quickly agreed. Uschi remained sympathetically silent. "Well, this is it then. Thank you for everything, Papa. Please try not to forget me because one day I'll come back here. I don't want to belong anywhere else."

My words carried a commitment made to both of us, and I said them with all the certainty someone my age could muster. Although not accepting my mother's decision as being right, I would honor her demand – until I was eighteen.

I took another glance at Papa, at the face I loved, every line special to me. Putting my arms around him in a tight, desperate hug I held unto him for a few more precious moments. Then I picked up my suitcase and walked quickly out the front door.

The house wouldn't be obscured from my view until I reached the bottom of the hill, but I knew that I would not look back. I also knew that my heart was breaking.

CHAPTER 12

A LEATHER-BOUND BOOK

Ouse Martins had built their nests under the roofline of my parent's garage. My friends and I believed that such seasonal visitors brought luck yet they certainly had not brought any to my family.

A few people might be aware of how things stood between my parents, although I knew it better than most. At times they did not speak with each other for weeks. I liked to think it was more than habit that kept them together but I had my doubts. Neither one understood much of what the other was saying nor cared to learn until they shared little of what was important. There were no arguments, just long stretches of silence with nothing to fill the void. Perhaps their marriage was not strong enough to bear the weight of their son's death.

I was often used as an intermediary and when opinions between them differed I usually sided with my father. But I pushed that awareness to the back of my mind.

Most of his time was spent managing his hotel. He only occasionally joined us for a meal. The large dining room felt lonely with just the three of us at a table big enough to seat twelve. It was my home. And money and good taste – not love – had decorated every room.

My father seemed to understand me, at least he listened and once in a while he even agreed with me. I had given up trying to imagine what a comfortable relationship with my mother would be like, but I was old enough to know what I had missed by not having it.

Thankfully, I could always rely on Martha. Unpretentious and practical, she had been working for my mother since before I was born. Almost a member of the family, Martha had become like a parent; there when I needed her. When I was little, running into her arms had seemed the most natural thing to do.

Years ago, when I shared my childish longing for a sibling she suggested that to get results I put some sugar on a small plate: cubes of sugar for a boy, castor sugar for a girl. It had all been somewhat confusing because my friend Rolf had eight siblings and he insisted that the stork had dropped off each one.

Knowing of my love for music, Martha's yearly birthday present was tickets to a concert by the famous Don Cossack Chorus which she and I attended together. She also took me on other outings. One was a visit to a Touring Flea Circus – if one could call it that. The little parasites even climbed a ladder and performed a number of other tricks. My favorite – when six fleas pulled a coach – the whole thing small enough to fit into a matchbox. We also went to an exhibit popular with young and old – that of a preserved beached whale. The young animal had washed up on shore and some enterprising man had preserved and put it on display.

Martha's behavior never changed. But lately my parents had acted rather secretively, or that was how their behavior appeared to me. And the fact that Martha did not offer a hint only increased my uneasiness. My mother had given away everything belonging to my brother – the remaining cars of his train set, his books and his stamp collection. What could possibly be going on? My questions, both silent and spoken, went unanswered.

When even Martha acted this vague there was no point in asking for an explanation. But I couldn't completely ignore the nagging feeling that there was something more to it, something larger and more predictive of future jolts.

There were changes at school as well. The whole family of one classmate was immigrating to Canada; the parents of another student were getting a divorce. Divorce was such a disruptive action. Would my own parents get one of those, which meant that our family would never be together again? And with whom would I live? Was I the last one to know? And what else were they keeping from me? Perhaps if I knew the right questions to ask, I would get the right answers.

Not knowing what to do with all the feelings inside me, I filled in the clean, blank pages of my diary with my thoughts. The maroon leather-bound book with the words *Diary* in gold script on the cover had been a present from an aunt. It had a lock. And to protect my privacy I carried the little brass key on a thin chain around my neck.

Months went by. We never mentioned it but surely Martha was aware of the tension in the house. She and I ate our meals together. My mother remained a vague figure in my life. I seldom saw her, though I heard her going in or out of her rooms.

When she once again disagreed with my wish to go live with Papa in Switzerland, as usual keeping me from what I wanted most, I had an idea. I would get to Malix on my own! My plan was not all that complex; the simpler, the less likely that it would need to be changed. With my decision made I became even more determined. But I would tell no one. Involving Martha, having her on my side, could almost guarantee my success; however, on this scheme I felt she was certain to agree with my mother. It was safer to pretend that nothing was going on.

It was impossible for me to leave anyway as I didn't have enough money for the train fare for both Artos and me. I would not go without him. Artos was well-behaved and I was sure Papa would not mind my bringing him with me.

Getting the necessary funds presented a problem. I had never lent a hand around the house. Because Martha and her helper cooked, cleaned, and picked up after my parents and me, there were no household chores for me to do. And that meant no allowance.

My friend Rolf Niemand helped by offering me his old job. He belonged to that family of nine children, and since the name Niemand meant nobody, I had always found that connection rather amusing. Rolf had worked for the owner of a lumberyard collecting money from customers who had bought lumber to build impressive pigeon lofts but somehow forgot to pay.

I applied for the job and rather pleased with my resourcefulness, I ventured forth. Evidently I was quite effective. A few of these men were scary-looking to someone my age, but they opened the door to me where they might not have done so for an adult bill collector.

The money-making enterprise lasted less than two months. My mother found out and put a stop to the endeavor. Undaunted, Rolf came up with yet another idea. Starting in November, the owner of the lumberyard sectioned off a corner of his lot and sold Christmas trees. More secretive now, I helped Rolf tie up trees for people to carry. With the money from that, and birthday and Christmas money I had saved, I finally had enough funds for a train ticket.

It would be such a relief to get away from everything. And there was no better chance than now, in a brief moment of possibility. Timing was everything and time was running out. My mother was giving me no choice. I had to act immediately. I had made a list of the people who might notice my absence and Martha was one of the few. She deserved something better from me and it was unfair to make her worry. But secrecy was important.

I knew that after I left the house I would need to make my way to the station as fast as possible. Hurriedly, I went to get my suitcase, which had been packed and hidden for weeks. But it wasn't in its hiding place. I searched frantically, yet couldn't find it anywhere. And then I saw it – standing next to my mother, by the front door.

Small as my chance might have been, it was gone now. A flat hopelessness overcame me, knowing that this is what happened when I let wishes venture out of my grasp.

How had my mother known? Careful to keep my plans to myself I had never said a word to anyone. There was only one explanation – she must have read my diary. She had no business doing so but that hadn't stopped her. Making it her business, she had known my intentions all along. While I was busy with my plans, she had been making plans of her own.

CHAPTER 13

THE OWNER'S DAUGHTER

M y father did not consider himself a religious man. I had never known him to set foot inside a church, but when it came to his principles he was unmovable. "If you have time to ask, you have time to say, 'Thank You'." And he applied that ideology to his relationship with God and people.

His values showed up in unexpected places. One of them concerned the hiring of new staff. Sharing a meal with any potential employee was part of the interview conducted by him. "You can tell a lot about someone by the way a person eats," he told me. "Food is a gift from our Maker and we should treat it with respect."

It was easy to recall the taxing sessions when he had drilled me on such things as the numerous steps needed to produce a loaf of bread – from the clearing of the ground, to the tilling, sowing, harvesting, and transporting the grain to the mill. I would never think of gulping down my food. The dining room was not to be treated as a refueling station.

There were other, less pleasant instructions.

On one occasion, my father and I had made plans to go horseback riding. My days formed themselves around those rare outings and I was fiercely protective of them. However, something important always came up and demanded his attention.

Irritated that he answered yet another phone call, again delaying our departure, I stood, impatiently tapping the side of my boot with my riding crop. I would never use a crop on a horse, but doing this made me feel terribly important and it surely emphasized my displeasure.

While waiting, I observed one of the employees being slow at his task and I took it upon myself to chastise him. The worker had said nothing. My father did. He quickly ended his phone conversation and turned to me. "Andrea, a moment of your time? Please!"

As soon as I entered his office, he closed the door and gave me a long appraising look. "I am troubled by what I just heard you say. You seem to have the wrong impression about authority and your role here. You are only twelve years old. What makes you think you have the right to correct my employee in such a manner?"

"But why shouldn't I? I am the owner's daughter," I answered, not so sure now and feeling faintly ill.

"That you are – but it is *my* hotel! I seem to have overlooked an important facet in your upbringing and it needs to be corrected. You leave for school at seven, yes? So starting tomorrow at five a.m., you will report to the kitchen. Someone will show you how to peel vegetables, carrots, potatoes etc. From there you'll transfer to the laundry room and so on, until you have spent a while in every department. If, at the end of that time you still feel inclined to order people about, you'll at least have some basis to draw on. You may hate my decision, but I trust that someday you'll understand and perhaps even thank me. Now, how about that ride?"

His words left me speechless. Perhaps I had been a little aggressive in my interaction with the staff, but this…? To say the least it was embarrassing. I didn't mind the work as much as I feared the staff's ridicule, yet my father held to his decision. Having spent much of my time away from home, there was much I did not know about him. Working with his employees, a number of them third generation, I learned some interesting facts. He had brought together a talented, dedicated team of people, knew each one by name, and frequently inquired after their families. They told him things and he listened, showing genuine interest. "You never become unpopular by asking people about themselves," he said.

My father's hotel was busy and the café with its comfortable chairs, chandeliers, polished wood, and large green plants remained a convenient location for meeting friends, recovering from the exertions of shopping, or just relaxing. Some of the customers came every day like clockwork, stepped through the large revolving doors, and stayed for hours, visiting and eating.

To my surprise, the staff and I became friends. Proud of what they were doing, they put in extra hours without complaining, but also insisted on having some fun. And my father agreed. "A certain amount of laughter is important for perspective."

One of the young men even took me for a spin on his brand new motorcycle. Learning of it, my mother had put an immediate stop to a repeat performance.

There was always work to do but some seasons were especially hectic. At those times, in a spirit of camaraderie, employees would eat meals together, and then it was back to our tasks. Tasks such as placing dabs of paper-thin gold leaf or sugared violets on hand-dipped chocolates before boxing them; or taking Spekulatius, (a thin traditional Christmas cookie, made from flour, butter and rich with spices), from still hot baking sheets, until blisters formed on my fingers.

None of my co-workers ever snickered or made unkind comments. And my father had been right. At the end of my six months, in-depth acquaintance with the family business I did not tell anyone what to do – but asked instead for their opinions.

CHAPTER 14

A SECOND LANGUAGE

fter nearly worrying myself to the edge of tranquility, I was informed that my parents were not seeking a divorce.

I felt no reassurance. Uncertainties, always ready for harvesting, had momentarily been deprived of oxygen. Yet bad things could still happen. Could, and probably would. However, having feared and then escaped disaster it was good to be safely back among accustomed doubts.

But I had been the subject of numerous discussions and I did not like the result. Deemed impossibly headstrong by my mother, she had enrolled me at a boarding school for high-spirited girls. And my father had supported the idea.

I would be one of two Lutheran students in a Catholic institution managed by nuns and the prospect of that depressed me even more. The parentally ordained establishment had not been chosen at random. My mother had been sent to such a place when she was a child.

Martha claimed that change meant things would improve. I could not imagine any good coming from something this upsetting and when I told her so she clicked her tongue in exasperation. "You'll survive."

The problem was that I didn't just want to survive, I wanted to live. Live and have a normal home life like other girls my age without feeling pangs of envy.

Leaving behind Artos had been even harder than leaving Martha. How could I let him know that I loved him, even if I wouldn't be there to play and take him on walks? He would have good care, just not the kind I had given.

I had promised Papa that I would return. Burying my face in Artos' neck I now made the same promise to him. He pressed close and licked my hands as if he understood. I hoped he did.

Like the other students I had arrived at the school with nothing more than was necessary — necessary as far as the nuns were concerned. And since we would all be dressed in the same uniform, that did not amount to much.

A group of red brick buildings stood on several acres of land interspersed with walkways, benches, trees and bushes. The property had its own small farm. Lay sisters performed kitchen duty and were responsible for a vegetable garden and an orchard.

There was a lecture hall, a library, conference room, laundry room, offices, kitchen, and a chapel. Students ate, studied, and slept all in the same building and were allowed little privacy.

The environment had its own customs and laughter was discouraged. Silence became a second language and I had the thought that speech could be employed only if a fire broke out.

The first few days were a blur of murmured rules and instructions of what was expected of me. My behavior was constantly reported on, even during compulsory chapel attendance. I didn't want to stand out, yet stand out I did. Saying or doing the wrong thing was a constant worry. Feeling swallowed up in the impersonal oppressive vacuum, there had been times I thought I might die of loneliness.

The sound of even one friendly voice would have brought comfort, but the other students treated me with yawning indifference. Their callousness burrowed deep and I always had the feeling of something unpleasant to come... again. I was nervous, and they were not blind to it. Knowledge was a weapon here. Everything depended on whom you knew and how well you blended in.

Uneasily, I watched the other students and did what they did. Just when I thought I had finally managed to get it right, someone contemptuously told me that I had fallen short again.

I certainly was not popular; to say I had friends would be an exaggeration. They tried to make me miserable enough that I would leave by my own choice. But they had underestimated me. Eventually, I learned to stand my ground, confronting their disapproval openly rather than retreat from it. But things greatly improved when Monika, one of the students, became my best friend. I did not have many; she actually was my only one.

When we first met, I didn't think she would want to have

anything to do with me; our backgrounds were not at all the same. Monika was Catholic, had doting parents, and called a large family her own. Laughter and hugs were a staple. And that only began to describe her life.

Yet she had become an important ally even if we didn't always understand each other. Intuitively overlooking our differences, we spent most of our free time together.

I adjusted to the school's inflexible traditions with a combination of defiance and resignation. Although some details had folded together, six months after my arrival at the school I was still struggling.

But I had observed and been duly impressed by the confident behavior of a transfer student. Although she was a year ahead of me, we attended two elective classes together. Pretty, bright and articulate, her long blond hair pulled back, Renate behaved as if she'd never had a moment's doubt about anything. Self-confidence could extend a horizon almost indefinitely and hers seemed to have no limits.

Some of the students wanted to be like her – others to be seen with her – and I? I copied her. Since I had no idea what I wanted to do with my life I saw no sense in starting the journey.

My only desire was to get away from my mother's controlling influence as soon as legally possible. Beyond that everything stretched in a haze.

I would have given anything for a share of Renate's confidence. Not coming to it on my own, I thought that the next best thing was to follow her example.

When she declared that no education was complete without some skill in the art of calligraphy and decided on an involved flowery French script, I did the same.

Here again the differences between us became noticeable. Renate accomplished her assignments with ease while I labored at the task, feeling more and more like a failure no matter how painstakingly I applied myself. The blank pages in my folder stared back, daring me to make the first move.

Mother Superior taught only one class every quarter. Once it became known that she would share her expertise with the calligraphy students, the class quickly filled up. She brought a fresh approach to an old subject, teaching us the history and evolution of writing, and which pens, paper and ink were best suited for specific projects.

Pupils appreciated that she treated us with respect, often making us come up with our own answers. We regarded her with an admiration bordering on reverence. A smile from her was almost like a benediction; being praised the ultimate reward.

To disappoint her was unthinkable, yet even after hours of practice, my penmanship remained uneven and lumpy.

Every so often, Mother Superior would check on our progress. That part of the morning brought sheer torture for me. I was aware of her, as she walked slowly up and down between the rows, pausing now and then to advise or correct.

For some time I managed to escape her discerning eyes, until the day when an uneasy sensation in the pit of my stomach told me that she would stop at my desk. Other students must have sensed it as well. Without exception they turned towards me. I tried to convince myself that the moment would pass, but while I was in it I felt awful. If only Mother Superior would keep going.

I tried to send her messages, such as 'Move on! Will you please move on! Don't speak to me. Assist someone appreciative of your help.' And that would mean just about everyone else in the class. I didn't want to be singled out this way. But the object of my silent plea remained oblivious to my concerns. St. Rita was supposed to be the patron saint of impossible dreams, only this sequence had nothing dreamlike in it. And maybe that was why she also did not respond to me.

"I could judge your work better if you did not cover it with your arm. May I see it, please?" Mother Superior asked.

Self-consciously I watched as she picked up the sheet of paper and considered my awkward creation.

"You might have better results with something more suited to you," she suggested. "Don't let fear eclipse possibilities. Have the courage to be yourself."

Her words made me feel as if I had been let out of prison. I immediately chose a different script and at the end of the term received an A+ from a teacher not known to give such marks.

I didn't know if Mother Superior remembered that occasion. I had never forgotten it.

CHAPTER 15

IN EVERY WAY THAT MATTERED

I had thought that being sent to boarding school was the worst that could happen to me. But I had been wrong. So very wrong.

I was on my way to my next class when one of the nuns informed me of an important telephone call.

"I'm sorry to tell you that... car accident... your father died instantly..." The voice at the other end of the line sounded like that of my father's secretary, but she was hard to understand.

Trying to make sense of what I was hearing I pressed the phone tightly against my ear. Her words were the stuff of a horrible nightmare yet I was awake. Awake and unwilling to believe them. Searching for an explanation I could hold unto

— hoping for one thing and refusing to accept another — I heard her say, "I am so sorry. Are you sure you're all right?"

"Dead," I told myself. "She tells me that my father is dead and she asks if I am all right?" I covered my mouth to suppress a sob. Nothing was right. Between morning and evening of an unexceptional day everything had changed. "I am fine," I answered, but even if I said it enough times nothing would ever would be the same again.

I suddenly felt very cold, making it difficult to think, to move — unwilling to move, because moving led to thinking. And that would bring back the awareness that my father wouldn't — couldn't return. I had counted on him always being a part of my life. And to have him gone? Just like that?

Slowly, some details were beginning to make sense. Two days ago my father had not called back when he said he would but I had not been worried. This was nothing out of the ordinary.

"I am going to be in touch," he had told me, and I believed him even though I had heard the same promise many times before.

To distract myself and make the time go faster, I had played games; if those big fat clouds stayed in the sky for only half the day he would call; or if I didn't step on any sidewalk cracks with my eyes closed. But for one reason or another, his plans had always been postponed.

He had missed performances, school Christmas programs, and other important events in my life all because of work. My mother had been there — my father — never.

Afterwards he would tell me that he had done his best to

be present. When he apologized, I again believed that things would change though it was getting more difficult to do.

"Never break a promise, even one just made," he said. But to me he did, and eventually I had adjusted my thinking. And now my grief was complicated by guilt. I was ashamed that despite knowing how hard my father worked, I had wanted more – more of his attention. How very little that mattered now.

I was not ready to fully absorb all that had happened. That came later when inevitability assembled itself. And with it the pain and a sorrow deeper than any I had ever known. Sorrow for all the days that I would not have with my father. All the things we would never do.

To whom could I go to for advice, take into my confidence? Who would help me make choices, tell me that I looked pretty in a new dress? Who would put a dab of shaving cream on my nose, go on the roller coaster with me? Between us there had never been any overt display of affection. So this had counted as his version of "I love you."

And then there was math. Strange that I would even think of such a totally irrelevant subject now. Math was a challenging subject for me and when my father was home he helped with assignments. It was not saying I never learned anything from my mother. She had drilled me on my times tables until I had them memorized. She also persisted until I could point out the countries of the world on a map and knew their capitols. When I mixed up Bucharest and Budapest she showed surprising patience and I had been happy for that momentary connection. But it was my father who made me feel that I needed to be no different than the way I was; that being a girl shouldn't place undue limitations on me.

I had returned home and on the day of the funeral I still felt numb; everything had gone by as if it happened to someone else. Nothing had prepared me for this emptiness. Nor was I able to bring the future into focus. In the absence of all that mattered – nothing mattered.

The brief graveside ceremony had followed tradition. Doing it properly helped as rituals were meant to do, or so I was told.

Afterwards, back at the restaurant, my mother had me serve coffee and tea to friends and acquaintances who had come to express their condolences. There were enough personnel to take care of this – all I wanted was to be alone for a while and face my own grief. But I played the role that had been written for me by my mother; the dutiful daughter, nodding and thanking our guests for their concern; smiling at dozens of unfamiliar faces until the muscles in my face ached. A few women had tried to explain that the accident was God's will and thought of the comments as consoling, but I found no comfort in their assurances.

I needed my father, but it hadn't been enough. And every day brought reminders of his permanent absence, exposing sharp edges that hurt, letting me know that the wound could not be ignored.

Many people had known my father, had loved him. With him gone, my home became a sad and somber place. His office, like everything else, seemed depleted, empty, yet I kept listening for the sound of his footsteps, at times telling myself that I heard them. Nothing made the facts bearable but one could cry only for so long and finally I had to accept the desperate reality.

Technically I was not an orphan, but that is what it felt like. I was alone – in every way that mattered.

After my brother Wolfgang's death we had never again mentioned him, as if my brother had not been a part of our family – any part of us. Now, in an echo of that earlier grief, my mother and I did not talk about my father. Not that we talked much about anything. And feelings and thoughts were seldom shared.

"It's not going to last, you know. Happiness never does," my mother said when I took a chance and told her about a positive experience I'd had. But that was her belief, and after twice hearing that debilitating remark I stopped sharing anything with her.

~~~

I returned to school a week after the funeral. Artos showed his dejection when I left and it had been wrenching for me too. We had gone on extra-long walks and played ball together. If he could have, he would have climbed into the car and come with me. So when I returned six months later for Martha's granddaughter's wedding he was beside himself with joy.

"This must be the season for weddings," Martha said. "I wouldn't be surprised if another couple did the same."

"Did the same?"

"Yes! Get married."

That just didn't make sense. My thoughts had been drifting. When they hit land they did so with a thud. Surely Martha was joking. Or was I hearing more than was being said? Nausea clawed at the back of my throat.

Her comment was simply too bizarre and disturbing to contemplate. She had said it without looking at me, as if she was just airing her thoughts, but in the kind of voice that meant she was thinking more than she was saying. And she had not specified to whom she was referring. Was she talking about my mother and the Englishman she had been dating? It was possible of course, but I didn't believe it for a minute. Martha once had suggested that it was inevitable; that someday my mother would remarry. But this had happened more quickly than I expected.

Not yet immune to shock, I drew in a quick, clenched breath. I thought everything that could happen had already happened. Martha had always been good at sizing up a situation, though in this she had to be wrong.

"But who else is there to get married?"

Martha sighed, confirming what I feared. There was a lot of information in that answer. And nothing about it was reassuring. To put it mildly, I was angry and confused. Had I missed every single warning sign?

"You are talking about my mother," I said, and Martha did not deny it.

Martha took pride in being German. Surely she would know that I saw my mother's marriage to an Englishman as a kind of betrayal.

"But he is English."

"I'm aware of it," she replied patiently.

Slowly, I learned some details. Since there would be no official announcement of their forthcoming nuptials I did not need to acknowledge Henry's existence. Sight unseen, I disliked him. And I certainly didn't want to make his acquaintance.

"But you have already met him," Martha insisted. "He's been to the house. He was helpful in evicting the Russian officer after your return from Passau."

And then I remembered. Unwilling to return to Moscow at the end of the war, a Russian officer had made himself at home on our estate while we were gone. As Düsseldorf was under British rule an English officer had settled the matter. And that officer was Henry.

For my mother to marry again was one thing; for her to marry someone like this man went far beyond that. He had to be almost fifty years old and that seemed ancient to me.

"He may be my mother's future husband, but he will not be the head of this family. Not the family that I belong to," I stated emphatically.

"Don't worry. Everything will work out."

Martha's remedy for any problem was a combination of food and verbal advice, but I was not hungry and her all-purpose response set my teeth on edge. It was all very well for her to say everything would work out. I had to do what I was told. Martha had a choice. She would go and live with her son and his two children and so would my Artos, leaving me to face my fears alone.

"Does that mean I would be allowed to stay with Papa?" I asked Martha

After a moment she said thoughtfully, "I don't have the answer to that. But I'm going to make myself clever and find out."

Making herself clever had not produced the required results. When Martha suggested to my mother that I live in Malix where I would be happier, my mother had refused. " She will not learn what she needs to know in some alpine village."

Talking to my mother in my present state seemed a self-destructive thing for me to do. I would confront her in the morning. And given the opportunity I would have, but she had left without saying a word as she so frequently did.

For the present, I would return to school. But my mother informed me that she would be moving to England, and that at the end of next year I also would live there. With her and Henry! At his place! The whole thing was absurd!

She knew that I didn't like change, or she could have if she had cared to think about it. I wondered, not for the first time, why I was so easy to reject. Surely somewhere out there a mother was waiting for me – a mother who would love me. When I was younger I had looked for her face in every woman I saw. But that was years ago.

"She has her life. This is my life. And I'm not going to England." I told Martha.

Martha's silence carried its own vocabulary but she was not one to keep quiet when things needed to be said. " Something good might happen. Give it a chance. If I didn't know better I'd say you're afraid."

"Of course I'm not afraid. Why should I be?" I laughed scornfully or what I thought was a passable imitation of it. "I've just never had the slightest desire to go to England. There is nothing I want to see there… nothing I want to do there."

"Andrea! Listen to me! Have I ever given you bad advice?"

Why was everyone always telling me to pay attention? "I am listening," I answered sullenly, my misery so huge I couldn't hide it.

"You'll be eighteen before long. That day will come sooner than you think. And then you'll have choices."

Martha, being the hopeful type, was trying to put a good face on things, but her insufficient platitudes did not comfort me.

So I was not supposed to fear the future; just accept and embrace uncertainty? And how long was long? To her maybe nothing at all. She had always found the best in me. I did not remember ever arguing with her and I didn't argue now – but when she reached for my hand I pushed her away.

Martha gave me a long level look. "What has come over you?"

I squinted against the light that had suddenly become intense.

"I don't know," I said quietly, wondering if she believed me. If she did, she shouldn't have, because for the first time I had just lied to her.

CHAPTER 16

THE PACKAGE

W hen I heard my name during mail call I did not respond at once. And then I heard it again. More loudly.

"Andrea, there is something here for you," Etta said, her tone adamant. Etta was the student assisting the nun in charge of incoming mail. Much impressed with her responsibility and the access to information it gave her, she gossiped the way the rest of us breathed.

Right now Etta had me at a disadvantage. I tried to act nonchalantly, as if her message didn't matter because someone had once played a joke by pretending a letter was waiting for me, but when I went to pick it up, I learned that it had been a prank.

For months after coming here I had checked the mail every

time it arrived, just in case. The fact that there was nothing for me shouldn't have come as a surprise. Somehow I must have displeased my mother yet again. Following our last separation she explained that I had not said goodbye to her properly. I didn't even remember the specifics. She paid attention to such details and being ignored was my punishment for that mistake. I would not receive any mail. Birthdays, holidays, all passed unmarked, until I finally had no expectations.

On one of our school's rare outings to a local fair, I had managed to buy a water pistol. Afterwards I didn't know why I had done so; I just liked the look of the clear lime green plastic. Knowing I could not keep it, I had entrusted it to Etta's care. She seemed competent to deal with such a request. That was before I understood that she had reported my infraction to Sister Maria Serena.

Etta and I had not been friends previously, and this had earned her my long-lasting resentment. It was understood among the students that you never – ever – informed on each other. Etta, convinced that no one would notice, frequently broke that rule.

Sister Maria Serena also led the choir. She considered herself an authority on things celestial, and according to her Etta was worthy of membership in angelic choirs. Etta was all freckles and she wore glasses; but yes, her voice was beautiful. Other than that, she could not lay claim to anything memorable.

To the despair of the choir mistress, I had never been able to carry a tune. I lacked such inspiring qualities and accepted my deficiency in that area. Yet I appreciated talent and in the blend of voices rising and dipping in unison – Etta's was the best – amazing in its clarity and power. The first time I heard her I couldn't believe that she was capable of producing such tones.

While singing, she became a different person. However, to her, a day without snitching was a day wasted. Her unfortunate practice of informing Sister Maria Serena of anyone ignoring school regulations created problems. But if outward appearances were acceptable, this nun did not look much deeper.

I continued to be Etta's favorite target; she was always on the look-out for any 'offenses', such as the evening I sneaked out after the lights had been turned off. It was not a wise thing to do but well worth the risk. There was a reason for my action. One of the work horses had given birth to a soft-nosed, whiskery foal and I simply couldn't stay away. I had become good at finding scraps of comfort, and this counted as one of them.

Pretending to be asleep after curfew had been one of the first things I'd learned at the school. It was unlikely that anyone would be up at this hour but wanting to be sure, I waited until it was dark outside. Then I tiptoed past a series of rooms and down the stairs carefully like a thief. By staying close to the wall I avoided any telltale creaks and slipped through the door.

After my eyes had adjusted to the darkness and judging it to be safe, I hurried across the yard, moving from shadow to shadow. Wind and rain splattered against my face. There was no moonlight, but I didn't need it to find my way to the barn.

When I entered the stall I hardly dared breathe. The foal, brown with a long white blaze and still new to its legs, wobbled unsteadily. Proud of her accomplishment and alert to every sound, the new mother had allowed me to brush her and her baby. Surely there was no harm in that.

I thought I had returned to my room before anyone became aware of my absence. But good luck had limitations. Someone had seen and informed Sister Maria Serena of my latest lapse.

Unburdened with imagination, in this nun's palette everything was black and white, just like the habit she wore. I preferred a dash of color. And that put us on a collision course.

My reprimand was up to her and she deemed two days in solitary confinement to be appropriate. If she had the power, she would insist that I stay in my room all the time. Evidently the *carpe diem* – seize the day exhortation, such as visiting the foal, only applied when it coincided with the rules of the school. The focus was on compliance – not thinking – with little emphasis on what counted in the long run.

I had always loved books and my frequent stays in solitary were put to good use. Books were my escape so it was not at all a lonely stretch. Especially since I had managed to convince Sister Maria Serena that I did not like reading when just the opposite was true. Surprisingly, she had accepted my protest as fact.

A few discrete questions confirmed that Etta had been the one to report my nighttime visit to the foal and when I confronted her with my suspicion, she had not denied it. If anything, she seemed rather pleased with herself.

That much snitching called for a response. Never one to let an excuse go to waste, I had retaliated by playing a number of pranks on her. From there it had grown into an active, mutual aversion. Was tricking me with news of a package her way of getting even? I didn't think she was all that inventive, though people could fool you.

One student counted on getting a card or letter almost

every day and Etta would know that I had never received anything.

"It's from Switzerland," Etta insisted. Even the bangs on her forehead quivered with importance. "It arrived for you."

Slowly I took the securely wrapped package from her. My name was written on the front. The stamps were Swiss all right, the handwriting Uschi's. Papa was a caring man, but somehow I couldn't visualize him putting a parcel together. This showed a woman's touch.

Uschi had not been particularly friendly towards me in Malix – could she have changed this much?

I pushed past the other students, forcing myself to walk casually, until I was out of sight before racing upstairs to my room. Unwilling to cut anything with scissors, I fumbled with the string that Uschi had so prudently saved and undid the multitude of knots. Eagerly, I tore away the heavy brown wrapping paper and what I saw brought tears to my eyes.

Ever practical, Uschi had sent bread, sausage, butter, and honey from Papa's bees. And with a sinking heart I knew that I would have to share it – all of it – with ninety-four other students. There was nothing secret about this requirement. Often quoted by the staff, I had lost count of the many times it was repeated.

Although obedience was an area of constant improving, sharing had never been a problem for me. But this was different. Inside this package were gifts from Malix and the memories they carried. This was not just food; this was nourishment on a much deeper level, providing a link with the only home I'd ever known. Priceless to me, without value to anyone else – and I didn't want to part with even one crumb.

Would that really be so terrible, or was it acceptable to be selfish once in a while? Sometimes it was hard to tell the difference. To keep the parcel's contents seemed right, even if I knew it was wrong. No one else knew what it contained and there really wasn't that much anyway – just enough for one other person.

In the end I asked my friend Monika to share the feast. When I explained my plan to her, she was hesitant. She had never rejoiced in my inventiveness because I tended to plunge into things willingly – frequently breaking the rules. She never even nudged them, following the letter of the law with an excess of caution.

"What trouble are you getting me into this time?" Monika looked alarmed. "When you have that look on your face you usually come up with something outrageous."

"Would I do anything like that?" I asked innocently.

"You know you would. We are not supposed to eat food upstairs," she warned. "Think of the mess we'll be in if we get caught. It makes me nervous."

My reluctant accomplice persisted with her questions until I wanted to scream and wondered if I had made a mistake involving her. There was no time to go over every detail – again. One could plan but one had to be flexible. Plans had a way of changing, but I had taken other risks. What was one more?

Monika groaned when she saw my expression. "You don't have to follow every idea in your head. And I wouldn't think less of you if you changed your mind."

But finally she gave in, somewhat amazed by her own daring. If her reluctance was a warning, it didn't come through loud enough. But then what were the chances that I would have listened? Determination can make you very certain about things.

"It's going to be all right." I assured her, less certain than I sounded, but that was what Monika wanted to hear.

"If we look like we know where we're going, no one will question us. We'll take what is left to the kitchen and put it into a cupboard or something. If anyone asks, I'll accept responsibility, absolving you of any wrong doing. Right now we're going to the linen room. No one is going to bother us there."

"Maybe," she said, chewing her lip as if she hadn't heard me. "I just need another moment."

My watch showed that we did not have many of those left. "In between classes the hallways are empty," I said, walking faster, "which is why it will work."

"Wait!" Monika held up her hand. "I thought I heard a noise. It's a sign," she said more urgently, the expression on her face squeezed together.

"I don't believe in signs!"

"There it is again!"

I jumped in before she could take another breath. "It's nothing – maybe a bird on the roof or something like that!"

Undetected, we took two plates from the kitchen and headed down the long hallway. We had made it this far but it wasn't yet time for congratulations. At last, after another quick look to be sure we were alone, we slipped into the linen room. Relieved, Monika and I grinned at each other. We had succeeded – and then it hit me – we had no knife! My plan had been foolproof! How could I have overlooked something as important as a knife?

Listening for sounds that shouldn't be there, I retraced our steps. I wouldn't want to explain to anyone why I was here. When I walked back through the door, Monika breathed a sigh of relief.

Quickly, we cut two thick slices of bread and covered them with butter. Then we carefully built up the sides higher than the center, creating a sort of moat effect through which nothing could escape. Next came a generous helping of honey. By the time it trickled in a golden ribbon from the spoon, my mouth was watering.

Everything tasted the way I remembered it, perhaps even a little better. I had only taken my third bite when the door was flung open, letting in light and a sudden rush of air. Disturbed dust motes danced crazily in the breeze. Blinking against the brightness I saw the disapproving frown of Sister Maria Serena. And behind her, the smirking face of Etta, looking very pleased with herself.

CHAPTER 17

A PIECE OF BREAD

"There she is, Sister," Etta announced, her words unrepentedly smug. "I told you I saw her. She always…"

This can't be happening, I thought. But of course it was. "Is there some problem?" I asked.

Sister Maria Serena motioned for Etta to be quiet, before she turned her attention to me. "I should say we have a problem. It seems there is no end to your talents. What possible reason could you have had in mind for your action? That is, if you thought of anyone but yourself?"

Stunned by her accusation I didn't know how to answer. "This bread is from the place where I used to stay."

"And this should matter why?" the nun asked in her typically brusque manner. "No doubt you have an explanation."

Bracing myself for an eruption, I watched her warily. "They sent it to me."

"They sent it to you! Whoever they are?" The tinge of sarcasm was impossible to miss.

"It came from Switzerland. From friends," I told her, thinking of any number of more satisfying things to say instead. At least a dozen answers vied for an opportunity to do so. Just giving in to it once would balance the score. But at the back of my mind I could hear Mother Superior's counsel, "Never speak words that make your lips ugly." That disqualified me, because the uncharitable thoughts I wanted to express to the Sister had the potential of permanently affecting my whole face.

"You still have not given me a reason! You clearly enjoyed this unexpected bounty. If it is so good why did you want to hide it from us?"

"There wasn't enough to share."

The look she gave me spoke volumes. Then, in case I'd not caught her meaning, she said it aloud. "That was not something for you to decide."

I felt as if I were being cross-examined and damning myself with every word I spoke.

The nun had a cautious, evasive face. There was something frightfully knowing about her. It was easy to picture her as a valued member of the Inquisition; if not a member, then definitely a dream crusher. I had only one dream and knew better than to let her get anywhere near it. I was still making my way through these thoughts when Sister Maria Serena interrupted. "I recognize troublemakers like you," she said. "And I am seldom, if ever, wrong,"

I suppressed a sigh. Last week, because I had been with the foal, I missed breakfast. Searching for something to eat, I found a warm pot of soup in the kitchen and was busy sampling its contents, when a chill touched the back of my neck. Turning around I met Sister Maria Serena's scowl. "What do you think you are you doing? You sample and you sample," she said crossly. "And when the pot is empty you still won't know how it tastes."

She had an impressive range of scathing looks. Occasionally they were intermingled with one of long-suffering. "You have spelled trouble from the beginning, and nothing has changed since then," she said.

Coming from her I took that as a compliment. So her memory was functioning. I knew what she was talking about. Months ago, I had made a face behind her back, and she had caught me in the act. And while I valued the stillness of enforced solitude, I was not going to be that rash again.

By now I was really annoyed. I had tried not to let it show, but enough was enough. What made her think she had the right to destroy this moment for me.

"I regret that I continually upset you," I said, tense with anger and failing to sound apologetic – failing because I didn't feel apologetic. "This was my idea. I don't want my friend to be punished for it. And as for you, Etta," I didn't even try to hide the scorn in my voice, "you can go now. I'm sure you'll be rewarded for your effort. And I'll try to remember it too," I added, treating her to my biggest smile.

For some seconds I allowed myself to enjoy the scandalized expression on the sister's face, deliberately keeping my eyes on her. If there was any blinking, I wasn't going to be first. Her jaw was moving as if she was grinding her teeth. It seemed an excessive reaction, but I liked being the reason. There was always a sense of urgency about her; so to just have her standing there was something new. When I briefly searched my conscience I found no remorse.

I understood that I didn't fit her image of what a good student should be. Individuality cast a dim light here. And I would always be something else…something less.

"I wonder how many other rules you have yet to break. Do you look for trouble or does it just find you? No, don't tell me. You have an aptitude for mayhem." Sister Maria Serena narrowed her eyes and rewarded me with an icy stare. Her hands were folded in her long wide sleeves but the gesture of piety did not fool me. Fighting off a yawn I waited.

As soon as her breathing returned to normal and she had regained her composure, she launched into another attack. It was the response I had expected.

Although I hadn't yet tested the farthest limits of my creativity, and my confidence was not exactly staggering, but for a few tempting moments I again wanted to say what I thought of her, of her malice, her cold-hearted lessons. I considered the consequences and quelled the impulse. Since there seemed to be no acceptable reply I said nothing. But it was a loud nothing. And she interpreted it correctly. Exasperated, she looked up at the ceiling.

I could have told her not to expect an answer from that direction. But good manners prevailed and I refrained from sharing my insight; yet another impulse that went unfulfilled. Surely there should have been some kind of ceremony to acknowledge the occasion.

"Are you listening?" The nun clapped her hands, making me jump. "And stand up straight! How many times do you need to be told?"

I stood straight, and I nodded. It was not an acceptable way to communicate, but at this moment poor manners would just have to suffer.

"Your attitude is not helping! Do you hear what I am telling you?" she asked sternly.

"Um...Um...Yes," I stuttered.

"I see you are verbally gifted in addition to your many other accomplishments." Sister Maria Serena gave me a withering look. "You are mumbling," she accused, her words precise and tightly wrapped.

I wasn't deaf, just distracted. And I hadn't answered because I did not want to make this confrontation worse. But I was mistaken in thinking that if I said nothing, I would be found innocent. I wrestled my thoughts into submission and turned my attention back to her. Though I didn't like her tone, it was time to tread carefully. Sister Maria Serena's eyebrows had drawn together until they nearly met. Most people used them as an expression; she used them as a means of communication. I could see her directing a whole orchestra that way.

"I hear you, Sister," I said, carefully choosing my tone – giving my best impression of the kind of person I despised – one suitably deferential. But she was not put off the scent so easily. Her eyes raked over me, taking in every aspect and still finding nothing to meet with her approval.

"Pride is a sin," she said bitterly, as if she were personally acquainted with it. "So do not think that a feeble sign of humility will save you from any consequences. You are arrogant, stubborn, and a bad influence on those around you."

There it was again – the indictment that I was taking the express road to damnation; my place in the afterlife assured. Sometimes it was nice to be considered predictable, but this was neither good nor flattering. I had engaged in nefarious activities, and a few may well have shortened this nun's life expectancy. But the truth was that she needed someone to blame, even when she had no evidence. Suspicion was enough, which in her view likely amounted to the same thing. Accusing me, the unappreciative heathen, had become second nature.

To Sister Maria Serena, unquestioning obedience was the tribulation of aspiring saints – the pathway to eventual salvation. Every act was measured by that standard. Convinced I could do something more useful with my time, I had spent considerable effort to distance myself from such restrictions. I would never be that malleable lump of clay – or want to pay the price.

"Clearly you have too much time on your hands. More homework will solve part of the problem and I expect you to obey," the Sister said sharply.

Her admonition soaked like water into desert sand. But she waited for my response and I gave it. Nodding, I was careful not to make eye contact and hoped she wouldn't notice my crossed fingers.

"There is never a need to be nasty to anyone, young lady, and believe me I use that term loosely," she said, "You are here as a favor to the Archbishop and you would do well to remember that."

Her sentences were filled with assessments she felt entitled to make. None of this was anything I didn't already know. It had just taken her longer to mention that detail. I was here on sufferance, but even from Sister Maria Serena the words stung. I let them pass, though not as easily as before. Fortunately, the bell rang just then. It was the best sound I had heard in minutes, saving me from having to explain myself any further.

"I think we understand each other. So, give me whatever you saw fit to hide from your friends." Annoyed, the Sister pointed at the sandwich.

Pinned under her gaze, my heart hammered wildly. Her demeanor made it clear that she would not accept an explanation, no matter how believable. What I had told her was the truth, but the look in her eyes made it seem a lie. She might see. She would never understand.

In the end, obedient to adult authority, I did as I was told. Slowly, I put my partially eaten piece of bread into the outstretched hand of the nun, knowing that I would never finish it, nor would I want to... now.

CHAPTER 18

IMPERIOUS LIKE A SHIP

No matter the circumstance, patience and I seldom read from the same page. Waiting gave me too much time to think. I had been in my room for over an hour when Etta gleefully informed me that I was to go and have a visit with Mother Superior.

That could mean only one thing – I was in trouble – the serious kind of trouble. Mother Superior was a nice enough person and liked by everyone, but I had broken an all-important rule, the one of sharing, and that carried consequences. I understood it. I didn't have to like it.

I was frequently in her office getting lectured for my latest transgression and by now I could find my way there asleep. This time I walked the long corridor much more slowly, one reluctant step at a time. I felt miserable and disheartened, grateful that no one saw me, my feet soundless on the linoleum floor.

But waiting for me at the office was thin-lipped, indignant Sister Maria Serena. "You can go in. Mother Superior is expecting you," she said in that curt tone of hers.

Of course I was expected and the reason for it – the school snitch and a nun who made it her business to stick her nose into everything. Having delivered her message and secure in the knowledge that she would be obeyed, she gave me one last disapproving look before she turned and sailed away, imperious like a ship on a wave of righteousness.

Nuns ought not to smirk, yet I could have sworn that Sister Maria Serena had done so. How could someone with a nice name like that be this spiteful? She certainly didn't live up to the *serene* portion. Maybe it had been wishful thinking on her part or unrealistic optimism when she had chosen it years—eons – ago.

I was doing some wishful thinking of my own, as in hoping for something that would postpone the upcoming conversation.

My last visit to Mother Superior's office had been because Etta and I had made a bet as to whether or not nuns were bald under their wimples. I had not been all that interested in unraveling the nuns' mysteries, but this was an exception. In this case such knowledge was especially valuable, because the loser of that wager would be a kind of 'gofer' for the winner. Every day! For a whole year! The way I saw it, Etta would have to shine my shoes and get me anything I wanted within reason, of course, but still... .

It was a foolish thought. Or was it? Could the chance of having the school snitch at my mercy be turned down? The enticing picture didn't leave me alone. Never one to shrink from a challenge – nor having the will to ignore it – I gave in to it. For a while the specifics remained elusive. Finally, a plan pushed its way to the surface.

After numerous modifications, it was ready to be put into action. I knew that it was somewhat on the risky side and I had become increasingly convinced that I'd made the wrong decision. The sensible thing would have been to walk away but I continued refining the details. After estimating the average height of the nuns I had placed a dark string head high above the width of the staircase and then rung the alarm bell.

The puzzle about hair lengths was solved at last. We had our answer when the nuns hurried out of their rooms. Caught by the string, a few wimples went flying. Unfortunately, Sister Maria Serena had been one of those at the receiving end of that prank. It had not endeared me to her. And Etta had proved to be an unwilling servant.

And now I was back again but glad that I had not given Sister Maria Serena the satisfaction of seeing me squirm.

I hesitated for a moment, took another deep breath and knocked for permission to enter Mother Superior's office. It was answered right away. Anxiously, I stepped into the room and closed the door behind me. She motioned to the straight-backed chair in front of her desk. "Please, have a seat. I will just be a moment." It was another indication that we were not going to have a friendly little chat.

Gently perfumed with the faint scent of candles and incense, the white walled room was spacious and orderly. Three tall windows looked out over a great expanse of lawn. The only sound came from the ticking of a clock. The stone floor was covered by a few rugs in rich colors of burgundy and blue.

Furnishings were limited and functional. Bookcases held volumes bound in dark leather. Her large desk was empty, but with enough scars and nicks to suggest that it had been there for a while. A large cross, a photograph of the current Pope, a framed painting of the Virgin Mary ascending to Heaven, and a few green plants in a corner softened the austerity of the room.

There was little to hold my attention. And maybe it was planned that way. Saint and sinner alike had to face Mother Superior without distraction of any kind, making all sit still and solemn in the chair of judgment. It gave the event an uncomfortably hushed and formal feeling.

I stopped myself. Someday not only my activities but my irreverent thoughts would get me into trouble. And I already had enough of those.

Mother Superior had been writing something. After several minutes she put down her pen and regarded me silently for a long moment

"The reason for this meeting has occurred quicker than I would have liked," she said. "Yet visiting with you is the only way to resolve this issue. Please know that I am not here to judge but to make sense of your behavior. I have some questions and I would like at least a few answers. Sister Maria Serena already shared her account," she continued, "however, I would like to hear your side. Today's action is entirely out of character. Do you have anything you want to say to explain yourself?"

Her eyes looked tired but she spoke firmly, like someone accustomed to solving problems. And I was sure that in her opinion I was one of them. Nothing I did would come as a great shock.

Mother Superior inclined her head. "I am aware that your father passed away recently. Is that what is upsetting you?" she asked.

Now we were on dangerous ground. Pain pressed like a fist against my throat; a warning not to spend too much time thinking about my loss. Losing my father had left a chasm in my life that I would never be able to step over. I still could not think of him in the past tense. So yes, I knew about grief. I knew how hollow a person could feel after losing someone they loved.

Could she understand even a small part of it? But more importantly, if I did say something it was certain that my mother would learn of it. And that would bring problems of a far worse kind. If she were asked, Mother Superior would find it difficult to lie. In fact she wouldn't do so. It was better for me to remain silent and not provide too much in the way of explanation. Half-truths and sins of omission seemed the better option.

"We are not as sheltered as you might imagine," Mother Superior said. "Life has a way of testing us wherever we are."

Sure it did! Was she serious? Nuns lived in sequestered surroundings. Gliding about in silent efficiency in their own *Sea of Tranquility*, opportunities for virtue were immense. By comparison my life was as unsettled as dandelion fluff in a fitful breeze.

Yet I would feel stifled in their closet-sized bedrooms, appropriately called cells. The nuns didn't even have to be concerned about what to wear on any given day. Or, heaven forbid, worry about running into someone wearing the same outfit. Even at my age, life had more variety than theirs. And I could always make additions.

I knew that my cynical side was showing and Mother Superior would be a stranger to that emotion. Dressed in black, there was a regal quietness about her. A white wimple framed her face. Over it she wore a black veil. Slender and tall, she made everything appear dignified. It was not the gold cross she wore that set her apart but rather the way she walked, ate her meals, and conveyed the weekly devotional.

We students frequently speculated why someone with her gifts and abilities would join a religious order and devote her entire life to it. I would never be capable of such soul-deep dedication. But maybe she was one of those people who had been born obedient.

"Perhaps I should find out if you intend to continue your present course of action?" Mother Superior inquired. "And we are discussing today's situation, not any transgressions of the past. Is that not so?"

Transgressions, as she called them, was a strong word to use for my random lapses, and not the one I would have chosen. Adventurous misconduct was the explanation I was leaning towards, but she had a point. A small whisper of hope threaded through my mind, and for an instant I was tempted to confide in her. Then just as quickly I decided against it.

In this environment one learned to withhold small pertinent truths. I was not skilled in the language of trust, but some things I knew for certain. You had to be careful with whom you shared anything important. Secrets were unpredictable allies, only making us feel safe. Mother Superior and I had nothing in common. My life was far removed from the order and peace she knew.

She must have sensed that I had misgivings about her sincerity. "I already know you are clever, Andrea," she said, "and you certainly don't lack daring. But even here, rules are not merely suggestions. They provide a structure for us to follow. We all abide by them and know what is expected of us. Yet there is reason to believe that you were the instigator of a prank only recently brought to my attention. Your imagination has an impressive reach. And though creativity is to be commended, in situations like this it cannot be encouraged."

A brief smile curved her mouth. "You have given us some never-to-be forgotten moments; although for the good of the school and in fairness to you, the other students, and the staff, it has to stop before it becomes too disruptive. I am relying on you to give me your promise and to keep it."

During the silence that followed, I tried to imagine the necessary changes. As far as my pranks were concerned, I supposed I could try to discontinue these supplementary activities. The trouble was that thoughts emerged without effort, like water bubbling up from a deep well, replenishing themselves automatically. Everything I needed for inspiration was within easy reach. A few weeks ago I had slipped an extra amount of starch into what was jokingly referred to as 'wimple water'. The wimples had dried as stiff as cardboard. They couldn't be ironed, and the sisters had to start the process all over again.

Sister Maria Serena referred to my 'gift of imagination' in uncharitable terms, but that is how I saw them. And often enough they worked to my advantage. The most recent – was when I'd taken as many of Etta's black socks as I could find and sewn each pair together at the toes.

My first idea had been to subject her pleated gray skirt – a part of our uniform – to the same treatment. But with that much sewing, I had decided that an effort spent on the socks would be more rewarding. When it was done I was satisfied. The small black stitches would take some time to undo. Petty, yes, and not a principled act, but I would take my revenge where I could find it. Eventually my creativity would bring diminishing returns, yet I had to admit that right then it felt good.

"What exactly is it you are searching for?" Mother Superior asked gently. It caught me off guard.

That was not difficult to answer. I wished to be in a place free of constant evaluation; a place that was familiar to me and where I didn't have to earn every moment. I missed Papa and my friend Ilse. I wanted to be with them, not here where everything was calibrated and organized down to the last minute. Even school bells dictated schedules.

My life was shrinking to the point where someday soon it could be contained in a thimble. In Malix, my days were largely unsupervised and uncluttered with expectations.

If the truth be told, I would willingly give up some of my independence, but I resented the heavy-handed manner with which it was taken away. Had Mother Superior any idea about the depth of resentment within me?

"You are not alone," Mother Superior said. "And I am not your enemy. I am sure there are things you could teach me. Can we not learn from each other?"

She leaned forward, searching for something in my face, then she stopped herself, as if she knew the answer but wanted the response coming from me.

"Since you are unwilling to cooperate, we will bring this

conversation to a close," she said, her tone reproving. "You are one of our most gifted students, and I had expected better of you. You leave me no option but to find a suitable reprimand for your behavior."

I saw that she was disappointed and shame plucked at the edges of my anger. The pursuit of justice ranked high on my list of activities. As soon as my one-sided conversation with Mother Superior was over, Etta would be the beneficiary of my undivided attention. It would be my pleasure and my duty to do so.

CHAPTER 19

A SUITABLE REPRIMAND

Still angry, I skipped the rest of my afternoon classes and helped Karl the grounds-keeper, rake leaves into deep piles. I felt comfortable working beside him. Associating with the 'hired help' as my mother called them went against her idea of proper manners. Even at home she became upset when I disregarded her wish, but it was not the main reason why I enjoyed Karl's company. I absorbed quite a bit of knowledge from him. For a little while I could almost stop thinking about the trouble awaiting me.

By the time the work was done, twilight covered everything in gray. It exactly matched my mood. Relieved that a trying day had come to an end, I couldn't wait to get to my room.

Enclosed in the parcel from Malix had been a note and a small metal canister. I had been allowed to keep both, but it was only at bedtime when everything was silent at last that I opened them.

First – the letter. Papa was not a letter writer. That task had also fallen to Uschi. It was easy for me to picture the two of them sitting at their kitchen table, discussing what should be included; carefully erasing then replacing a sentence until it said what they wanted me to know. I hungrily read and re-read the lines, even though I knew each word after the first time. The pages would soon begin to tear, but for right now they gave assurance that someone cared, that I had not become inconsequential.

Next – the container. Inside was one of Papa's blue and white checkered handkerchiefs. It still had the familiar combined scents of animals, of hay and straw, and his pipe smoke. Uschi must have taken it to the barn and left it there for a few days. After it had absorbed enough scents, she had placed it in a small canister and sent it to me in a package.

When I held it to my face a yearning for Malix swept up like a wave. With no one to hear or judge me, I wept tears of anger and pain and whatever else tears are made of until I was empty; the handkerchief clenched in my hand, my only source of comfort. Night swallowed the day but not my loneliness.

In the morning the meaning of Mother Superior's 'suitable reprimand' became clear. If anyone had asked me to describe my punishment, I would have said it was right up there in the nightmare category. Only someone with Sister Maria Serena's way of thinking could put such a penalty into effect.

It was customary for students and teachers to take our meals in the dining hall at long tables set up in a horseshoe shape. Today the configuration was different. A smaller table had been set up at the open end. And to my dismay I saw that on it was a large silver platter holding my sandwich.

We all stood before our chairs, taking our seats after a nod from Sister Maria Serena. When she stood up to speak, her finely honed self-righteousness intact, I realized what was coming.

"At this esteemed institution," she began, "we pride ourselves not only on the academic achievements of you, our students, but on your integrity. We have no secrets from each other. Or should I say we did not have any, because regrettably one of you has fallen short of our standards. By acting in a deliberate and selfish manner she has dishonored a tradition long held dear."

Sister Maria Serena paused as though she had to explain something that shouldn't need to be explained. Her parents had served as missionaries in China and she sometimes shared information learned there with us, such as the Chinese *one hundred kinds of silence*. I didn't know if that was based on fact, but it surely felt as if she were making her captive audience experience ninety-nine versions of them.

"After painful deliberation on our part," she said, one word at a time, as if sentences had not yet been invented, "It has been decided that the student in question will stand at this table. She saw nothing wrong in eating this sandwich in secret. Let us see how comfortable she is eating it while facing her peers. There will be no other food for her until she has complied."

Her voice grew louder – or perhaps the silence grew. As a rule, Sister Maria Serena talked at such a high speed that it was hard to understand her without total concentration. But today she imparted her information in a clear and condescending tone. And since the hall echoed at the slightest sound, her message carried all the way to the back.

At first there had been a few snickers, but when she finally stopped, the room was tense and uncomfortable, with some students exchanging nervous glances. Mealtimes in the dining hall were seldom noisy. Today it was deathly quiet.

Looking along the rows, Sister Maria Serena asked "Any questions?" As if she didn't know that no one would dare raise their hand. Not here. But the students' minds were busy. I could see it in their eyes. Although conscious of some drama in the air, they had learned not to express a thought; were not expected to do so. This nun would not want competition.

Her words, full of reproach, hung in the air. Had they come from Mother Superior, they would have been less harsh, but it was Sister Maria Serena who had delivered the verdict. Devoid of subtlety, she might as well have mentioned my name. A few of those present were still trying to make sense of what was going on, but the vast majority of students already knew. There was small hope of such an event not circulating. And since my sandwich and I were prominently displayed, no one needed to guess the identity of the culprit.

I'd had better days, but thank goodness at least the first phase of my penance was behind me. Score one for Sister Maria Serena. Only she knew what the next chapter would deliver.

I spent the evening somewhere between discontent and self-pity. Self-pity was not all that productive, however, I decided to indulge myself anyway. I must have slept some time during the night, but when it was time to get up I did not feel rested.

The nightmare of the previous day continued. If anything, it became more challenging as the hours wore on. I went to class with the others, but starting with breakfast while the other students were eating, I again stood and faced them, full of undigested anxiety, defiant and afraid all the same. Hardly inconspicuous, I tried to look calm and avoid any show of weakness. I was far from it, though I wouldn't give anyone the satisfaction of discovering that little detail.

I knew their names yet I wouldn't call them friends. They kept their distance, avoiding me as if I were contagious. A few had deliberately turned away. It hurt but at the same time it made it easier. Also easier was the absence of Mother Superior.

At lunch and again at dinner I stood tethered to my assigned spot; my misery level somewhere between uncomfortable and excruciating. This was certainly the worst consequence of my action. But I had no regrets.

Given the chance I would do it again. If Sister Maria Serena expected me to hang my head in contrition, she had underestimated me. I was already suffering enough. Any lengthy posture of meekness would just make my neck ache so that simply was not feasible. I could feel her watching me without overtly doing so, if such a thing were possible. But hers would be a long wait. I didn't view this as a challenge of wills, though she might see it that way.

Out of my reach, the dining hall's straight-backed chairs had never looked so good. And to think that not long ago I had wished to be free from their hard surface. Sister Maria Serena insisted the chairs were that way for a reason. We had to sit on them with straight backs and on the edge. Character building, she called it.

Standing in the potent quiet I was building something as well – something with tools readily available in the revenge department. Thankfully meals never lasted long, yet they gave me enough time to promise dire consequences in the way I glared at Etta. Was it my imagination or did the freckles on her face turn pale?

As the hours went by, only marginally less trying than those of the day before, I also thought of my friend Monika. To my relief, her punishment had been more appropriate to the offense. Her sentence: five essays on the topic of unselfishness. Books dealing with the lives of saints should provide a fertile research ground. Our teachers had nothing but praise for the saints' many good qualities and held them up to us as examples to follow. For them the keeping of commandments had presented no difficulty. And here I was, wrestling with my conscience over a piece of bread.

Day finally surrendered to evening but my anger was still at a low boil. When Monika came to see me, I asked if I had missed anything noteworthy. "No. But everyone is talking about the deep trouble you're in." She didn't say, "I told you somebody would notice," because she was too good a friend.

I wasn't in the mood to talk nor was my misery keen to have company. But when I saw that Monika had saved a good portion of her food for me, I started to laugh.

"What's so funny?" Monika asked, not sure what to make of my reaction.

"A lay sister secretly brings me something to eat and now you do the same. If I gain weight on this specific diet, one horrid nun will be very puzzled. You know the one I mean – the chief source of piety in the place. It almost makes me want to try it."

My friend had quietly accepted Sister Maria Serena's punishment and even now was far more charitable towards her than I. "I wish you wouldn't talk like that," she said. "Sister Maria Serena is only worried because she is in charge of us. She has to be aware of everything and that includes paying attention to details."

I could rely on Monika to be my conscience but that did not mean I always agreed with her. She truly believed that this sister negotiated with heaven on our behalf. I had a different and equally strong opinion.

"Oh, please, you must be joking. Memory is no problem for her. She is old enough to recollect the flood and minute facts of what has happened since then. She's never been the forgive-and-forget type. Maybe she was born sour. Or maybe she is nasty for the fun of it. Anyway, I'm just doing what she expects. On my part that is only polite."

Monika gave me a knowing look. "You can see how well that worked."

"You're right," I admitted. "I'm in enough trouble. But tell me what I should do. Everything that interests me is outside these walls. Have I mentioned how much I hate it here?"

"Several times," she assured me. "But where would you go?"

"Honestly, I don't know. After two years at this place I should be used to it and I'm not. I was caught the last time I tried to go to Malix. My mother is in control. At least until I'm eighteen. Too bad I can't go into hiding like the nuns. But I'm temperamentally unsuited for their schedule of getting up at dawn and spending hours in prayer. I just don't seem to have the humility they require."

"Among other things," Monika agreed. "But now I'd better leave. You're not going to do anything stupid, right?"

I nodded, with as little commitment as possible. "Define stupid."

Monika rolled her eyes. "You think too much. You know that? I'll try to come back tomorrow. And stop worrying. The worst is behind you."

Perhaps she knew more than I did. Unable to sleep, I stared at the walls and tried hard to believe her.

The next two days were dismal carbon copies of the first. By now my poor piece of bread, still on the platter, was turning in on itself.

For breakfast on the third day I was allowed to re-join the other students. I never learned what happened to my sandwich.

CHAPTER 20

CERCA TROVA

"Mother Superior would like to see you," Sister Maria Serena said, shooting me a reproving glance.

I bit my lips, willing myself not to answer and by now smart enough to know what thoughts I needed to keep to myself.

How could this sharp-tongued misery muffin be in so many different places at once? The nun didn't actually tiptoe, but it felt like it the way she managed to appear abruptly out of nowhere.

Since the last incident I had tried to avoid her and because of it our paths had crossed less often. It also kept me from being a target. But now the school's self-appointed conscience keeper was here again.

She had a habit of muttering to herself as she walked away, but audible enough for the target of her remarks to hear. And I was not hard of hearing.

I took another deep breath. Was she trying to humiliate me, or just being her disgruntled self? In the past, I had allowed myself to be intimidated. But I had gained some knowledge and her predictable words, worn away by frequent usage, had lost their power.

Given the opportunity Mother Superior would probably ask me to change my attitude towards Sister Maria Serena, or at least try to find a shred of sympathy for the nun. That would take a substantial adjustment. Total forgiveness was unrealistic; even understanding her might not be possible – at any rate not for me.

Other than telling me to report to Mother Superior, Sister Maria Serena had said nothing.

For her this was unusual, because no matter how small a student's infraction, she would know details. And it was the reason why something in her attitude made me uneasy.

It had been almost two months since I had spoken to Martha and there hadn't been any hint of a problem. And the same was true here at the school. My mind did a rapid inventory of misdeeds I had committed lately. With the exception of a little bit of mopping up, I had done nothing to draw undue attention to myself.

My association with Etta was progressing well, especially after I decided that I should find out why she acted so despicably. I'd had a lot of practice in overcoming my fears. I knew what it was like to be measured and found wanting. Perhaps Etta also suffered from feelings of inadequacy and coped with them in another way – her way.

When Mother Superior first suggested that Etta and I become friends, I had almost laughed at the idea. Snitches did not bring out the best in me. I didn't like them and Etta was the one to invite my anger. By comparison my relationships with the other students had been relatively effortless.

Irmgard, one of my few friends, was physically challenged. She could only walk with the aid of crutches yet I had never seen her other than cheerful. With a delightfully wicked sense of humor, though also a little shy, she was fun to be around – in stark contrast to Etta.

But there was no denying that Mother Superior's words had prodded my conscience.

Where Etta was concerned I felt the heavy hand of guilt on my shoulder. I had to admit to being part of the problem. And I would be letting down Mother Superior, myself – and maybe even God – if I didn't make amends.

For the first little while Etta flinched whenever I came near her. I had never hit anyone in my life, so I was not sure why she would respond that way. Whatever the cause, she still knew better than to antagonize me. It took a while before we learned to tolerate each other in a wary, superficial truce. Etta would never be my friend, nor I hers, but there was no reason for us to remain adversaries.

Familiar with the long hallway to Mother Superior's office, I once again took my time getting there. My visits had become habitual. But I sensed that today was an exception and I tried to shake off my feelings of imminent doom. It was unusual to get a summons from her during class time.

"Your mother left a message for you. It seems that your time with us is coming to an end. You are to go to England." Mother Superior paused, allowing me to absorb the information. "The necessary tickets have been purchased for you. I have them here. Your mother's chauffeur will pick you up in two hours."

I listened with a strange detachment. The words flowed over me as I faced the fact that my mother had once again overturned my life.

My mother. Always my mother. No wonder I associated any bad news with her. It didn't help that she never said anything to me directly. Messages had always come through a third party, as they did now. Frankly, I was surprised that she herself had made the call.

"Regrettably, she will not be there to welcome you," Mother Superior continued. "She is accompanying your stepfather on a business trip to Hong Kong and hopes you'll understand."

There were instructions on what I needed to pack, but given the limits on what students owned I did not have very much. There were also instructions as to what was expected of me once I reached Great Britain. Moving there eliminated all plans for a return to Malix. And the loss of that hope was devastating. I had already been enrolled at a school in England and the thought of it stretched before me like a long prison sentence.

It was one thing to experience a journey of one's choosing. It was quite different to be plunged into it because of someone else's decision. I had successfully traversed the grim terrain of this boarding school. Loneliness is a tutor and I had many lessons to my credit, but I was not eager to continue with that kind of education. Would another round of misery really accomplish anything?

Having spent much of my life traveling alone, the journey itself was not the problem. The problem was the journey's end, because no matter how many times I told myself not to be afraid, I had a good idea of what awaited me on the other side of the channel. Compared to that future, staying here at this school no longer seemed so unbearable.

In a way I had known another upheaval was coming. I was used to it, if one could ever get used to unpredictability. Now, there was no more guesswork and I was too tired for anger. Thrown off balance for a moment, but not shocked – not really. Although the randomness of my mother's actions had never made sense to me, I recognized a pattern. It was the one constant in my life.

What made her keep me at arm's length? Something about her was unreachable and I didn't how to find it. Had she decided not to care in case she lost me just as she had lost my brother? Was it something in me and had she done the same with my father? And when and how had she learned to do it so well? There had to be a reason. There were always reasons, I just didn't understand most of them.

Everything in my future seemed disturbingly bleak. I absolutely dreaded having to start all over in yet another country. Surrounded again by strangers, where I knew nothing but words; knew nothing of the day-to-day living. Feeling out of place, a moving target without defenses, left me too vulnerable. And a litany of assurances would change nothing, even if they came from Mother Superior. I was tired of listening to people who had no idea about what I was feeling.

I had readied myself for a lecture; instead there was silence, measured and still. But it was not the kind of silence associated with the lack of sound. In the quiet there was a form of peace.

"My dear child," Mother Superior said at last. "You will discover that life does not always appear to be fair. Now and then we human beings fall short of each other's expectations. It cannot be helped because none of us are perfect. But whatever your future holds, don't disappoint yourself, Andrea. Life is a journey with a destination. And you have one chance in it... one precious chance holding untold possibilities.

"We are all part of something bigger than ourselves. Do not throw away this gift of grace by pursuing unimportant matters. Not everything needs to be a battlefield. Reach for goals that are worth reaching for."

There was unspoken advice layered between her words. She wanted me to recognize that some things needed to unfold in their own time and in their own way. Her remarks carried no reproach. We both knew they were not made in reference to my school activities. Perhaps Mother Superior had not been so insulated by her position after all. She must have understood the tangle of anger and loneliness I had felt. And I suddenly realized that it was more than a surface understanding.

It was all so clear now. Why had I not seen this before and how long had it been there? Blind to the obvious, what else had I failed to notice? Our association could definitely have been less trying, because what she thought of me mattered more than I wanted to admit. Right then I would have promised anything to thank her for her kindness, for never giving up on me, or automatically believing the worst. I felt a surge of gratitude – and an impulsive and unfamiliar wish to hug her – but there were invisible barriers one did not cross.

"We shall miss you. Please keep in touch with us. We would like to know of your whereabouts." A wry smile touched Mother Superior's face. "Eventually even Sister Maria Serena might agree that it is dull around here without you."

Tears blurred my eyes and I tried to blink them away. Mother Superior had stood by me even though my mutinous behavior must have caused her a fair amount of anxiety. At least with me gone, the school would be quiet again.

If Mother Superior sensed my emotional state she did not acknowledge it.

"Your car will be here shortly," she said. "It is time for you to leave but before you do I would like to give you something to remember us by."

Coming into the office I had noticed a paperweight on her otherwise empty desk. Mother Superior stood up, took the paperweight and placed it in my hands. "It belonged to my father. He was an enthusiastic student of history and gave this to me when I assumed my current responsibilities. And now I would like you to have it."

Taken by surprise I was speechless. How could she part with something so valued? I wanted to tell her that I could not accept such extraordinary generosity, but a glance at her eyes told me that she would not take no for an answer.

"Thank you," I said quietly, knowing I would never be able to thank her enough. And not only for this gift.

I studied the weight more closely. Written in minute calligraphy on parchment, but magnified by the heavy glass, were the words CERCA TROVA.

"There is some history connected with them. Do you know

what they mean?" Mother Superior asked.

I shook my head. Was I letting her down again, now of all times? I really didn't remember learning anything about this specific topic. Perhaps it had been covered during one of my numerous stints in solitary.

"You have read about the life of the great genius, Leonardo da Vinci, yes?" she continued.

"Yes," I whispered, glad that I was able to offer this, no matter how insignificant, but wishing I could think of something else to add.

Yet it was enough for Mother Superior, and she nodded in approval. "Good. Then you will recall his painting of the Battle of Anghiari. The original is believed to have been lost, however, fragments of copies made by other artists have survived. And that is how we come by those words seen on a flag.

"CERCA TROVA means 'He who seeks, finds.' I have tried to live by these words. I am afraid not always successfully and I expect you to do better. I see myself in you, although I don't believe I was ever quite as fiery and strong-minded. But I would like to think that if I'd had a daughter she would have been like you. Go with God, my child. I will keep you in my thoughts, and you will always be in my prayers. Be strong and have faith."

She did not utter anything else but for a moment, and a moment only, her hand on my head said everything. Then it was gone, leaving me aware of its sudden absence.

"Please… Forgive me," I managed.

I looked at her, and this time my tears would not be stopped.

CHAPTER 21

NESTS IN THE IVY

Gathering my few belongings had not taken long. Everything had fit into one suitcase.

While packing I had tried to answer Monika's questions to the best of my ability. There was not much to tell when I myself had no answers as to what was going to happen next – I just knew what I feared.

In what seemed like no time at all I was on a train and heading north. Looking out the window, I saw small towns and villages strung along the river. Green meadows and farmland divided plough-furrowed fields with Lombardy poplars marking the boundaries. Mountains reminded me of tawny-haired lions, their paws resting in the valleys; the Rhine raced along, wild and swift.

At last I arrived in Hoek van Holland. Tickets in hand I

walked with other passengers through the noise and commotion of the harbor. The air smelled of fuel, oil and ropes.

Then came the call to board for the eight hour overnight ferry boat ride to Harwich, England; one of the means to connect the Continent with Great Britain.

The rumble of engines vibrated under my feet. In a whirl of activity, whistles, shouted commands, and cars clattering past, the ships horn blasted, the ferry came to life with a shudder and lurched into the restless, unsettling heave of the English Channel. Whitecaps turned over without rhythm. The horizon was invisible, earth and sky faded into a gray nothingness. And each mile put distance between Malix and my uncertain future.

Following instructions I found my cabin and soon the hypnotic hum of the ferry's engines lulled me to sleep. The uneventful crossing was followed by a train ride to the city of Norwich.

Sarah and Jeff Newman, Henry's sister and brother-in-law, picked me up at the train station and took me to Henry's farm. Hill Farm to be correct, located twelve miles from Norwich.

Sarah was a cheerful, matronly type with an enthusiastic laugh, blue eyes in a kind honest face and brown hair.

"Is this your first visit to England? I hope you will like it here," she said in a convincing tone. "You can always call me if you need anything. I'm here and happy to help. But right now let's have a look around, shall we?"

I did not know what I had been expecting. What I found was a gracious, red brick, two-story house set in an expansive lawn. A large bronze beech tree, planted so long ago that its branches brushed the ground, had a space all to itself. A ha-ha divided the sheltered formal garden filled with rosebushes.

A graveled driveway led to the double front doors. Entering, I saw a large grandfather clock; the living room was on the left, the farm office, a butler pantry, a kitchen and the dining room were on the right. Big windows provided a lot of light.

A curving staircase went to the upper floor, with a cascading runner covering the steps. Bedrooms opened up on both sides of a carpeted hallway (a total of seven and each with its own fireplace). A window in a large bathroom had the best view of the valley.

The ground-level back door led to the scullery where it was always cool. Pheasants and other game birds would hang there for a few days, until it was decided to cook them.

Thick-stemmed ivy thrived unchallenged on the walls of an old potting shed; a convenient place for birds to build their nests. A vegetable plot showed off its peas, lettuce, onions, broccoli and brussel sprouts. A fig tree, trained to grow along a wall, utilized the afternoon sunshine. Herring-bone patterned walkways separated one section from another.

A hedgehog and a number of cats who lived in the barn shared saucers of milk. Shep, a black and white border collie, tolerated them all. He helped bring in the herd of brown and white Ayrshire cows from the pasture. There were one hundred and forty-five of them and given their numbers, they were milked by machine.

Three small barns housed new calves that were being bottle fed, then taught to drink from a pail. Some of the outbuildings looked as if they had evolved over time. A central courtyard, formed by the house's walls and those of other farm buildings, was enclosed by a double gate.

I didn't know all that much about farms, English or otherwise, but I could tell that this one was owned by someone who did.

After introducing me to the housekeeper, a stout solid woman named Mrs. Gray, Sarah left. Mrs. Gray's first name was Nellie but no one called her that. She had moved here from Scotland and her speech was laced with the accent of that country. Economical, she seldom said a lot, as if she had decided to spend only a certain amount of words on any given day.

Amazingly, she could touch the ground in front of her with her hands flat and keeping her knees perfectly straight. "Watch me," she said out of the clear blue. "Can you do that?" And proceeded to demonstrate. I thought it was remarkable. And just to be on the safe side I told her that this feat was impossible for me since I hadn't tried it since sometime around kindergarten.

The large kitchen was Mrs. Gray's territory. Here she turned out hearty meals on the kitchen's large red Aga stove. In the mornings the sideboard, almost bowed by the heft of plenty, was covered with dishes of eggs, fried potatoes, bacon, sausages, tomatoes and mushrooms. There was always a large pot of porridge served with heavy cream. The rest of the offerings included toast and Dundee marmalade, a dark, bitter orange jam. I especially liked her crumpets, scones, and bannocks – warm, flaky biscuits eaten with butter and homemade jam. Once in a while there would be smoked kippers poached in milk.

Mrs. Gray wasted nothing. Apples, their flesh wrinkled from storage, were considered good to eat and transformed into dishes such as apple flummery or delicately flavored Eve's

Pudding. A treacle tart, lemon custard or shortbread could also be dessert.

On Friday evenings the eagerly awaited fish and chip van arrived at the farm. The driver had a standing order for news-paper wrapped fish and chips and we always ate them in ap-preciative silence.

I learned that Henry hired day laborers when needed and that he also had two tenant farmers, Ken and Mr. Simpson. Ken, in his mid-thirties, and the younger of the two, took care of the cows.

Of slight build and not too tall, he was amazingly strong for his size. His looks were unremarkable until he smiled his slow-moving river kind of smile, with wrinkles forming a star-burst at the corners of his blue-gray eyes. His eyelashes were sparse and even a mustache struggled to take hold on his nar-row face. Untroubled, Ken was the kind of person who didn't worry about tomorrow until it arrived. As far as I could tell, ambition did not crowd his days. At least he showed no out-ward sign of it.

~~~

Hill Farm had its own bus stop. While getting ready for my first day at school I had missed the bus to take me into Nor-wich. Mrs. Gray, watching from a window, noticed my dilemma and coached me in the fine art of hitchhiking.

Not having done this before, I skeptically held out my hand. At this early hour not many vehicles moved on the country road. A few of them drove past until finally a farmer in his small truck stopped right next to me. In the back were five full grown pigs on their way to market.

Viewing the odorous collection I had my doubts about entering the vehicle, but I didn't have the heart to decline the ride – not after the man had been nice enough to stop. Pride warred with practicality and I climbed in.

Nothing looked as if had been cleaned since it was new. The vinyl passenger seat was cracked and badly stained; fish and chip papers and crumpled candy wrappers were everywhere.

"Make yourself comfortable," the farmer said, smiling apologetically as he brushed the debris to the floor. I found his gesture oddly touching.

Wind, dust and engine exhaust rushed through the open window, making me choke and adding to my already disheveled appearance. The farmer didn't seem talkative, which was fine.

When we arrived in Norwich thirty minutes later, I took a realistic glance at myself in a mirror and boarded the next bus back to Hill Farm. I needed someone to laugh with me.

Ken was already at the milk shed, I could hear the clutter of pails. Only he was not alone. He was talking to a man with a deep authoritative voice. Surely it couldn't be Henry?

Henry was not expected until later in the month yet there he was, standing right next to Ken, and I felt a moment's irritation at finding him there.

"This is quite a surprise." Henry cleared his throat, but to me it sounded suspiciously like a chuckle.

Ken didn't have a mean bone in him, but after taking one glance at me he burst out laughing. It broke the strained, uncomfortable silence. "Eau de Oink. There has to be a market for it," he gasped.

Given the circumstances, it was kind of funny and perhaps years from now I would see it that way. Right now my mouth was dry, but I kept the smile on my face no matter how much it wanted to slide off. The reunion with Henry, if one could call it that after only one brief meeting, had happened without preparation on my part. And his demeanor didn't help.

So this was my mother's new husband. A few inches over six feet tall, with dark hair, steady gray eyes and smooth skin, his jaw strong and slightly squared. I could see why she would find him attractive. And it was just one more reason I didn't like him.

There had to be a code of behavior governing something like the present situation. I just didn't know what it could be. Mother Superior was fond of saying, "When you leave a room, leave a good impression." It was too late for that in this case. The whole experience was a miserable start to what I was convinced would be a miserable relationship.

Feeling silly at best, I squared my shoulders, gathered up what remained of my dignity and left the shed. One thing was certain! I would not stay here for long! No matter who or what would try to stand in my way.

CHAPTER 22

A HORSE NAMED MAJOR

To me, my father was irreplaceable and I was determined to honor his memory. Nothing could fill the space where he was supposed to be. Even so, some of my memories were becoming harder to recall no matter how hard I tried to hold on to them. I guessed that my mother had already totally forgotten him or she could not have fallen in love with a man who had fought against us in a war not that long ago.

At Hill Farm, everything I saw reminded me of Malix. But for the foreseeable future my life was going to be exactly as it was now with me remaining on the edge of things. Yesterday was the same as today, as tomorrow, and the chain of days after that would be.

And then something completely unexpected happened –

something that broke the monotony.

"He goes by the name of Major," Henry said, "and he'll be in the pasture or that stall over there. He's yours if you can manage him."

A short while ago I would have considered his comment to be fighting words and responded angrily. But one look at the gorgeous four-legged creature standing next to Henry and I was lost. How could I not be?

With the exception of a white blaze down his forehead, Major was all black. I had not been on a horse for a few years and I had told myself that I didn't miss it. I had been wrong. Major had a beautifully shaped head and eyes so deep and dark they appeared almost liquid. To say that I liked him seemed inadequate. I had known him less than five minutes and I already adored him. My love of horses was one of the few things that had not changed. When my father was alive I'd had a horse of my own, but it was stabled at a riding academy and someone always had to drive me there.

Major had watched me with calm, confident eyes. Now he lowered his head as if giving me permission to touch him. Slowly, I reached out and let him get my scent; his velvety lips soft against my hand.

I knew enough about horses to recognize quality when I saw it. And Major was quality. There was nothing at all wrong with him...but everything wrong with the man who had given him to me.

Henry Peverell. I called him Henry. I had forced myself to practice the name so that it would come more naturally. So far without success. Legally he was my stepfather – as in one long step removed. And as much enthusiasm as I brought to the relationship, it might as well have been a thousand miles. He was a complication I didn't need right now… or at any time. Just thinking about the new dynamics made me feel uncomfortable. I didn't like Henry and had no wish to be in his debt. But this was not only about debt.

"Here, let Major have one of these apples," Henry suggested. "He would eat them by the bushel if we allowed it. Why don't you take him out for a ride…get acquainted?"

Filled with eagerness yet about to refuse, I paused and bit my lip. Something told me that Henry was used to being obeyed. Trying not to let my excitement show and scolding myself for being weak, I did as he suggested.

As if all of this were not enough, Henry had chosen Major's saddle, the bit – everything – with care and it fit perfectly. Somehow his attention to detail did not surprise me.

It took me two tries to tighten the cinch with fingers that were suddenly clumsy. Henry's gift was generous and thoughtful and I should have been happy. But it didn't make up for all the changes that had happened with nothing to hold me in place.

I wanted things to go back the way they used to be. I was not ready to give him my trust and I resented his intrusion into my life. Yet problems could not be wished away, no matter how hard one tried. I might as well save my energy until I could do something effective about it.

"Thank you," I told him awkwardly.

Henry gave me a knowing glance. Not offended – amused – as if he had all but seen the thoughts written on my forehead. I wondered uneasily how he could be so sure.

And then I remembered. He was married to my mother. She wouldn't have told him much about me, just whatever served her purpose. And that was a concern.

Being obligated did not bring out the best in me. There were days when I felt I would choke on my resentment. Anger, at first a constant visitor, became my new best friend. I wasn't about to let it go. Caring for Major provided a welcome diversion, giving me something to do and think about. I brushed him with long, slow strokes until his coat gleamed. There was little else to claim my time and he happily absorbed each hour I wanted to share.

I frequently went to the pasture seeking solace and needing to convince myself that he was really there. He was simply amazing. Unable to keep an emotional distance, I loved him with a fierce possessive love, every regal inch of him, and at seventeen hands he was not a small horse.

Before long it felt as if we had known each other for years. Major seemed to sense my moods. His eyes, innocent yet somehow aware, made me want to talk to him. He was the most attentive listener I'd ever met, and I had a lot to tell him – he just didn't have any answers.

In some ways life in my new surroundings was not so different from the one in Malix. Because of my experiences in that village, livestock and barns here were oddly comforting and I decided to focus on what I knew. So when Ken asked me to accompany him on a tour of the farm I gratefully accepted. I liked his calm and unhurried manner. Cheery and optimistic, he never resorted to showy actions and I always knew exactly where I stood with him.

Ken was happy to explain the more detailed workings of

the large complex. On the way back to the house we passed the livestock area. Henry kept a few Aberdeen Angus, stocky, black-coated animals. The majority of the cattle in Henry's dairy herd were Ayrshires, a reddish-brown and white Scottish Breed.

Confined in a stall was the biggest bull I had ever seen, also of the Ayrshire strain, but there was nothing *airy* about him and I approached hesitantly. The way he turned his head and glared at us was a little unnerving.

We stood for a moment observing each other. I had no trouble picturing his ability to cause harm and was glad to be on the other side of a sturdy steel gate.

"Are you comfortable around him?" I asked Ken.

Ken thoughtfully tugged at his earlobe. "No, can't say I am. I keep my distance because that one is mean even on a good day and it doesn't take a lot to get on his bad side. When you're out riding, it might be smart for you and Major to avoid his territory," he suggested. "The bull isn't always fenced in and he can run fast. You won't be able to dodge him. Take my advice. There's no need to make life more exciting than it is."

As if to lend credibility to Ken's words, the bull butted his huge head against the gate. The impact was strong enough to make the ground shake and I thought it prudent to move back a few steps.

"Are you saying he would attack us?" I asked, alarmed. "Nothing can happen to Major!"

Ken gave me the rueful look country people bestow on city people, and he clearly thought I belonged to the latter category. "Well...," he answered somewhat evasively. "It all depends on his mood. You know, if he likes you or not. But the end is usually quick." He lifted one shoulder in a shrug and flashed me a mischievous smile.

I nodded and smiled back, knowing that I had made a friend.

CHAPTER 23

DRIVING LESSONS

lthough the calendar said it was the season of renewal, that eagerly awaited time was slow to take hold. Until suddenly, spring, with all its magic, traveled in overnight – making its intoxicating presence felt.

The air was like a soft caress and the countryside seemed dressed in soft-hued garments. First, delicate snowdrops and chaliced crocuses appeared. Daffodils standing like proud exclamation points bloomed with a sense of purpose. Buds softened stark branches. The color of leaves started to deepen and meadows were covered with the fuzzy green of new grass. Then came May and with it the scented clouds of creamy hawthorn blossoms.

Finally it was summer, my favorite time of the year because it meant no school. For weeks the air had been so still it barely moved, and nights brought little relief.

Thunderflies – small black insects whose bite was out of proportion to their size, ignored anyone else – but chose me as their favorite landing spot. They were a predictor of a storm two or three days before it arrived and frequently proved more reliable than the weather service with all its technical equipment.

My relationship with Henry remained strained and gray. Gray as fog and just as difficult to pin down. Though minimal courtesies were maintained, mostly we avoided each other.

Henry was proficient at everything he did. Perhaps all landowners were. But he was the only one I had met. He knew how to milk the cows, and he knew how to drive every piece of machinery on the estate. What he didn't know was how much I disliked living here. I had no responsibilities and there was nothing to make me feel useful.

I once overheard Henry's sister Sarah refer to me as a "poor lamb." And she had told him that he needed to be patient with me. I liked Sarah. She had been friendly right from the beginning. But I was not poor – and I wasn't a lamb. And what I didn't need from anyone was pity.

Time stared me in the face. With Mrs. Gray having everything under control there was little for me to do. I did not think she was all that aware of me but I learned otherwise. "If you want to do something productive, you can help in the garden," Mrs. Gray offered unexpectedly. To her this meant weeding, and I was not too enthusiastic about that specific task.

However, when she mentioned that a garden path could be improved with a brick-edged border, I quickly volunteered. There were bricks available from the remnants of an old shed.

They just needed the cement taken off to make them usable.

When Henry heard of my suggestion he gave me a dubious look, as if it were something I couldn't possibly manage. "I am no stranger to hard work. You English aren't the only people who know how to do things," I snapped.

"Indeed," he said, sounding faintly surprised.

I stole a glance at him, fully expecting him to be offended, but if he was, he didn't show it. I regretted the words as soon as they crossed my lips. I had thought I was past the anger but here it was again. In a calmer frame of mind I could have told him that after World War II many German children had gone into the wreckage of bombed-out buildings and done this very thing; my friends and I among them.

Day after day, using our fathers' hammers, we had chipped the cement off bricks, loaded them onto a wagon and sold them for pennies to a man who would then resell the material to a builder; beginning the process of rebuilding the nation.

I still remembered the painful blisters and the tiredness, but above all the sense of accomplishment we felt. Lining a garden path would not be more exhausting.

~~~

Harvest time did not decrease the pace of life at the farm. If anything, it became more hectic. Making maximum use of every moment of daylight, the field hands had been up since dawn. Even Ken's help was needed. That left Mrs. Gray and me to do the milking.

Within minutes we had developed an effective system. My job was letting the cows in and out of the milking shed. I washed their udders and swept the floor. Then Mrs. Gray took over. There was a calm give-and-take between her and the bovines.

The day hadn't yet made up its mind as to what else it would bring when Henry propelled it into a direction. "Andrea! Where are you?" he called. "We need you! The men are waiting. I'll explain on the way."

We quickly walked to his large sugar beet field on the other side of the highway. If I understood Henry correctly, I was to drive a tractor with a trailer attached. Not only that, but I had to make sure that the trailer remained parallel with the conveyor belt as the sugar beets came tumbling down. "When would you like me to start?" I asked, forcing assurance into my words.

Henry raised an eyebrow, which was not the answer I wanted. "Now!" he said. "We are understaffed. Get up there and drive the thing!"

His crisp words held no advice for me. Henry expected me to do this right now? I could hear the engine already running and I didn't know whether to laugh or cry. I had wanted to be useful but not in an area where I had no experience. And it was a little late to suddenly discover a previously hidden talent.

Competent, it wouldn't occur to Henry that I knew nothing about operating a tractor. Even Ken's children were familiar with all kinds of heavy equipment; knew the purpose of each knob and lever. I did not. Precious little of what the nuns had taught me was of use here. The convent school hadn't offered a course dealing with machinery. At any rate, in Germany it was illegal to drive until age twenty-one and I was seventeen. But there was no time to explain this to Henry. He would see it as an excuse and a short-lived one at that.

I felt self-conscious and angry. After months of not having me do anything, Henry had put me on the spot. But I recognized a test – a challenge – when I saw one and I intended to pass it. Forcing myself not to show the slightest hesitation, I climbed up, whispered a quick prayer, and released the brake as if I had done it many times before.

Henry gave me an appraising glance. "All set?" he asked. After another quick look he stood back with a satisfied nod. "Jolly good, then. I'll take that as a yes. I'll see you in a little while."

A sympathetic chuckle let me know that I was not alone. Aware of my predicament, Ken understood immediately. "Are you all right?" he asked, wiping the sweat from his face.

"No. I'm pretending, but I'll be fine," I said to myself as much as anyone else.

"Not to worry. You'll get the hang of it." Ken's genuine words made all the difference.

With Henry in charge, things went with military precision and in spite of myself, I was impressed. There was never anything uncertain or unprepared about him.

The overcast day had begun warm and soon turned muggy, filling up with heat as if with liquid. The hours took on a pace and rhythm of their own. Working mechanically I lost track of time, knowing only that I was focused on the task ahead and the number of rows left to do.

By the time we finished, the sun was sinking into a late afternoon. It fell slowly at this time of year – and when it did, it floated like a blood-red lantern over the valley.

Exhausted, and with a sense of relief I shut off the engine and rested my head on the steering wheel. Arms, legs, hands, everything ached, yet I was more content than I could remember. Though not without some anxious moments on my part, everything had gone smoothly enough. Along with the others in our small committed group I had accomplished something worthwhile. It was good to be useful – to belong – even in a momentary way.

Lightning bolts do not produce a storm, but they definitely contribute their share of drama, and thunder was quick to applaud the display. Watching, I smelled the rain on the hot thirsty earth before I saw it. At first it spattered in polka dots tapping politely. But soon the sky opened up and the deluge began until it came in bands that swept across the countryside; almost as if it were raining on the rain itself. Before long, gutters spat streams of water. Nature's cycles and circles dictated when people worked the land. We had finished this harvest just in time.

"Nicely done! That was quite an achievement. You have more than proven yourself," Henry told me at dinner. And I thought I saw something like amusement in his expression. "You could have panicked, but you didn't. Instinct served you well. And by the way, I was not taking chances. I knew you were capable."

I hadn't had enough compliments in my life to know how to acknowledge them graciously, and one given by Henry raised my suspicions. Yet I was also absurdly pleased by his approval.

CHAPTER 24

PRESENT ARRANGEMENTS

D ays and weeks funneled into each other. Slowly, the space between the familiar and the new became smaller. At times I even appreciated Henry. Our relationship had lightened since the 'day of the test'. I didn't want to praise him for more sterling qualities than he deserved, but I had become more comfortable around him. By avoiding any subject that could cause conflict we managed to have some argument-free conversations.

Even so, I wanted to move to Malix. Papa's home was a place where I would be free of my mother's constant criticism of me and comparisons to my brother. They weren't always spoken, but were there nevertheless. I had nothing useful to offer; had none of the attributes my mother valued. In her eyes my brother remained the ultimate example, perhaps even more so as time passed.

Her hope that I would grow to be like Wolfgang would not be realized, because I knew that I was incapable of being that person.

I also had loved him, so in my own way I even understood her grief. Yet I wanted my mother's approval so much it felt as if I must not have tried hard enough to earn it, when just the opposite was true. For a time, years ago, I had followed my father's suggestion and made a greater effort to please her, hoping that would help. If I could be good enough, patient enough, maybe, just maybe, I would finally succeed.

But nothing I did had been acceptable. It was much like an uneven step I couldn't help stumbling over. When anything I did turned out well I knew there were forces different from mine at work.

To someone like my mother this was inconceivable. "But to do it right is so easy," she said. And for her it was. I continued to be an embarrassment. Social standing and appearances were what mattered. And I could not satisfy her requirements.

She had been a confusing influence. Her approval mattered but not as much as it once had. When I thought of her it was with gratitude, resentment and sadness. And every shade of emotion in between.

There were old wounds, and the new, and at times I still felt duty-bound to justify my existence. A son mattered in my family, a son who would take over the business. I understood that very well. I was not the child my mother wished for, but I was the one she had been given, with feelings and wishes of my own. As it turned out, neither she nor I got our wish. I had longed to share that fact with her more than once, but our connection was too fragile to take even this slight a strain.

My staying at Hill Farm created a strain of another kind. Perhaps if I talked to her and carefully presented a request about leaving she would give her permission.

This time I intended to leave nothing to chance.

She and I finally made an appointment to meet and discuss the matter of Malix.

I had faced her before. Not often, because I inevitably up feeling diminished, and the result of the interaction stayed with me for days.

With her flawless manners and perfect make-up, my mother always made me feel earthbound. With her, nothing was left to chance. Not a strand of her shiny, well-cut hair was out of place. On this day she wore a charcoal-colored wool jacket, a soft gray blouse, a matching strand of pearls, gold earrings, a black wool skirt, and black pumps on her feet.

Knowing that my mother would search for something to criticize, I also had dressed with particular care.

A frown was an unusual visitor on her face; seeing it there now gave me an idea what the answer would be before I finished asking if she had changed her mind about my going to Malix. Her unapproachable elegance in place, my mother drummed her fingers on the arms of her chair. Silence, heavy and awkward, spoke volumes. And my mother could make silence speak louder than words. She did not look pleased and her eyes held a warning that I caught immediately.

"I see no need to alter the present arrangement," she told me with some impatience. "You suffer from an appalling lack of reasoning. Have you learned nothing over the past years?"

She would not give her permission. And that was what this conversation was truly about – the same words, just a different setting. I had practiced for hours, rehearsing the suggestions in my head, yet the discussion was concluded before it began.

I had not expected her to respond with enthusiasm, but today a strong sense of injustice hit me. Aware that this important moment was slipping away and stung by her casual dismissal, I took a deep breath and allowed my voice to change its mind. It didn't.

"But why can't I stay with Papa? You don't care about me," I blurted out with helpless anger. There. I'd said it.

My mother held up her hand. "I'll pretend I didn't hear that, but not another word. Isn't it enough that I tell you? I believe I heard myself say 'no'. There are lots of reasons. I take no pleasure in having to point them out, but let me make them clear – again – so there will be no further confusion. Your insistence of living in Malix is sheer nonsense. Sometimes I wonder if you are truly aware of your responsibilities."

Her words scraped to an unsatisfying end. And just like that, the subject was closed. I wondered if she had even listened to what I said.

'Lucky me, just what I need,' I thought, as Henry came into the room, no doubt ready to give his opinion.

My mother turned to him with an exasperated sigh. "Why must everything I tell her be met with stubborn resistance? She is obsessed with this village and it must be stopped."

An amused smile formed on Henry's lips and there was humor in his eyes.

"Can we look at it another way? What is wrong in letting

Andrea live where she'll be happy?" he asked. "She may not go about things the right way and occasionally her behavior does create problems, but have you always been an angel?"

My mother laughed. I looked at her with sad detachment and had trouble reconciling the image of the emotionally remote woman I knew her to be, with this cheerful, laughing person. I couldn't remember the last time I had heard her sound this carefree – perhaps never.

Knowing or guessing something, and seeing it were different matters. What I had not at first understood, I now grasped all too clearly. With Henry she came alive. My mother did not need Henry's permission to do anything – nor he, hers, but they valued each other's opinions. And his face lit up when he looked at her. He held out his hand toward my mother in obvious affection, as if she was the most important person in the universe. And to him she probably was. So much for English reserve. I might as well not be in the room.

Hurt and angry I turned away to keep from seeing more. Martha had been wrong. Time did not heal all wounds.

CHAPTER 25

MR. SIMPSON

H enry owned quite a bit of land and his holdings
needed constant attention. Every morning he went
over the day's projects with Mr. Simpson, the farm
foreman. Though Henry had ideas of his own, I didn't miss
the fact that when Mr. Simpson talked, Henry listened. "You
find people who know what they are doing and leave them to
do it," he enlightened me.

Mr. Simpson was a modest man, average in height, with a
stocky figure. The weathered skin of his face held a network
of wrinkles. Bushy eyebrows shadowed his faded blue eyes. He
had been a member of the British Navy; his mannerisms were
a little formal and he always addressed Henry as Sir.

He referred to himself as a jack-of-all-trades. His hands,
unused to inactivity, were gray with ground in oil and grease.

Even with swollen, painful-looking knuckles he could fix just about anything. Given the amount of machinery and the number of stables and barns on the property, there was always something in need of repair. He was also adept at cutting a long unbroken S from the skin of any apple.

In his spare time he liked to go pheasant hunting, never returning empty-handed. During the war years it had been a necessity, helping to put much needed food on the table. These days it was a more of a hobby, but he had done it for so long that he would not give it up now.

Gun casually held in the crook of his arm, solid, dependable, Mr. Simpson walked with the rolling gait of a man who had spent much of his life on the high seas. I liked going with him. Not that I was allowed to shoot anything or even carry a weapon, but the outing did get me away from the house.

Recently widowed, Mr. Simpson seemed pleased to have my company. "You'll have to be patient with me," he said. "Getting older means making a few adjustments. I'm not as nimble as I used to be. But from the neck up I'm OK."

He was a person more likely to smile than to laugh, even when something was quite funny. His good hearing ear was on the left side so that is where I walked, wearing the necessary Wellington boots.

We followed the fence line before striking out across the fields. Because of the high water level the ground was soft and marshy and there were drainage ditches for us to navigate. The sky looked like a gray sheet pulled clear to the horizon. But it was early enough not to be humid yet and it felt good to be out in the fresh air.

A few crows hopped away on twig-thin legs, however, they

were not the birds we were after. And a pheasant, drumming into sudden flight was also safe from us.

"I need to warm up first," Mr. Simpson explained.

We walked in silence. This was nothing new. No one could accuse my companion of talking just to keep the conversation going. He was a listening more than a talking man. If he had nothing to say he said nothing. And he never answered a question quickly when slowly was an option.

But today's silence was enough to start my misgivings.

That was the trouble with these kinds of thoughts. Martha called them intuition and she depended on them. She hadn't yet convinced me of that, though I had to agree that such things could be disturbingly correct even when they came out of nowhere. At other times they could be totally wrong; especially if you let fear enter first. Fear could distort anything.

Mr. Simpson cleared his throat, the way he did before he moved into a verbal mode.

"Courage doesn't necessarily come from being ignorant, you know," he said bluntly. "What you see depends on which eyes you see with. It probably wouldn't hurt you to listen to the colonel. He's usually right. How much do you actually know about him?"

So he was aware of my feelings concerning Henry. I thought I had heard something odd in Mr. Simpson's gravelly voice. A chill went over me that had nothing to do with any temperature.

I felt the seriousness of his question, but I couldn't understand why it should matter.

"Other than that he managed to ruin my life?" I asked, immediately on the defensive.

"You don't really believe that."

"Yes! I do!"

Mr. Simpson lifted up his hand. "You need to stop right there. There's a lot he hasn't told you."

Mr. Simpson was right. From what I could tell, Henry kept his business and his private life separate, seldom speaking about himself in a personal sense. It was easy to think that he knew nothing of disappointments and pain simply because he didn't show it.

But how was that my fault? He and I lived in an uneasy truce, both pretending not to notice each other, yet I had to admit that given the way I behaved towards him he had shown remarkable restraint in his interactions with me.

Mr. Simpson took off his cap and scratched his head. His hair had receded and he seldom let the sun reach what he referred to it as his thinking spot. "The colonel lost two members of his family in the war. His first wife died during an air raid in London. His brother was killed at the Front."

There was a sad weight to his words and oh, the effect they had. I stared at him in horror. Surely there had to be some mistake. Wouldn't I have learned something about this by now? What about my mother? Was she aware? And if so, why hadn't she mentioned it? No! None of this could be true, though the expression in Mr. Simpson's eyes told me that it was. No one could have faked the sadness there.

"How could this be? He, I mean Henry, never said anything," I stammered.

"Well, he wouldn't, would he? No purpose in that. What with him being a gentleman and knowing you had nothing to do with it. You were a child. Anyway, he isn't a person who lives in the past. He thinks people are basically good. Can't say I do, but he does. That's all there's to it."

His words were mortifying and I felt ashamed that I'd been so incredibly selfish. I should have known but concerned with my own problems, my own fears, I hadn't been particularly thoughtful or considerate of anyone else. I didn't want to realize all these things about myself. But here was Mr. Simpson holding up a mirror leaving me no escape--no choice but to look at its reflection.

The tragic, uncomfortable truth would always hover at the periphery. Complicated, subtle – waiting to be remembered – waiting to remind me. Pretending it didn't exist was not going to work. I had lived with a burden of guilt ever since Uschi had spewed her venom about all things German. And something of the poison had remained.

I had tried not to bring it closer, hoping that I didn't have to deal with it. Yet here it was again. It was what I expected; it was what I dreaded. And all of it was painfully familiar.

After leaving Switzerland I had tried to build up some armor against any accusations, knowing that English people would be more than justified in voicing them. It was what had scared me the most about coming here. Though I never admitted it to her, Martha had guessed correctly.

But no defense could cope with something like this. It would always be an outsider's sadness, no matter how much I thought I could feel or understand it. And, as before, I couldn't scrub the guilt from my skin, couldn't leach it out of my veins.

"I am sorry. So very sorry," I whispered.

Though the regret weighed heavily it was not enough. It would never be enough. There were some things that couldn't be undone no matter how many apologies were offered. My words would not make a difference, but I had to say them anyway.

Of the many other heart-stopping tragedies I had heard and read about, Henry's loss was the most personal. Everything I had learned in school was useless in the face of this information. There hadn't been a course covering this either and how could there be?

Why would any nation feel justified in doing something this horrible? My country rightfully claimed musical geniuses like Beethoven, Handel, Bach and Brahms. And I had seen how good people could be when life had been reduced to basics. During the war we were cold and there was a shortage of hope. Yet friends, neighbors, even strangers, shared food and clothing and looked after each other's children, making do as they struggled to get from one day to the next and helped when they were able.

Whenever sirens warned of yet another air raid, my brother had to be carried down treacherously steep and narrow wooden steps into a basement used as a shelter. We never knew how long we would have to stay there, but were aware that eventually he had to be carried back up. My mother could never have managed without the assistance of caring individuals; none of them the callous monsters described by Uschi.

How could both – the good and the bad – find room in the same nation? How could my countrymen have adopted someone like Hitler and his beliefs? I had wrestled with that question for years but had never received a satisfactory answer.

Very likely no acceptable explanation would be found in England, although there were many reminders of the war. Every town and village had its own memorial. One would have to be willfully blind not to notice them. I understood why men would fight for a place, fight to keep their way of life unchanged and intact, and I cringed whenever I saw these sad, silent reminders of countless deaths. Perhaps someday, mercifully, the scars would be less visible. Afraid of condemnation, I never let their effect show on my face.

There was more to Henry's story and I needed to hear it, but the disclosure was too grim and right now my mind shrank from further information. There were questions I didn't want to ask, while others didn't bear thinking about. It wasn't that I didn't understand. It was that I understood some things all too well.

And then I felt ashamed that I didn't have the courage to learn more. What kind of a coward did that make me? Millions had lived through devastating loss and destruction and I shied away from just listening?

Mr. Simpson stood next to me, awkwardly protective. "I thought you should know. You were bound to hear about it at some point. It wasn't said to hurt you."

I could hear that he was trying to be careful. "You didn't. I wish…"

There was another laden silence, but I knew that he was not angry with me. Perhaps we had just run out of small things to say, and the big subjects were too painful to talk about.

Concern deepened the lines in his face. "Maybe we'd better go home."

"Yes," I said quietly. "It's been a long day."

CHAPTER 26

COMMITMENT TO PRIORITIES

Y esterday's conversation with Mr. Simpson had left me confused. And there were reasons. The people I knew were good, hardworking individuals, shouldering each day's responsibilities with fortitude and resilience. Even so I had automatically expected signs of animosity or contempt. Yet what I had received was a quiet acceptance. That said a lot about this nation.

Anticipating the worst, I had braced myself, but my fears were unfounded. I had never been the target of anyone's justifiable anger. Just the opposite was true. At times I could have wept at the kindness shown me. How did they do it, given their firsthand experience of war, the wounds still raw.

No one had let me feel the pain of their personal loss. No one had talked to me about the destruction of large parts of their country. By *my* people – and *my* people they were.

Henry's sister and her husband, other members of their family, my teachers, fellow students at school, farm workers, shopkeepers, none of them had ever spoken an unkind word to me or given a hostile or wary look. It was almost like a friendly, collective decision.

But could I trust it? I was used to not being liked and lowering my guard carried risks. Would it not be safer to maintain a tenuous connection and not see anyone as my friend? I just couldn't make sense of it all.

English people had lived through so much yet there was nothing reserved in their interaction with me. They smiled and said "Hello, luv," even though we had just met.

They had welcomed me into their homes and into their families in a sincere, warm kind of inclusiveness. And it was more than a surface courtesy. I had found friendships where I didn't expect them. Could the past really be forgotten? If not, then somehow overcome with time?

The English nation was known for its generosity. It was inspiring to learn that Coventry and Kiel became sister cities in 1947 – a mere two years after the end of the war when much of the rubble hadn't been removed in either place.

Difficult as it was for me to believe, this kind of behavior – the calm, the civility – came naturally, from within the people and not because of an edict from Buckingham Palace. Her Majesty Queen Elizabeth II had power, but not that much.

I remembered reading a newspaper article about a lady who was invited to a garden party given by the Queen. Upon her return from this momentous occasion her friends asked how she had behaved in such an unaccustomed, white-gloved setting. "Why," she answered, "I was myself. I acted no differently than on any other day or with anyone else."

I had forgotten why this lady was being honored. I had never forgotten her reply. At a young age she had made a deliberate commitment to her priorities. There would be no shift from the person she was inside to the one she showed to the world.

It gave me a lot to think about.

~~~

"There you are," Henry said. "Mr. Simpson told me I would find you with your horse."

I had been grooming Major. Startled, I lifted my head and saw Henry quietly watching me. Absorbed in my thoughts I had not heard him approach.

"Might I have a word with you?" he asked. "You and I need to talk. I've been rather busy..."

Though I knew little of his schedule, the remark did not seem like an overstatement.

"I had quite an enlightening conversation with a neighbor," Henry continued. "He lives in Mulbarton and he told me that last week a girl dressed in black and riding a black horse all but flew through the village. Whoever it was must have been in a mighty hurry."

Mulbarton was more a village than a small town, and only a few miles from Hill Farm. On our way through the center, Major and I had startled some ducks floating serenely on the smooth skin of the village pond. The ducks had protested in a wing-flapping frenzy. By the time they had settled down again we were long gone.

Henry had not said it accusingly and there was no point in my denying the truth. I also knew who had told him. The owner of Mulbarton's grocery store had jokingly called me black devil on more than one occasion. There wasn't a lot of creativity in his description as my boots, my blouse, jodhpurs, everything, including my horse, were indeed black.

"I did that," I admitted. "I was to meet someone and I didn't want to be late."

Henry waited patiently for me to go on.

"We did go fast, but Major wasn't hurt," I explained. "I made sure we stayed mostly on the grass."

"Oh, well, that's all right, then."

Still, if anything had happened, it would have been my doing. And the consequences could have been serious. If the same thought had occurred to Henry he did not say it out loud. Expecting a more negative response I studied his face, but he just smiled and patted me on the back. "Next time it might be a good idea to leave a little earlier, don't you think?"

Henry and I had been talking for a while, and it was too long for Shep. Henry called him Trottle Trousers. The dog adored his master and answered to both names.

Shep had appointed himself to watch out for me. Normally, his chin between his paws, he would lie there quietly watchful. Today, his eyes pleading, he circled impatiently.

Major also waited for deliverance. He shifted his weight

and tossed his head, restless with unspent energy. Although I was also eager to leave, I patted his neck to quiet him.

But Henry was not finished. Instead of excusing himself he went on. "Tell me more about this place. Malix, is it?" I'm listening, his tone said – but it was an invitation, not a demand. "I hope you don't mind my asking,"

I did mind, but what could I say? I might as well answer him. To do so would take more time than I had, or perhaps more accurately, than I wanted to give. But if I didn't take care of it now I would only have to do so later.

"What would you like to know? There isn't much to tell."

"Is that so? Then talk to me about what you do know. Tell me why you don't want to be here."

I blinked, taken by surprise and not quite knowing what to do with that kind of honesty. Though not indifferent to what I had learned about him, this was a topic I didn't want to discuss. Not with him. Something in Henry's voice said that he had noticed my unhappiness. If he understood at least that part, why was he asking a question to which the answer should have been obvious.

My one wish was to return to Malix and it was not up to him to let me go there. Perhaps if things were different between us...but they weren't.

Henry ended our conversation without insisting on an answer. He did not strike me as the kind of man who would take the convenient way out and tell a lie. To a degree, his quiet comment of "I'll see what I can do" had helped.

It was only a shard of hope but I clung to it all the same.

CHAPTER 27

CATHERINE

I met Anton Held because of Henry's sister Sarah. Sarah had introduced us while she and I were on a shopping trip in downtown Norwich. "You have something in common. He is German too," she said by way of explanation.

Anton was a handsome man with blond hair, blue eyes and high cheekbones. He had a firm chin, strong nose and a generous mouth and judging from his laugh lines, was quick to smile. A small scar on his right eyebrow gave him a slightly roguish look.

I knew that he had a woman in his life because he had told me that her name was Catherine. Whether she was his wife or not, I had never seen the need to ask. It wasn't my business anyway. What mattered was that they were happy together.

When he took me to meet Catherine, she was sitting on a

lawn chair, a light blanket covered her legs. Her posture was erect and graceful, like that of a dancer. She was slender, with collar-length auburn hair cut in a practical way. Arched eyebrows framed hazel eyes in a fine-featured face. Holding my hand in a firm grip, her smile warm and genuine, she said, "I don't suppose you and I need a formal introduction. Anton has told me a lot about you."

And then realization hit me. There was no doubt – I knew her. Or at least I had heard of her. Fame was a byproduct of doing something well. But in this case it was more than that. Everyone in the equine community was familiar with Catherine Houghton's tragic story. A severe riding accident had cost her the use of both legs. The rider responsible was able to walk away; Catherine the only one seriously injured. A lesser person might have placed blame for causing the accident. She did not. Her first concern had been for her horse. To her relief, her mount suffered only a few cuts and bruises.

People spoke of her with admiration and respect. But no one had told me about her connection with Anton. And to have her here, sitting poised and confident in front of me, had a tinge of unreality about it. Not in my most unlikely fantasy could I have imagined such a meeting and I tried to observe her unobtrusively. So this is what a legend looked like.

"Well, have I passed inspection?" Catherine asked, her distinct upper-class voice wryly amused as she observed my thought process.

A flush of hot embarrassment swept over my face. I could feel the heat deepening the color I already had. Years ago Martha had assured me that my blushing would stop when I got older. Just how old would I have to be before that happened? This blush-inducing experience took feeling awkward to whole new level.

I could not have looked away if I had wanted to. But I also didn't want to meet her eyes while trying to conceal my awareness of her plight. Angry for being so transparent, I stuttered an utterly ridiculous, "It's nice to make your acquaintance. I've heard a lot about you too."

What an inane thing for me to say. I wanted to bite off my tongue. Surely I could have thought of something better than the first thing that popped into my head. But it didn't faze Catherine.

"Have you? Come now," she laughed, not looking for an apology. "No harm done. No offense taken," she assured me and my fears evaporated.

Before long we were chatting easily. In mere minutes we waded past trivialities and struck for the deep. It was like the continuation of a relationship begun in another lifetime.

CHAPTER 28

A SANCTUARY

C atherine had offered no clarification about her accident. "I'm sorry. I thought you knew," Anton told me
some weeks later.

Not sure whether his comment was in reference to her mis-
fortune or their living together, I said nothing. There had to
be quite a story there, but that would have to wait until they
wanted to share it with me.

An educated woman, Catherine could recite whole passages
of poetry from any number of authors. But for me, a highlight
was to hear her read from some of G. K. Chesterton's works,
particularly from his 'Ballad of the White Horse.' Anton had a
preference for Rupert Brooke, Goethe and Schiller.

If it were true that things once lost are better left in the past, Catherine ignored that specific script. Evidence of the life she had known was visible throughout the house.

"Anton and I like to collect things," she explained. "We are pack rats."

Their two-storey thatched roof cottage made of weathered stone was comfortably furnished and larger than it looked from the outside. The main room had beamed ceilings. Softly lit oil paintings and watercolors of horses hung on white-washed walls. Photographs, a visual history of her life with Anton as well as her accomplishments, graced the piano. Shelves filled to over-flowing held pewter mugs, trophies, books and magazines. Meals were eaten in the large open kitchen at a trestle table flanked by benches. A parlor, study, bedroom, two bathrooms and a guest room completed their abode.

French doors opened onto a large flagstone patio. The stone floor was a bit uneven, but Catherine had prevented Anton from making it level for her.

"None of us are without some rough spots," she said. "It's the flaws that give us character."

Catherine and Anton owned a healthy supply of optimism and it was what drew me to them.

Both in their thirties, and different in temperament, they were uniquely themselves yet also the same. Reassured by their actions, their home had become a sanctuary – a refuge from the turbulent uncertainty my life had been. With an innate sense of compassion my friends were giving me what I could not give myself. Taking hold of it with both hands, I did not feel so alone and adrift anymore. I frequently wondered if they knew how much such kindness meant. Just being around them made everything brighter, better. It was nothing that could be found in the contents of a first aid kit, but it healed all the same. Whatever else the week held, I could look forward to time spent in their company.

At the boarding school there had not been all that much to smile about. Having almost forgotten what it was like to talk and think without restrictions, I found my new relationships liberating and I laughed more than I had in months.

Once in a while we were joined by Catherine and Anton's other friends and I liked them immediately. A remarkably diverse group, they made me feel as if they really wanted to get to know me; the first people to say 'yes' to me – their acceptance seamlessly unconditional.

I had steeled myself against intrusive, detailed inquiries. There hadn't been any, which was good, because there were no answers I wanted to give. And I never volunteered.

So this was what friendship and trust felt like – a brimming dish that I intended to carry without spilling a single drop.

"Friends mean a lot, especially those that have been on a journey with us," Catherine shared. "I strongly believe in the need for connection."

A skilled conversationalist, she served as the group's tranquil unruffled center, keeping strong-willed exchanges at a reasonable level. We joked and argued good-naturedly over international and domestic politics. Plays, TV programs, movies and favorite books were other subjects that would often lead to deep discussions. Everyone involved generously allowed the others to shine without resentment. Not a moment spent with this intriguingly rich mix was boring and I appreciated the experience.

I had always been drawn to those who's knowledge was more extensive than mine. Bright and dynamic, these people encouraged me to think differently about what I saw or heard. Whisked to a new kind of understanding I watched and tried to learn from them all that I had never been taught, absorbing everything like a sponge, adding or replacing knowledge. There was no lack of good advice, so mostly I just listened – especially as I had no particular views on many subjects and was unfamiliar with others.

But because of my frequent stay in solitary 'contemplating my sins', I had acquired some knowledge. Now I was reaping the benefits of the many hours spent alone with books. If Sister Maria Serena had been here I would have thanked her for so tirelessly giving me that opportunity.

~~~

Aware of Catherine's interest in my life, I tried to recall all the adventures I could. She especially liked the 'sewing of the socks' and the 'wimple water adventure'. Comparing our boarding school experiences made us laugh. Catherine even had her own version of Sister Maria Serena. People were people.

I had never shared my past with anyone, and doing so now made it seem as if it had happened to someone else.

"I was alone a lot. I did some wild things to get my mother's attention, and made sure she learned of it," I said slowly. "You know – riding fast – skiing fast – going out alone in my kayak."

"You don't get along with her?" Catherine asked gently, like a doctor probing a wound.

"We have a complicated relationship. She sees me as a disruptive force because I don't play by her rules. With her, the correct behavior for every occasion is written in stone. And I'm not talking about having to speak French at breakfast, English at lunch, and German in the evening.

"But she can be very charming. My friends have always liked her, and I pretended not to be jealous, but I was. Perhaps I am not giving you an entirely fair description of her because there were some well-intentioned redemptive moments.

Once she bought me a pair of black jeans. Jeans were popular at school and these had a five inch cuff of red, white and black plaid. I was thrilled, but when I modeled them for my father, he said that I needn't bother coming into the dining room as long as I wore something so unsuitable for a girl. That day and for a quite a few afterwards I ate my meals with Martha at the kitchen table."

I had never harbored a lot of daughterly feelings towards my mother. Now with my friend, the confessional floodgates opened up. Yet even as I recalled painful experiences, I somehow felt disloyal. It was hard to explain, because as much as I thought I hated her, she was my mother.

"And now there is this new situation," I muttered.

"I'm listening," Catherine answered, and I knew that she truly was.

"I've realized that my mother and Henry are happy together. They speak more than one language. Just a look is often enough, if you know what I mean. With my parents there were these long hollow silences. So it wasn't words that hurt but the lack of them. I've wondered if they ever shared any kind of communication. Shared it before my brother's illness that left him, a sturdy blond, blue eyed little boy, crippled by polio at such a young age.

"Had they shared it before Germany declared war on its neighbors? Shared it before the bombs fell and my father was away for much of the time, leaving my mother responsible for a fourteen year old and a newborn?"

Catherine cradled the cup of tea between her hands and blew across the steaming surface.

"I'm so sorry. I had no idea," she said.

CHAPTER 29

A FEATHERED GIFT

W hen I shared my tractor/trailer driving experience with my friends, Anton confidently declared, "That is something we're going to change. I'll teach you how to drive."

And now he remembered that promise. Navigating on meandering, narrow country lanes bordered by tall green hedgerows seemed a lot more ambitious than guiding a tractor across an empty field. But I couldn't think of a polite way to refuse. I also felt bad that Catherine would be staying home during this excursion.

"You people drive on the wrong side of the road," I offered.

"Oh, that. No problem," Anton didn't bother to hide a smile. "We'll make allowances for it, give the other motorists the right of way and seek refuge in a farmer's turnout."

He took us to an abandoned runway at Hethel Airfield. Small plants and grasses pushed through cracks and potholes in the cement. A few starlings walked, a slight swivel in their short steps, before they rose nervously into the air.

I was nervous as well, yet Anton didn't seem the least apprehensive.

After what he considered to be a successful lesson we went back to the house for tea and sandwiches. The conversation dealt with knowledge of different languages. Catherine was in her element and asked what I thought.

"Knowing a language is good but it does not necessarily translate into perfect communication," I said. "I can tell you that there are differences between the English spoken here and the one I was taught in Germany. On my first visit to Norwich I was puzzled by store window displays proudly proclaiming, 'We Have a Gift for Everyone'. As this was around Christmas time it was understandable, because in English a gift is a present. But in German the word means poison. And that is not the only difference. In German, the word *hell* means *light*. Here it means…well…you know what."

Catherine chuckled. "You must be learning our ways. And it looks as if you've already made a conquest. Anton tells me you have a young man interested in you."

"Newell? Oh, no. He's nice enough and he means well, in a trying way. He watches my every move; it makes it so I can't breathe."

Newell, hired by Henry to help anyone needing assistance, was on the skinny side and maybe a year or two older than I. His blond shaggy hair hung straight down over his eyes. He blinked constantly as if sending out Morse code. If there were a message, I had no idea what it could be.

"I simply don't understand him because he swallows half his words. He's not exactly speaking the Queen's English, is he? There are sentences I still don't put together correctly, but then I wasn't born here. At least that's my excuse."

I could tell that Catherine was trying hard not to laugh. "But is it getting better?"

"Not yet. In class I made a mistake spelling the words *whole* and *hole*, and the teacher was quite annoyed."

"Don't take it too hard. Nobody is perfect. What exactly are you studying?" Catherine wanted to know. "Remind me."

"Oh, you know. The usual." I answered evasively. Was hers a casual question or had something I said raised an alarm? Had she found out about my deliberate attempt to sabotage my academic performance? To my relief she just nodded, letting the matter go – and I tried to clear a space where my conscience could operate.

~~~

I was becoming more accustomed to my surroundings. At times my loneliness retreated, before it stepped out again as sharp and insistent as before.

With my friends' gentle urging I expanded my relationships. At the students' club I was introduced to Brian, an American pilot stationed at Lakenheath Air Force Base. He was good-looking in an open, boyish way with kind blue eyes and blond hair. When he gave a quick and infectious smile his teeth showed white and straight.

"Hi. You aren't from here, are you?" he inquired.

"No, I'm from Germany."

"I thought I recognized the accent. You speak very well. My name is Brian."

His behavior was very polite, so when he asked me to join him for a dance I agreed. Broad shouldered and long limbed, he moved with natural grace and I found it easy to follow him around the floor.

Brian told me that his parents and an older brother lived in Dallas, Texas, and went on to explain that his brother had been a tremendous influence in his life.

"Coincidentally, I had an older brother as well," I said. "For a while after the war he worked as a translator. I was a little girl then and I remember playing on the sidewalk outside his office when two GI's in a jeep drove up. The young men in their green fatigues and black boots looked like tall trees growing into the sky. To my amazement they rolled not one, but two rolls of Lifesavers on the sidewalk towards me. I had no idea what the shiny, multicolored presents in my hand were, but they had come from America so I just knew they had to be good. Thrilled, I ran inside to tell my brother. When he asked me if remembered to say thank you I realized that I had forgotten those important words. By the time I reached the street again the soldiers had left. I never learned their names, yet I often think of them."

"It's good to hear that. We aren't liked everywhere, you know," Brian commented.

"But why not? Your country has performed many acts of kindness. My father said that with the Marshall Plan, America saved western civilization; that it helped put Europe back on its feet. I had my first banana because of that program. Of course we also received cornmeal and dried pea soup. Both tasted horrible. Perhaps the women at school didn't have eggs or a ham to prepare them correctly. But the thought of someone on the other side of the world caring enough to send food and other much needed items to us really touched me."

Brian had a temporary membership at the club and visited whenever he was on leave. I soon realized that our meetings were not accidental. He made it a point to find me and after the third week we spent evenings together. I should have known that it could not continue this way.

"You dance very well and I enjoy our time here, but perhaps we should add some variety. How about going to the movies with me?" Brian asked one evening.

Dancing within the confines of the club was one thing. I was less sure of being seen with him in public. Some of the male students had expressed resentment of the 'Yanks taking away our girls.' I wasn't one of 'their girls', but I thought it best to avoid any unpleasant encounter.

Delaying my decision worked only for awhile. I recognized the hurt in Brian's eyes and soon excuses sounded lame even to my own ears. But I had an idea. If Brian picked me up and I contrived to be late we would arrive at the theater after the film had started. And if we left before it was over, and if I were lucky, no one would see us.

Everything went as planned. The place was full and we quickly found our seats. But twenty minutes into the movie the reel broke and for half an hour the theater was lit up brighter than daylight. And there we were together, for all to see.

Ashamed of my subterfuge I never went out with Brian again.

After that episode, Catherine decided it was time for me to meet her twenty-three year old nephew, David. The family resemblance was easy to see. He had light brown hair, hazel eyes, and was gregarious and confident.

Even at his age he looked the perfect English gentleman. Tall, an inch or two over six feet, with a supple athletic body honed from playing soccer, he was studying international law with plans to eventually take over his father's practice.

Within weeks David and I began seeing each other. On our first date he had taken me to a village named Wreningham and a favorite pub of his called *The Bird In Hand*. In existence since around 1805, the pub was acknowledged to be the best in the area. White walls and dark wooden beams created the setting. Beer, spirits and hearty country food were served in this unpretentious atmosphere. A dartboard begged for friendly competition.

David told me an interesting tale about how the pub acquired its name. Evidently long ago a witch had lived in Wreningham. When she found out that witch hunters were looking for her, she turned herself into a wren and flew away.

"That's funny," I laughed. "I think one of her descendants came to see me."

And then I shared how one morning not long after my arrival at Hill Farm, a wren had found its way through the open kitchen window. There had been seven of us sitting at the breakfast table but the small bird landed on the rim of *my* cup. It stayed there for just a moment before it flew away again. As I had not told anyone that it was my birthday, the feathered, unexpected visit was a special gift.

CHAPTER 30

AN OLIVE BRANCH

W ashing down the holding area on a dairy farm was a twice-daily occurrence. The cows were finished, so to speak, but there was still more for me to do.

Putting on my Wellingtons and armed with a sturdy broom I went to work, hoping all the while my mother would see me. And knowing that if she did she couldn't object. Not really.

We had different ideas about appropriate behavior. But this was farm work and it needed to get done. By the time I was finished, the yard could not have been cleaner. Every inch had been scrubbed and then hosed down.

"You're getting quite good at the job," Ken observed. "And by the way, Henry wants to see you in his study. And he doesn't look happy," he added cryptically.

I didn't like what Ken was implying, but when I glanced at him, he merely shook his head. One thing I knew. I was tired of more changes and challenges, and not at all receptive for another Socrates spouting unsolicited advice, trying to teach me about life, teach me about anything.

Henry was first on the list of people I did not want to engage in conversation. Chances were that it would be about something I didn't want to hear – like making an absurd demand about improving my grades. But that could be my conscience speaking.

So once again my mother would say nothing to me, leaving Henry to deal with the problem. Years ago she had done the same thing – leaving my father to pass on her requests. Why should that come as a surprise after everything she had done or not done? We rarely saw each other.

She enjoyed spending time with Sarah. Both were involved in arts and charitable causes. On the second Wednesday of every month they and some other ladies met for tea. And today was the second Wednesday.

The library lamps cast warm circles of light into Henry's study. He must have stepped out, giving me a chance to look around.

Surrounding a large desk were floor-to-ceiling bookcases with a ladder on a track for reaching the top shelf. An arrangement of leather chairs and a sofa were drawn up on either side of a fireplace. Regimental prints and those of hunting scenes, dogs, and horses, hung on the paneled walls. It was a place to linger, but I had not been brought here to enjoy myself.

Entering the room, Henry cut an impressive figure. His military bearing was unmistakable in uniform or dressed in every day well-cut clothes: checked shirt, cavalry twill trousers, and a tweed jacket. His favorite jacket had suede patches on the elbows. My mother had bought him a new one, but Henry smiled apologetically and continued wearing the old.

Not sure in the way I needed to be sure, I waited for him to speak. Did he really think that any interference on his end was going to make a difference? Because interference was how I would see it.

"I am not your father and I certainly don't want to replace him. But I have watched you and I will not permit your behavior... not while you're under my roof," Henry said, his tone noticeably crisp. "I'm aware that you don't like me. You have made that clear on several occasions, so it's nothing new. But no matter what you think of me, you will neither treat your mother with disrespect, nor will you deliberately antagonize her. None of us are perfect, but we are responsible. And the way you have been acting does not fit who you are."

Henry must have seen me wielding the broom and understood my intent for doing so. What he said was true. My behavior was less than stellar. I didn't even know what I wanted to prove anymore. Sometimes I argued even though I basically agreed with him. Making a list of his shortcomings had occupied me for a while. But the anger didn't last through the day as it once had.

What I knew of him in the light of Mr. Simpson's revelation had made a difference. Now I wondered what I could have learned if I had not been so angry and defensive.

Sitting there in his study, my thoughts went back to when he had invited me to go with him to the Norwich livestock market. It had been good to see him friendly and relaxed. He was partial to Ayrshire cattle and mentioned that the characteristics of a well-bred animal were a straight back, straight belly, and good clean colors.

Henry and I had walked around the field, viewed the livestock, talked to his farmer friends, and eventually ate lunch.

To my delight, he had bought eight pink, squealing piglets. It almost made me like him for a moment. And then he told me it was my job to see that they were fed, watered and had clean straw. That was all right with me. The piglets did extremely well but we were puzzled why one gained weight much more quickly than the others. I soon understood the reason. This piglet, jouncing along, ears and short tail flopping, knew exactly what he wanted and where to obtain it. The culprit squeezed through the loose slats in the fence surrounding the cows in the sickbay and expertly took his nourishment from them. But the little guy had not made allowance for its increasing girth.

One day he became stuck and his secret was out. While trying on my own to find a solution, I had kept my discovery to myself. In the end, ignoring the correlation between indulgence and longevity, this piglet was the first one to go to market.

Once again I went back to my thoughts, remembering the time when Henry had taken my mother and me on a four day trip to London. We had visited the majestic Westminster Abbey, the Tower of London, several museums, had seen the Rosetta stone, admired the Elgin Marbles and enjoyed high tea at Harrods's.

Henry had done kind things. Perhaps I owed him another chance. A peace offering might also change his opinion of me (a slender possibility) but then it was better than nothing.

"I haven't thanked you for coming to my defense when I wanted to go to Malix," I said cautiously.

Henry checked his watch, as if he had a hundred things to do before the sun set. And very likely he did.

"It seemed like the most practical thing to do," he said absently. He held my eyes for a moment longer, and then he shrugged as if it didn't matter to him one way or another.

His answer hurt. Why had I even tried to appease him? Just about the time I thought that things between us could change, he acted like this. I had to face the fact that we were not communicating and it would be a good idea to accept it. My previous course of action, that of detesting him, was best. We would just carry on our own form of battle. I willed the tears back into my eyes as my olive branch went quietly up in smoke.

"What was that all about?" Ken wanted to know.

I summoned a smile. "Family problems."

"Oh, right. I'd almost forgotten," Ken said and walked away. He did not say anything else, but I had the feeling that he understood. Understood all too well.

~~~

Henry also formed opinions about other people. Ken frequently showed up late for work and grinned an apology. He was good with excuses and I would have forgiven him, but Henry was not pleased and let it be known.

One day, when an expectant cow was not with the others, I had saddled Major and gone looking for her. I had found her out in the pasture, and a calf, only minutes old, by her side.

Later, I heard Henry tell my mother, "If my dairy man cared as much about our animals as Andrea does, we would be in good shape."

Two weeks after that conversation Ken was replaced. I didn't realize how much I had come to depend on him until he was gone.

CHAPTER 31

NOT TO FORGET

D ays went by without incident. Although the after-
math of my interaction with Henry could have been
worse, I was aware of his presence and I didn't speak
to him unless necessary. And in the following weeks I spent
even more of my time with Anton and Catherine. Their approval was important to me.

The competent, self-appointed custodians of my future
had an uncanny way of cutting through a problem. Especially
Catherine! Pragmatic, her plans were larger than mine.

"I have given your academic situation some thought. You
know the one we discussed the other day. And I think I have a
solution. If I taught you several hours a week you'd catch up
on your class assignments very quickly. I have a schedule
mapped out – subject to your approval, of course."

"That sounds interesting. Someday we'll do it," I said impulsively.

Catherine didn't hesitate for a second. "Good. Then it's decided."

"Just a minute. What is decided?" I asked, as the implication began to sink in. "We do what now? Why would I want to study in addition to my classes at school?"

Catherine looked up at me. "Surely I have explained that," she said.

"Somewhat. But this can't be fun for you." I said, stalling.

"Won't that be a waste of your time?"

"Not in the slightest. Nothing worthwhile is ever a waste. We can discuss other details later, but three times a week, we start at eight o'clock in the morning!"

"Eight o'clock?" I gasped. I was a teenager, and teenagers didn't believe that anything before nine a.m. actually existed. "You can't be serious," I told her.

Catherine shrugged. "I'm always serious when it comes to things like this."

"I don't believe you mentioned that before."

"Did I not? Well, you know now. Perhaps we can compromise. What do you consider to be a reasonable time?"

"Not eight o'clock. The birds haven't even begun to sing by then," I protested. "I was thinking more like around ten."

"What a remarkable concept," Catherine said, amused. "So you think you're a bird? And a very late bird at that? For your information, birds start singing much earlier than that, so that's not the best of arguments to make." She gave me an indulgent nod but the reprimand was unmistakable. Perhaps feeling that she should qualify her statement, she asked, "Or would you rather not do this?"

Her plan of teaching me was ambitious and I didn't bother to conceal my doubt but I bowed to Catherine's talent of persuasion. "It's all right," I said, with as much enthusiasm as I could muster. "This is the place to start."

Catherine smiled. "How astute of you… I find that very reassuring."

"I just hope you know what you're getting yourself into. But then Anton said that you bring a lot of perseverance to anything you do."

A flicker of surprise showed on Catherine's face. "He did, did he? What a nice compliment. Then I suppose I'd better live up to it. So let's not wait until another day. But before I forget, I have another task for you." She pointed her chin in the direction of her desk. "Nothing too involved," she added when she saw the alarm in my eyes.

Waiting on the desk was a reading list of the classics and other books she considered necessary for my enlightenment. In total there were a hundred volumes.

I gave her a disbelieving look. "That's a daunting number. Are you sure you haven't missed any?"

"I don't believe so," Catherine said, scanning her copy of the list. "I think for now that's all. And, of course, there is your other homework."

"Of course," I repeated ironically. "But are you telling me there could be more of them? More beyond the first hundred?

I'm fond of reading, but this many? That almost borders on cruelty!"

She glanced at me, her smile conspicuously absent. "The problem lies in your definition. Yes, there will be more. This is just an abbreviated version. I suggest you study them in your free time. I'll give you the first five books to take home now. Let me know when you're finished and I'll select the next lot."

I just about choked at Catherine's words. Did she really believe that each book held a secret and that it was up to the reader to find it? When I skimmed over the titles I saw that I was familiar with a few, but plowing through all of them would take me forever. And I lacked the motivation to go on an extensive treasure hunt.

"Are you all right?" Catherine asked innocently.

"No, I can't say that I am," I admitted.

"Oh, dear. A shame, that. I trust it's nothing fatal," she commented, her tone laden with false sympathy. " So do we have an agreement?"

Although the 'agreement' would not take that much of my time, I already regretted my decision. Yet not able to come up with a rebuttal, I said nothing. Everything was happening too fast. Looking for support, I sent a silent plea to Anton, but none was visible.

"This should be fascinating," Anton said, with a gleam of humor in his eyes. "In the game of chess it would be called an opening move." His smile widened into a boyish grin. "I'm glad you're not objecting to the course, Andrea. Take it from me, an educated woman is very attractive, at least in my humble opinion."

"What a treat. A German with a humble opinion." Catherine looked at him with affection.

Their eyes met in a private moment of understanding; long enough to acknowledge the past with a wry smile.

Anton held up his hands. "I believe I've just been insulted and complimented in the same breath. And since I don't know whether to be offended or amused I'm going to ignore it."

At first, my friends' reference to Anton's German background and the war had surprised me. It wasn't ignored, nor was it belabored, but even so I hadn't quite known how to interpret their candor.

I knew that the nations of Europe shared a troubled history of old feuds, deep-rooted traditional prejudices, alliances and broken promises. For decades, political relations had been anything but peaceful. Relationships, especially those between England and Germany, had carried their share of challenging, at times devastating, conflicts. It was a lot to overcome.

By now I more easily understood my friends' verbal give and take. Perhaps being used to each other's ways of expression and spoken without abrasion, potentially inflammatory remarks were permitted.

Anton had been a member of a German Medical Corps. After he was taken prisoner of war and sent to England he had worked in a hospital. He and Catherine had met there and renewed their relationship after his release. "She was easy enough to find. All I had to do was follow the trail of admirers," Anton smiled.

He had completely embraced the English way of life. Catherine's family had not embraced him, nor had they trusted him. Catherine's condition required frequent care and you could only entrust someone you respected with this important task.

Her relatives were loyal to their country. It was dear to them and they showed it by rejecting Anton, closing their ranks against the unwelcome intruder. A brother-in-law expressed their opinion with thinly veiled hostility. "Tell us why," he had demanded of Catherine. "What do you see in this German? It's because he's a medic, right?"

Catherine's love for her country was no less deep and profound than that of her family, and she had expected support from them in her choice of the man she loved. She refused to back down, and after that exchange she had not spoken to her relatives for weeks.

"Catherine's family live in Coventry," Anton explained. And then he reminded me that in November of 1940 much of that city, including the historic Coventry Cathedral, had been destroyed by the Luftwaffe. "With everything that happened, you can't blame people for their strong feelings. But it's better now. I've grown on them. We're all doing things a little differently... not to forget, but to put it behind us," he said quietly.

Anton could, without saying a word, put up a 'no trespassing' sign. It was there now. Soldiers involved in the war had experienced more than any human being should have and they didn't talk about it, as if the past were too dangerous to touch, even with words. I had noticed it in my father, Henry, and Mr. Simpson.

Their silence masked horrible events. I would never know the brutal details. But I did try to imagine what I would feel if I were in Anton's place – leaving everything behind – another challenge that couldn't have been easy.

"It was not so much a matter of going or staying," Anton said. "It's a matter of belonging. We all need a place that feels like home. I was born in Dresden."

His comment clarified some more things. Dresden, a city in East Germany, had been heavily bombed by RAF and American planes in the final weeks of WW II. The whole area was now under Soviet control, making his return out of the question.

Anton put his arm around Catherine. "There were only memories to go back to...so staying here was the right thing. It was for me. And I know I made the right decision because I've never regretted it."

CHAPTER 32

ALL THE KING'S HORSES

"You have the distinction of being my first student,"
Catherine had said without hesitation. If anyone
wanted an example of a strong will, she more than
qualified. There was the private Catherine and the one on duty
with drill sergeant tendencies.

I endured what was probably the most mentally exhausting
time of my life, something akin to an athletic event. Catherine's
questions – she referred to them as a winnowing process –
made it clear that only thoughtful answers were acceptable. Re-
laxation would not have a place in my immediate future.

After exploring the meager sum of my knowledge she outlined a challenging objective. "It doesn't have to be all perfection," she said, and then she required exactly that. Her verdict
provided a certain amount of discomfort, yet sprinkled

throughout her lesson were bits of personal wisdom and stories about people she admired and horses and dogs she had owned. It was the first time she had talked about herself to any degree and it brought a welcome break before my trial (as I liked to think of it) continued.

When, hours later, Anton walked into the room with the makings of an English tea – plates of fancy watercress and cucumber sandwiches and tempting treats – I was ready to contact the appropriate authorities and submit his name for sainthood.

"I don't want to get in the way but am I wrong in thinking that you ladies could use some refreshments and stop for a few minutes?" he asked.

My friends made allowance for my liking a cup of Earl Grey, sweet and strong. When Anton poured, I was touched that he remembered my preference. He liked to cook and Catherine and I were fond of his creations, but at this moment she was not happy with the interruption.

"You had to do that, did you?" Catherine asked, rubbing her temples. "I sincerely hope there is a reason for it."

The question was meant for Anton. "I am doing this for your own good," he answered calmly. "Has anyone ever pointed out that you drive yourself too hard? Surely Andrea doesn't have to learn everything in one afternoon. You can't shave a plucked chicken."

Noticing my bewilderment, Catherine said, "You'll have to forgive him. That is his expression for 'enough is enough'. It's a cultural thing. I guess not all things translate well."

Earlier she had been in a pensive mood. But something disquieting had entered the conversation and made its presence felt. In Anton's eyes, Catherine was just about perfect and I didn't want the harmony between them disturbed because of me.

"Just a minute, please," I said, "Let's not give up yet. If I remember my fairy tales correctly, some enterprising lad fooled a giant. He made the giant believe that he could squeeze water out of a stone. The impossible can happen."

"Aren't you a wealth of good cheer? That was accomplished through trickery," Catherine told me with a note of exasperation. "Here, we deal with reality. From where I sit, the two don't have anything in common and you know it. Neither fairy tales nor nursery rhymes, as in 'all the king's horses and all the king's men' can fix this problem. Welcome to my world." And she gestured impatiently to her legs.

Her tone held an unusual brittleness. It was very much out of character and as close to a complaint as I had ever heard her express.

Anton didn't appear at all surprised by her outburst. He seemed to understand or maybe he read something in her eyes.

"We just have to change the odds then," he said quietly, moving the focus into safer territory. "Perhaps we'll continue this at another time. It's up to you, Catherine, but I think you should stop for today. Please," he added, "you need to rest."

"Rest? How can I rest?" she said, almost as if she felt the need for an argument. "I'm all right. You're the one that needs a rest, always having to take care of me. But I'll think about it." There was a brief silence and then she spoke again. "No," she said emphatically.

Anton was not convinced. "Did you really mean no? Is that

wise?" There was concern in his question. "You're upset."

"Yes, something along those lines, but I'm fine now." Catherine gave him a weary smile. Her frustration had vanished as quickly as it had appeared. "The day has had some difficult patches. Let's not add anything to it." She reached up and brought her palm to rest against his face. "You are the soul of tact, my noble Held," she said, making tender use of his last name.

The German name Held means hero, and Anton smiled good-humoredly. "And you're too good to me," she told him, her eyes unusually bright. "Sometimes I'm not sure I deserve you. I'm sorry for earlier. That just about went pear-shaped. Silly of me, really. If it's all right with Andrea I would like for us to continue."

Earlier, Anton had started a fire to take the chill from the air. Now he walked to the fireplace, put a new log of fragrant apple wood on the glowing embers and adjusted it with the tongs. The light from the flames sent shadows wavering against the walls. One of the logs snapped, and a burst of sparks flew up the chimney like a panicked flock of birds. The sound broke the silence in the room.

"But I agree with Anton. We should do this at another time and…" I said.

"I'm not finished," Catherine interrupted. She picked up her cup of tea and set it down again without tasting it. "Clever, very clever, you two, trying to distract me. I hope there isn't more where that came from… because, unfortunately for you, none of it will work."

I looked at Anton and could tell that our thoughts were the same. He shook his head almost imperceptibly at me and gave

Catherine a quick smile.

"Well, there you are, then. Undoubtedly you are right," he told her. "As usual, you're a step ahead of anyone else."

His remark once more steered the conversation unto a less contentious track. If he was troubled by Catherine's decision, he concealed it well.

"Yes, I suppose that's true." Catherine leaned back and slowly stretched her arms over her head. "You see... I have my ways. Timing... it's all about timing," she assured him, her dry humor coming to the surface again.

"Having a plan is always good," Anton agreed calmly. It was all he said, but it was enough. We laughed and the lesson continued.

CHAPTER 33

EDGELESS FREEDOM

M y mother had never been comfortable around animals. I liked all of them. They gave so much and asked for so little in return, especially horses. I could hear Major's nickered greeting before I even entered the barn.

After last night's storm a crisp clean morning had not so much dawned as that it had merely stopped being dark. Raindrops silvered each leaf and nature showed more variations of green than I could name. The clouds had moved on and the sky was clear – a good time for me to saddle Major and get in some exercise. There was a riding competition taking place at the end of the week. Any additional preparation could only help.

I was getting Major ready when Catherine called with an invitation to join her and Anton for lunch today. I kept my answer deliberately vague and told her that I had a lot of work to do. That much was true; it was just not the kind of work she thought. While talking to her my explanation seemed acceptable. Now I was much less certain.

Because of intensive treatments for her condition we had not seen each other since I visited her studio some weeks back. As a student, Catherine had attended school in Italy; Florence to be exact. Now, with more time on her hands, she was painting again. Her landscapes were good enough to be exhibited in a Norwich gallery.

"I'm glad you like it," she said, when I admired a half-finished canvas standing on an easel. Even at this stage her talent was evident.

"Do you paint?" She had asked.

"No, I never have. I'm all thumbs as they say."

"You're nothing of the sort,' Catherine insisted. "You're just creative in other ways."

I had to smile. "Sister Maria Serena would agree with you there. But I'd rather discuss your latest work. This fascinates me. How do you know when it's completed?"

"You just know."

"That's something, isn't it? A lot, actually. Couldn't it take the place of... ?"

Catherine hadn't pretended to misunderstand. "Yes, it's something, but not enough. Not nearly enough," she said fiercely. "My life has changed, but I won't give up."

I tried to do my best when competing, but it was Catherine who had lived for the sport.

Eager to learn from a champion, I had asked for a film clip of Catherine in competition. She was known for having mastered the discipline and I watched in awe as she achieved her objective. The performance was ambitious, but Catherine created an art form as horse and rider flowed over the course like water. Movements were precise yet also graceful and fluid; reminding me of a well-choreographed ballet. The only hindrance – gravity.

Centered and quiet, she harnessed the vitality of her mount. Though fearless, the jumps were never reckless. I could see the horse's muscles tensing as it gathered strength and then in a single explosive motion clear the barrier. Capable of soothing the most skittish, uncooperative horse, Catherine didn't rush her mount into the next sequence. Patience, trust and a thorough knowledge of an animal made the difference. Harmony between horse and rider created the whole. When it was over there was a look of pure joy on her face.

But only so much could be absorbed by watching someone. Other competitors had to consciously think about the process. Catherine, oblivious of everyone and everything else, performed it with the ease brought by hundreds of repetitions. She had done this from the time she was young. And it showed.

Trophies, silver cups, the many ribbons, all were visible evidence of her accomplishments; being successful – a frequent event in her life.

So very gifted and respected by her peers, she had come to the attention of the British Olympic team. That is why her accident had been such a heartbreak. I never brought up the subject and did my best to skirt around the issue, especially considering her recent surgery. The one question on Catherine's mind had been, "How soon can I ride?"

When her doctor had advised her not to expect a miracle, none of us had to ask details. We knew. Tragedies such as this seldom reversed themselves. And indeed the operation had not gone as well as my friend had wanted. Her condition might never become worse but a change for the better, though not unheard of, seemed unlikely.

The only time Catherine allowed herself to cry was when she was told that she would never walk again. I sent flowers and had once visited her in the hospital. After that we had only spoken briefly on the phone. There were reasons why and I was aware of all of them. But right now I needed to concentrate on what I was doing.

A gentle nudge was all Major needed to set out.

In the distance a woodpecker tapped a rhythmic tattoo. Close by a pheasant shouted his alarm as he whirred off to a safer place. Those and the creak of Major's saddle and harness were the only sounds.

There was something intoxicating about a morning rich with the scent of the earth, gently sloping pastures as far as the eye could see, and the edgeless freedom to explore them. Happiness engulfed me and I laughed for the simple joy of it. With no one to interrupt my solitude, I could pursue my thoughts without distraction. Somewhere I had read that few moments were perfect, but this was coming close.

It hadn't taken any coaxing for eager-to-please Shep to accompany us. He might not always be in sight, but he was always near. Ecstatic, he ran back and forth, stopping only to explore a strange or new scent. Occupied with less weighty concerns than keeping a herd of tenacious cows in line, Shep looked for trouble and frequently found it. His whole body quivered with each discovery.

"Sometimes you're a terrible disappointment to me," I told him laughingly when he arrived, covered in mud, to check on our progress. He wagged his tail, and cocked his ears the way he did when he listened intently, and then he raced away again. Major shared our enthusiasm. Used to admiration and sure he deserved it, he held his head proudly, as if he owned everything visible. There was something superb about the way he moved; his long strides casual… his strength restrained.

It was only when being around other horses that he showed his competitive side. Yet despite his ambitious temperament and size he was easy to control. With his muscles warmed up I could let him go more quickly and for a little while I let him run as fast as he wanted, his hooves drumming the ground, before I slowed him to a walk.

Seeing things from a rider's vantage point gave me a different perspective. Small wonder Catherine loved this sport. She had ridden since she could walk. I had come to it later than that, but I certainly shared her passion now.

The sun had climbed higher in the sky, revealing the contours of the countryside. Reluctant to put an end to the outing, we turned back. Major knew the way home with the accuracy of a compass needle. By the time we reached the farm it was well past noon. It seemed like only thirty minutes but my watch confirmed that we had been gone for several hours.

Surprised to see Anton's car in the yard I kicked my feet free of the stirrups and slid to the ground. But it felt as if my heart reached terra firma before I did.

What was Anton doing here? Nothing was planned for today. There had to be a simple explanation. My stomach clenched in an unfriendly way. Suddenly uncomfortable I walked towards him.

"Hello," I called, pretending to be calm and relaxed. "Is everything all right?"

"You went riding this morning," Anton stated the obvious.

"Yes," I answered. I didn't give him any more details, because I didn't think they were necessary.

And then I saw that he had not come alone. Catherine was there. In the passenger seat. Any hope I might have had that this visit was purely coincidental died right then.

Mortified, I stroked the lopsided star on Major's forehead as if he were my only concern. I had not expected to see Catherine. Her presence certainly complicated matters. And I didn't like complications of any kind, especially those of my own making. "You're here too. Have you been waiting long?" I asked, sounding subdued even to myself.

For a few seconds Catherine and I stared at each other.

This was the very thing I'd wanted to avoid. How long had she been aware of my subterfuge? I had intentionally only entered competitions of little interest to her. Though what had made me think I could hide those activities, especially as the names of participants were always listed in the paper?

She looked at me with knowing eyes; disconcerting because I had tried so hard not to bring up anything connected with her past. And that definitely included horses.

The same was true of my experiences during a recent trip to Florence, an art lover's city if there ever was one. I had reveled in going to museums and galleries but kept those visits to myself as well. Worried that they might cause her distress I had not shared any of these things. I had convinced myself that it was because I did not want to add to her sorrow.

But the truth was that I had hidden behind my fears. It had taken time to admit to myself that I avoided talking about her accident because I didn't know how to deal with someone else's pain – not something this life-altering. And now she was here.

"The newspaper says there is a gymkhana this weekend," Catherine told me gently.

There it was at last, out in the open and I began to understand what had brought her here. "It looks as if you have things under control," she added.

I cleared my throat. "I'm working on it."

Catherine had been holding a riding crop. When she handed it to me she didn't need to tell me that this was her own. "I thought you could make use of it. I don't want it to go to waste."

Her action distressed me. Competing had been everything to her. To love something so much had to be terrifying, the loss of it... devastating. Though I would never fully grasp the daily difficulties confronting her, the battles she fought and what they cost, I knew enough. If she thought that she'd lost a significant part of her life's purpose, what would happen then? For someone like her time would offer only a slow erosion of the spirit.

Was this what was she telling me? Was this her way of giving up? I pushed the thought aside, not even wanting to contemplate it. Not trusting myself to speak I stayed silent until I had my emotions under control. But whatever her plan, I needed to apologize for my behavior. "I really am sorry... I shouldn't have done that...," I floundered on. "I thought you wouldn't want to know..."

I struggled for a little while longer to salvage or at least clarify my original intent. Yet no excuse made my actions acceptable. And there was nowhere for me to hide. I had managed to get myself into this on my own, as was the case with most of my dilemmas.

In need of absolution and unsure of where to go from here, I waited for something – anything – that would fill the silence. Anton would describe it as a gap in the seam of communication. He had tactfully excused himself and stood some distance away, letting us do our own mending.

Catherine had listened to my stumbling explanation without interrupting. For long tense moments she did not answer. Silence took shape and almost became visible, thick enough to cut. Was she ever going to say anything?

"I haven't forgotten what it was like to ride." Catherine let out a breath as if releasing an image. "I remember. I remember it very well. Sometimes I even think I can still feel my legs, foolish as that may sound. And I dare say I'll never forget any of my experiences, even without the cups on my mantle to remind me. Being around horses has always been like medicine."

As if understanding her words, Major lowered his head and chuffed gently against her shoulder.

"When we know each other better you'll see that I don't need to be protected..."

Catherine's voice faltered as if needing to collect herself for a moment. It was so brief that only someone listening closely would have heard it.

"Everyone has something to overcome. This seems to be my lot," she continued without a note of bitterness. "It isn't a walk I wanted, but it's the path I'm on. And I'm not going to float through life like a passenger. I was, and am, proud of my accomplishments. However, now my goal is to concentrate on what can be achieved. If I focus too much on the injury, I will lose even more. I may not have control over everything, but this I can do. Will do!"

Again she paused, as if sorting through her own cautions. "I appreciate your reasons for trying to shield me but most things can't be solved by avoiding them. I'm aware of my boundaries, but they will not determine the course of my life. I'm English… this is how we do things. So I would ask you, please, not to deny me the joy of sharing your accomplishments."

The faintest touch of a smile appeared at the corners of her mouth. "You can also tell me of your losses, though we'll leave that for now." She paused, her eyes thoughtful. "Each thing we do is a choice."

"We have choices?" I asked, wanting to prolong the conversation, relieved that Catherine was speaking to me.

"Yes. But whether we have the courage to exercise them is a different matter. Nor does any of this come with assurances."

I didn't like those odds, though put that way I reluctantly agreed. Catherine's comment had been in keeping with what I knew of her personality. Thank goodness my fears had been groundless.

"Now, tell me something," she said, her tone so casual that

I immediately put up my guard. "How are you doing at school?"

The suddenness of her question was unconnected to anything we had discussed. On the surface it lacked specifics; instinct told me there was more to it. Some people circled around a subject like a dog trying to find a comfortable place. Catherine's way was brisk and to the point, and I liked her directness – most of the time.

"Well enough," I answered cautiously.

An exaggeration, perhaps, but that did not make it untrue. And that was the hard part – knowing it had strayed in that direction. Catherine had been honest with me and that should have called for honesty in return. Although my answer was the best I could manage, it was tinged by several shades of guilt. Guilt because I was entering into the domain of yet another deception when she and I had only just resolved the most recent one. And guilt because I once again didn't feel free to share my reasons with her. I felt myself sinking deeper into duplicity, but what choice did I have? Self-interest was a powerful force. Which was important in itself.

"Good," Catherine nodded. To my relief she did not elaborate and I wondered why.

CHAPTER 34

NOT YOUR AVERAGE BEAR

W ith a strategic lack of detail, and the fervent hope that she would not find out the rest of the story, I had told Catherine an abbreviated version of the truth.

Sometimes I wished that I had been more forthcoming right from the beginning. I was tired of not trusting and not really knowing what to do next. Every once in a while my conscience reminded me that I was living something of a double life. 'This won't be for long,' I thought, excusing my action. 'It isn't hurting anyone,' I consoled myself.

Catherine was my mentor, an older wiser friend. It was hard not telling her what I was doing. Keeping my academic performance secret was becoming a bigger burden than I thought it would be. Yet I didn't want to risk our relationship. For the moment, everyone knew as much as they needed to know. Self-protection seemed wise and appropriate.

My plan proceeded simply and effectively, and I considered it to be rather ingenious. If I did poorly in school I would be dismissed. And the logical outcome of that would be my return to Switzerland. To patiently wait and hope might be good enough for saints and nuns – it had never worked for me.

By going to various stables and arriving at different times no one had questioned why I was there and not in school, allowing me to stick to the truth as closely as possible.

From what I could tell, grown-ups were too busy with their own lives to check up on me. By moving in a low bubble of attention, I was confident that discovery would be unlikely.

But now, to my dismay, a complication had crept up. Anton and I would need to talk. Soon!

The opportunity came when he took me home early one evening. Twilight covered the countryside like soft gray wings.

Anton was an avid birdwatcher, and was sharing with me his latest findings. After a few minutes, he asked quietly, "Is there something you want to tell me? I might be able to help."

"It's nothing, really," I said.

Not wanting to be truthful right then, I postponed my answer with a question of my own.

"How do you decide who you want to be?" I asked.

Anton looked surprised. "That is the easy part. You figure out whom you admire and try to emulate that person. I don't pretend that I get it right every day. I have thoughts enough, but I don't know all the answers. Actually, I'm just learning the questions," he said frankly.

"Catherine can tell you that I'm guilty of choosing foolish little habits and routines and becoming intensely loyal to them, and that I huff and puff if something gets in the way. She doesn't get lost in the unimportant. Being around her makes me aware of priorities and why certain things matter." Anton smiled. "What is given is not always received, but I like to think that I've absorbed some of her wisdom."

"You sound like my father. I was robbed of the time we could have had together. I miss him, and I wish I'd said then how much I love him."

"Don't you think he knows?" Anton asked quietly.

I was stunned, not because of his words but because he had said them.

Except that Anton and Catherine did not belong to the same faith, I was unaware of his religious convictions. He had once told me that 'He was undecided because religion is deceptive, like quicksand', and that his belief in a deity was tenuous.

Having been exposed to the dark side of humanity did he consider himself to be an atheist?

"On some matters I might have opinions; others I'm sure of," he informed me. "During those years in the trenches survival was a hope, not a certainty. If God spoke, it wasn't in that place. So it's not that I rejected him. He just didn't seem all that available. That's why I trust in what I can see. My religion is the outdoors. Nature can teach you a lot and it's what I answer to. This is different from what you expected," he added thoughtfully.

"Yes, it is."

Anton seemed to understand, and with understanding

came comfort. I could only hope that he would bring empathy to the explanation I was about to give.

"Catherine wants to buy more textbooks," I blurted out. "I don't see how I can continue my studies with her. She is putting in too much time and I don't want to become a burden."

"That is a very thin excuse," Anton insisted. "I know that people are not always comfortable when receiving help from someone they don't know that well, but you know us! Nietzsche, one of our countrymen said, 'That which does not kill us makes us stronger.' Is the real issue pride?" he said, not unkindly, but laying the burden of answering squarely on my shoulders.

For now, I had to let him believe that this was indeed the reason. "Yes, I suppose so," I said, wishing my emotions would leave my face alone.

Anton glanced briefly in my direction and then concentrated on the road again. "Not to be rude, but why is that? Used in the right context, pride is a good thing. So here's another lesson – few things are demeaning unless you make them so in your mind. While we're on that subject, how is school, and how are the lessons going with Catherine – or do I want to know?"

"Let's not talk about the first. And the second is harder than I expected. Catherine's technique is effective. I just don't share her confidence in my role as her student."

Anton nodded. "It's early days yet. If discouragement weren't so seductive, people wouldn't give in to it so easily. But I have a request. Hopefully it will make you feel better as well, but this isn't about you. This is about Catherine. The world would be a boring place if we all had the same gifts and Catherine is not your average bear. She has achieved every goal she has set for herself. She'll conquer and build a meaning around this struggle as well. Even now she plans to instruct other riders a few days a week. People keep asking her, but the doctor agrees with me that right now it would be too physically demanding. Her injuries haven't healed nearly enough, but she won't be stopped for long. So that's where you come in."

"I'm not entirely selfless. You could be a big help to me." There was a hint of a challenge when he continued. "Have you even considered that Catherine teaching you subjects – stimulating, yet unrelated to anything concerning horses – might be the very thing she needs to do? It may not be what you want… but it will be good for her. And that should matter. So hear me out and don't say no right away."

I eyed him cautiously. "You are worried about her."

"Yes! Yes, I am! Many of us try to figure out reasons to get up in the morning. Catherine has always known where to go, and when, and how – she still does. It's just that at the moment she could use some help. I've tried where I can, but this requires the efforts of more than one person. So that's where you come in. All you need to do is apply yourself in a serious way and convince her that you're worth her time. If she wants to buy textbooks, you need to let her do that. Look on the bright side. You just might forget your own problems, and that alone should be worth it."

I had wondered what Anton would ask, and when the answer came, it didn't surprise me. Now was clearly not a time for beating around the bush. He could be funny, at times irreverent, and his straightforward demand may have lacked a poetic edge – but there was nothing obscure about his loyalties. He proceeded to tell me that whenever his mother felt disheartened, she baked bread or cookies, and shared them with friends and neighbors.

"You don't cook or bake, do you? ...Well then?" he asked, with his usual matter-of-fact directness. Polite, but adamant. "You're tough and you're tenacious, in a way not so different from Catherine. I expect you to get this done."

I didn't want that responsibility, nor could I recall ever having been coerced so effectively. Sometimes honesty could make things worse, but Anton didn't care much for compromise and from anyone else his words would have felt harsh. Yet he had the ability of saying things and making them sound as if they were just information to be passed on – even when blithely issuing ultimatums.

"When you put it that way it makes sense. Why didn't you tell me this before?" I wanted to know.

Anton shrugged. "Would you have paid attention earlier? You forget I was your age not so long ago."

"There is that. Don't you get tired of being right all the time?"

"It's a gift," he said, amused, rather than offended by the question. "Though now and then it does get boring."

I laughed. I couldn't help it. I liked his understated grasp on what was real.

"There's one more thing," Anton added. "Let's keep this conversation between us. The woman I love is extremely intelligent and it doesn't take her long to become suspicious."

CHAPTER 35

PILGRIMAGE IN HUMILITY

I n the past, my approach to scholastic requirements had been significantly lax. I was seventeen and had missed even more classes then were noted on the attendance roster. The amount of information Catherine expected me to digest covered a wide range of topics and there was nothing casual about it.

Although she taught me for only a few hours every week, she set a blistering pace, using structure both visible and invisible as if she had done it a thousand times. And very likely she had – in effort and dedication – with her beloved horses. I had seen her interact with her four-legged friends and had the suspicion that she now used the same methods with me.

"You're very good at this," I commented, hoping for a short break. "Do you always have this much stamina? Because

kly, I can't keep up with you. You're running circles around
e."

Suddenly, I remembered. Embarrassed, I looked at her wheelchair and told myself — not for the first time — that I needed to think before I spoke. "I'm sorry. I could have phrased that better."

Catherine reached out and touched my arm. "Don't be. You have no idea how much I needed to hear this."

I liked and admired her. She was brilliant, funny and humble, and she conquered each day with cheerful toughness. Watching, I gained a new appreciation for small moments.

Her expectations became my conscience and eventually the hard work showed results. Even so, there was no sudden vault to perfection. If anyone needed a big dose of confidence, I qualified. On days when I thought my head would burst with learning and memorizing, I wondered if it would not be better to go back and attend school full time. The Cambridge textbooks Catherine used in our sessions were intended for twenty-two year old students. And to these she added knowledge absorbed in the course of living.

Frequently my commitment to the task was not sufficient enough to please her. "I need you to muster some enthusiasm. Obligations don't diminish with time. My job would be easier if you applied yourself," she requested.

To her credit, she most often focused on what I did right, not on my mistakes. Failure earned me a gentle correction... a raised eyebrow meant, "This needs work." At other times admonishment arrived with the force of a whirlwind, sanding me down, and I was told about my lack in no uncertain terms. "If you don't pay attention you miss a lot of things."

I frequently endured a refresher course. And although I did not relish these pilgrimages in humility I realized their importance.

Comfortable within silence, Catherine embraced it, but she also liked to talk about deep things. At Cambridge, philosophy had been one of her favorite subjects.

Her tool of choice was enthusiasm. I had never met anyone so persistent in giving shape and purpose to each moment. There were no limitations to what she found important. Everything had potential; nothing was ordinary. And out of the goodness of her heart she invited me to walk in that sphere and take some of the journey with her – letting me learn what was important at my own pace – with only the occasional push. The nutritious soil of approval did its work and after a while it felt as if I had grown a few inches.

"I surely could have used someone like you at my previous place of enlightenment," I grumbled. Recalling the caged misery of boarding school made me cringe even now.

"You are giving me too much credit," Catherine said gently. "But I'm here. Don't think about the past. Be aware of the present and make it your own."

I had tried to adapt to challenging circumstances since I was a child. Catherine was doing so now in her own situation, but she didn't carry the resentment that was such a part of me.

My coach and mentor never ignored what needed tending and made sure I absorbed a number of essential skills along the way; how to achieve, how to behave. There were no shortcuts.

"Balance is crucial to everything we do," Catherine instructed pointedly. "It's easy to be tolerant when you're about to get what you want. But things need to be kept in perspective. I have no patience with impatience. Many a good horse has been ruined that way."

I was familiar with the concept; I just had not always put it into practice. Thank goodness I couldn't be blamed for that specific wrongdoing where animals were concerned, yet I could see that I would have to add patience to my mandatory collection of virtues.

"But how should I do this?"

"It's your playground. You decide," came Catherine's terse reply.

CHAPTER 36

THE COLOR GRAY

y next unpleasant exchange with Henry took place after I returned from the paddock. Riding Major always brightened my day and I was in a very good mood.

The mail must already have come because Henry stood in the yard reading a letter. And then he motioned me towards him.

That did not bode well, nor was it a particularly encouraging start to this interaction. What could be on his mind now? My fears came rushing back, bringing their relatives with them. And it was a large family. I had survived the unpleasant chat from a few weeks ago, but the memory of it remained.

"That's the spirit," Henry said. A smile tweaked the corners of his mouth as he scanned the lines. "You're full of surprises. I have to say I'm impressed."

He turned to the next page and I watched him as he studied that one as well. Henry looked puzzled for a moment, then his eyes narrowed and I saw a frown replace his smile.

"Apparently you've missed the majority of your classes, yet you're doing very well in your exams..." he said, the pause slightly wrong. "Rather peculiar, wouldn't you say? How do you think that happened?"

Henry held out the piece of paper for me to see. He was calm but any trace of good humor had disappeared.

Quick bursts of conflicting thoughts went through my mind. This was serious business and I put on my most serious expression. Clearly some response from me was expected, but I tried to act as if I was just as puzzled as he, as if I didn't understand his well-founded suspicion, didn't know the content of the letter, and had no idea how the school had arrived at its assumption. I was familiar with the kind of epistle Sister Maria Serena wrote – wordy, but no substance. This one, however, had not been sent by her.

I could have told Henry that the reason I did well on my exams was because most anything I heard or read stuck in my mind. Yes, I was somewhat behind in a few of my assignments, but was that enough to warrant this much fuss? Although my attendance at lectures had clearly not been frequent enough, until now my ruse could be counted successful. But deep down I knew that the day of facing the consequences of my action would come. So perhaps this was the conversation that had been waiting to happen. In a way I was relieved to have my deception out in the open. I just didn't like the messenger.

Excuses piled up while I tried to decide what the best answer might be.

A lie might deflect further questions and momentarily protect my defenses. There was a difference between an outright
lie and leaving the truth undisturbed, but I doubted that Henry
would agree with any elastic definition. He preferred logic. He
could just about read my mind anyway and was far too perceptive to be misled.

His patience was unravelling. Frown lines showed on his
face and the set of his jaw spoke volumes. "Is this true then?"
he asked.

"It probably is," I answered, my tone carefully neutral. I
looked down as if I had discovered something fascinating on
the ground in front of me. My voice sounded steady and I
wondered at that, because inside I was shaking. I did not lack
negotiating skills, but this was beyond my ability.

"You've certainly revealed a new aspect of your character
and I have to admit that I feel let down. Just exactly what were
you thinking?" Henry asked in a brusque, no-nonsense way.
"Because that's the center of the question, isn't it? And please
do not dismiss my question with some offhand answer."

If I needed assurance that my future was going to be bleak,
he was standing right in front of me. And I could guess what
he expected me to do. I'd heard it all before. I also knew I didn't
want to do it. Had I not earned the right to take life a little easier?

Surely I deserved some diversion. I was tired of having
everything arranged by others; always conforming to someone
else's requirements; having to say the right thing – do the right
thing – never dishonor the family name. There were things I
wanted to do, and to live at the whim and mercy of other people was no way to live at all. And all that studying – as if studying would improve, or add anything.

"I am curious," Henry said. "You didn't pick up this much knowledge on your own. Who has been teaching you?"

I searched for a plausible reply and decided to tell the truth. Somehow I had to stop this day from plunging into an even greater decline. I had not wanted to involve Catherine because that would mean a lecture from her. But I had no better explanation and it wouldn't take long for him to get that information on his own.

"A friend of mine thought it would be helpful."

Henry was silent, no doubt analyzing and weighing my words after I had told him the bare minimum about my interaction with Catherine and Anton.

"The results might be acceptable," he finally said. "But let me be specific. I'm not happy with the method. Not at all happy," he repeated. A tiny pulse throbbed in his temple. "So what are you going to do about it? Let me know when you've come to a suitable decision. Your definition of appropriate behavior seems to have a wide range of meaning."

I looked at his face with his aquiline nose and his arrogant jaw. I resented him, resented everything about him. How could resentment be cold and burning at the same time? There was, unfortunately, some truth to his accusation but it didn't make me feel any better.

"Must I give you an answer immediately?" I wanted to know.

Henry frowned. "What could you possibly have to consider?"

I was eager to get away, but the question curled open, and behind this one there would be others. "All right. You don't have to say anything else. I will attend school. All of my classes," I amended. Resistant to authority, I also responded to it. I wasn't too thrilled about ultimatums, but in this case, surrendering to the inescapable was the only way to end the interrogation.

Henry locked eyes with me and seconds stuttered by, each one an hour long.

"Very well," he said at last. "We're in agreement, then, on something. I admit that I don't understand your motive, but we won't discuss the subject any further." His eyes narrowed just a little. "I'll be checking on your progress. Is that understood? Don't make me speak more plainly," he snapped.

"Yes! Sir!" I answered firmly. If I'd dared to salute I would have done so. Instead I nodded and hoped it was enough. I may not like him, but I would take his warning seriously. The alarming moment had passed. I had no idea how much of anything he would share with my mother. Very likely he still considered that an option but I was too tired to worry about it.

Henry turned on his heel with his usual briskness and walked towards the house. Perhaps in his mind he had said all that needed to be said.

"Probably just as well," I muttered, trying to hide my guilty relief. "I feel much better already."

I thought he might close the doors behind him with an emphatic boom; he was that angry. Yet he did so – gently. He undoubtedly had heard me, but diplomatically acted as if he hadn't.

I almost felt sorry for him …but not enough. It wasn't my responsibility to make him feel comfortable with the way things were. I hadn't asked to come here. And I certainly didn't need his approval, I thought angrily. And then I realized that I had been looking for it all the same.

~~~

"Andrea, dear, what's going on?" Catherine asked. "You didn't just come for a visit."

From experience I knew that her question was not casual. I cleared my throat and wondered if that came across as hesitating. I had already told her about the positive results of my tests. But I had kept the less admirable part, that of skipping school, to myself because she would require an explanation.

"I had a run in with Henry," I admitted reluctantly. "He brings out the worst in me. So I gave him another reason."

Catherine was watching me with thinly veiled amusement. "How good a reason? And I want to hear all of it."

"I'd just as soon forget it. It's a long story," I replied evasively, not quite certain how to begin describing it, even if I had wanted to. "It's complicated."

"I'm sure," she said drily. "Things tend to get that way. But that's all right," she assured me. "I think I can bear it. I'm not going anywhere."

Encouraged by a few gentle prompts I summarized the encounter, omitting nothing important and feeling less heavy with each sentence I spoke.

"You didn't," she said, when I was finished.

I cringed. "I'm afraid I did."

"You have had an eventful day." Catherine made no effort to hide her thoughts. "Are you serious?" Her smile grew into rich warm laughter. It was infectious and I reluctantly laughed with her, until it overwhelmed us and we couldn't stop.

"How on earth did you manage something like that?" Catherine asked after we had recovered. "You live long enough and you see it all. I must stop underestimating you. That's what you had in mind?" Her mouth twitched and she appeared suspiciously close to laughter again. "Let's see if I have this right. For months you've fudged on your school attendance? And you truly believed you could make this work?"

"Pretty much," I admitted. "It seemed the thing to do at the time."

"Now I have another question," Catherine said. There was nothing new about that. She always had questions. Perceptive, not intrusive, and I had come to expect them. "Why didn't you just tell us? Anton and I could have worked something out."

The short answer was that the topic had not readily presented itself nor had I been all that eager to hunt it down. But I had to agree with her, telling my friends would have been the safer course of action although that was hindsight.

"What do you suggest I do?" I asked.

Catherine exhaled noisily, somewhere between amusement and exasperation. "For starters, let's try something different than what you have been doing." She shifted to find a more comfortable spot. But I knew that her mind was at this very moment sorting through any number of ideas.

"I may have an answer to the problem," she said with deceptive simplicity. "Instead of teaching you only a few classes a week, I could instruct you every day."

Catherine's offer had caught me unprepared. Finding myself with a decision I really didn't want to make I nodded, because I couldn't say anything without saying too much. As much as I liked my friends, there were old concerns I was not eager to share. But perhaps it was time I trusted someone. The need to be secretive would be over and I was more tempted by her proposal than I wanted to admit. "You're willing to teach all of my classes? You won't mind?"

My favorite Samaritan looked at me in surprise. "Of course I'll teach you. None of us will ever learn all there is to know. But you are in danger of squandering your talents and I will not permit it."

How could I squander my talents if I didn't even know what they were, or what I could achieve? But if she said I had potential, who was I to disagree.

"Someone has to take you in hand, keep an eye on you, so to speak," Catherine continued, "and I'll make it my responsibility. But before we even try to scale that summit, is there anything else you need to tell me?"

"No. There's nothing else, now that you know this."

She gave me an encouraging smile. "Oh, well, that's a comfort. I'm glad you decided to accept my suggestion. Of course this needs to be cleared with the school – and your mother."

"She is busy. And if I talk to Henry, he may not believe me."

When Catherine offered to speak with him and share her idea, I was relieved. "You're really serious about this," I remarked, when she and Anton returned from that meeting.

"Very much so," Catherine said. "Henry and I worked out the details. I even guaranteed your success – so no excuses."

"I owe you…for talking to him."

"I know," she laughed. "I'm sure I'll find something for you to express your appreciation. Trust me, the price will be high."

It seemed as if there was no end to my obligations. Just the thought of fulfilling them exhausted me. "It's not fair," I muttered.

Catherine looked at me. "Sometimes life is like that. But you're not in any position to argue the point, are you? And ignoring the facts does not change them — nor will it make Henry go away. At some point you may have to make peace with that. I don't know everything, but I think there is room in this for more than one side. For Henry also, this is a different experience. Few things come with instructions. There is much he has to weigh — to consider."

That sounded reasonable enough. Logic was logic, no matter how far it was from what I wanted to hear. But my resentment ran deep and I lived in a satisfying blend of smoldering anger and self-pity, prepared to find fault with anything Henry did.

"Nobody has laid out a crumb of trails I could follow either. I've really tried to like him and I'm nice most of the time. Anyway, it isn't important," I said with a casual shrug, although I couldn't totally hide the hurt in my voice.

"Perceptions are perceptions," Catherine said. "After a while it becomes comfortable to lie to yourself about your motives. It's tempting to blame someone else, but solutions to problems rarely get solved that way. If things don't go right at first you may have to come back to them another day. Discuss it with Henry. Acceptance is a form of forgiveness. Although I don't think he has done anything necessitating your forgiveness. He is not the enemy and punishing you is not on his mind.

He has your welfare at heart."

"Well, he doesn't!" I protested. "He doesn't care at all. I'm not sure he is capable of it. Anyway… I absolutely, positively… do not need that man interfering in my life! "

"You're so young and already filled with so much anger." Catherine's voice held deep pity. "Hopefully, one of these days, you'll see that anger is a wasted emotion; wasted, because it turns everything gray. Thoughts in that color leave little room for objectivity. It was one of the lessons my accident taught me. And if I teach you nothing else, I hope you'll learn that."

CHAPTER 37

A CAPTURED WAVE

I never subjected my relationship with David to detailed scrutiny. I trusted him. He was very thoughtful, and for the first time in a long time I felt as if someone was taking care of me.

He and I could talk for hours, moving easily from one subject to another. It didn't matter if the topic was of little consequence or great importance. We shared a mutual enjoyment of the arts, attended plays together, went horseback riding, and took long drives exploring the surrounding areas.

David referred to them as 'Tours in search of the picturesque,' and I had joked about having my own guide. "Anything to keep a valued customer happy," he answered.

He also remembered my liking for anything connected to the sea, especially food. One day, he took me to the market below Norwich City Hall. Rows of stalls, covered with striped awnings, featured a range of merchandise.

The market was already crowded, but David was eager to introduce me to the taste of cockles and whelks. Searching, we found some for sale in a stall tucked away in a corner. A woman – her face puckered like a frosted apple – sold us the salty morsels.

We had already visited Ely, Bury St. Edmunds, Runnymede, and the memorial commemorating the signing of the Magna Carta. Today we had no specific objective.

"Shall we see where the road leads us?" David wanted to know. "How about meandering to the coast?"

I smiled. "Meandering sounds just right, but didn't you tell me that you had to study for a test? I wouldn't want to get in the way of your scholastic requirements."

"How thoughtful of you, but not to worry. All is well."

Speaking seemed superfluous. David ably handled the wheel and we drove in quiet contentment.

"Everything is so peaceful. I could lose myself in such mo-ments," I said, when we were close to our destination.

"Catherine feels the same way," David told me. "The coast was one of her favorite places. She's always loved the sea, the tang of the air, and the sound of the waves hurling themselves against the shore."

Then Catherine had endured her own storm. And that tragedy was never far from my mind. Her traumatic loss had not come slowly, with time enough to adjust, if that were even possible. Fate, with merciless indifference, had reduced the thousand details of living from one perfect moment to the splintered next – and left her to cope.

I remembered watching the film of her in competition; the passion and vitality she had brought to everything. But to live the present way required different abilities. Now even minor acts took some thought.

I wanted to offer her something, though what could it be? Every idea seemed trivial.

"You are being very contemplative, plumbing deep thoughts again. Am I right?" David asked. "I can tell when you're somewhere else. It's not much of a compliment to me if I can't hold your attention."

"I was just wondering..." I said.

"Wondering what?"

"Stop the car, please," I requested. "I have an idea."

Without waiting for my explanation he pulled over to the side and turned off the ignition. To the right of us, set back from the road, was a small house. One of its windows was covered with cardboard; through another, a television flickered dimly. If houses had feelings, this one was probably disheartened. At some point it must have been white, but time and weather had scoured off the paint. Now it stood there, rundown and shabby. Only weeds, rusted-out automobile parts, and a washing machine that had seen better days, kept it company.

"Discolored, like a pear bruised around the edges," David commented.

His description made me laugh. He liked to do that, having once told me that sometimes I was too serious. "Not gloomy, just too somber."

We sat quietly, watching gulls call to each other as they wheeled and turned with the wind.

David and I exchanged a smile. "Well?" he asked at last.

My mind had been busy but I was not ready to share my plan. It might be a useless gesture and I wasn't naive or arrogant enough to think that it would change anything for Catherine. Yet it was all that came to me right now. I quickly stepped out of the car before my confidence evaporated.

"I'll be right back," I told David.

Nothing about the property in front of me looked inviting, but it was as if a thought led me by the hand, my feet seemingly moving of their own volition. A path paved with flat irregular stones pointed to the door. Somewhere in the distance a dog barked in a half-hearted, conversational kind of way. I fully expected a less friendly associate of his to be in close proximity. There were plenty of hiding places and the low, sagging fence surrounding the place would offer me little protection.

When I was a little girl, I had been bitten by a dog. Not eager to repeat that experience I walked in tense, careful steps, all the while telling myself that dogs could scent fear and that I should relax. That was easier said than done and to my relief I arrived safely at the house.

I had already knocked at the door several times, and was about to turn away when it was opened by a heavyset man, a sleeveless shirt straining over his substantial girth.

"Excuse me. I wonder if you might have an empty bottle you could give me?" I asked self-consciously.

The man grunted something that could have been an answer. Without disturbing the cigarette clinging to the corner of his mouth, he reached back into the room and handed me what I had asked for.

"Thank you very much. I want to give this to a friend of mine," I said, embarrassed to share something this personal, yet needing to let him know all the same. "She used to come here as a child, but now she's in a wheelchair. We want to take the memory of the shore to her with some shells, seawater and sand…"

Still not saying anything, the man took the bottle out of my hands and shuffled back into the room. Not quite sure what to do, I decided to wait. I could hear him tossing aside odds and ends and rummaging around in some boxes. There was the rustling of paper and then he came back with another bottle. Made of delicate pale green glass, and wider at the bottom than at the top, it looked like a captured wave.

"I don't know how to thank you for this," I told the man. "It's perfect."

He lifted his hand in silent acknowledgement and closed the door behind him.

David made use of his artistic abilities and arranged swaying seaweed, shells and other aquatic odds and ends, and then we carefully filled the bottle with water. The result looked beautiful and was just what the day needed to make it feel complete. All the way to Catherine's home I held the miniature seascape like a prized possession.

When we arrived there we saw no sign of my friends until we walked around the back. On the patio Anton sat in Catherine's wheelchair holding her on his lap, her head on his chest.

In a rich tenor voice, Anton was singing *Unforgettable You*, as he slowly rolled the wheelchair in a semblance of a dance; shifting in subtle ways to accommodate each other as if it was the most natural thing to do.

I had the impression that we had disturbed not a conversation but a communion. My friends shared everything that mattered: the laughter and the tears. It was impossible not to be moved by their devotion. I liked their open affection, the way they interacted with each other. Yet in the honesty of this moment, I felt as though David and I were out of place. David coughed politely; I tried to look away out of respect

Catherine and Anton were not embarrassed. "Just showing you young people how it's done," Anton laughed.

With traffic a faint, far-away noise, their home was truly an oasis. Nothing unpleasant intruded here. What their property lacked in size, it made up for in other ways.

Raised garden beds produced plentiful vegetables and fragrant herbs. Gnarled branches of apple trees were laden with fruit. The patio was bordered by a low stone wall topped with flower boxes holding a variety of bright, vibrant blossoms. Anything served as containers – such as an old boot and a dented milk pail. Climbing roses, hybrid tea roses; roses of every hue gave off a light, delicate fragrance. They seemed to be her favorite; the rose garden her favorite place.

When I complimented Catherine on the beauty of the setting, she quickly gave Anton the credit. "He has a fondness for anything that grows and treats it with respect. He sees the connection, how everything gives something back. Anton is a good man, kind and interesting with a lively sense of humor. Nobody who lives life the way he does will ever get old; wiser, yes, but not old. And he makes me feel safe. In my condition there's little room for pretense. I love him. Love is very much about friendship…about understanding. We each have our idiosyncrasies, but in all the ways that matter, we're not different."

"And he's easygoing, right?" I dared ask.

"Easygoing?" Catherine seemed amused by my question. She gave a small shrug, indicating that she was not necessarily of the same opinion – not all the time. "That's just an act he puts on for you. Anton isn't always quietly contemplative.

"He has strong opinions and can be very stubborn. No one forces him to do anything he doesn't want to do. I don't often push him in such a direction." Catherine turned away and looked out over the garden. She had a way of withdrawing into a far place and then coming back. "Please don't get me wrong. In his own way he tries to move heaven and earth for me; holding me up when down would be easier. But most importantly, he takes the thorns from my roses."

Lightly said – not lightly meant. And behind that truth there was a bigger one. What mattered to my friends were the small daily considerations. Important things not always verbalized, but read all the same.

I did not need convincing. Anton nurtured hardy plants and those vulnerable to incautious care. I had seen him cut thorns from stems; wicked things, sharp like scimitars, so that Catherine could hold the flowers, put them in a vase and arrange them the way she wished. There was something very revealing in his gesture.

"Beauty doesn't always lie in the noticeable, but oh, I adore my flowers." Catherine gently touched the bushes with her fingertips as she passed them.

Knowing that my mother's favorite bloom was the rose, I had deliberately chosen carnations as mine. But here, enveloped by the heady scent of Catherine's flowers I was willing to change my mind.

After a late lunch, Catherine insisted that Anton show us his latest triumph – irises from Germany. They had arrived months ago as knobby, unremarkable rhizomes. Now they were in full glorious display, and both David and I made sure to express our appreciation for their beauty.

Glancing back towards the open patio doors we saw Catherine carefully, deliberately stand before she came to an abrupt, unbalanced halt.

Immediately Anton was there, catching her, holding her in his arms – making it appear as if he had planned to do this very thing all along.

"It's all right. I'm here," he said. "I've got you."

Catherine's face was pale, the skin stretched tightly over her cheekbones. She made a frustrated sound in her throat. Fiercely independent, too proud and stubborn to express any feelings aloud, this was the most she would permit herself. Everything seemed poised as if waiting for something of comfort.

Anton looked at Catherine the way he always looked at her. He held her hand for a long moment before lifting it to his lips.

"You promised you wouldn't run away," he gently scolded her before he turned to me.

"I couldn't live without Catherine," he said. "I wouldn't want to and she knows it."

A tender expression swept over his face. He said nothing

more. The raw emotion was all in his eyes. Having conquered the stretches, my friends bore the burdens together, but never referred to them by that name.

Visibly struggling with her own tears, Catherine drew in her breath and exhaled slowly.

"People can't survive without hope. I know I can't." Her words were so quiet they almost seemed to disappear into the silence.

CHAPTER 38

ELOQUENT MESSENGERS

A hot summer had turned into a gentle autumn. Fields were covered with golden harvest stubble and days were becoming shorter and cooler, telling of winter not far away. A few leaves drifted uncertainly in the still air as if surprised by their momentary weightlessness.

My 'rehabilitation', as Anton called it, followed its own well-established pattern.

Learning spontaneously a few hours a week had been fun, but since Catherine and Henry had come to an understanding about how my education would proceed, the way she taught had changed.

Catherine was a tolerant person and brought a forgiving perspective to most topics, yet when it came to our curriculum she showed no leniency. Whether the subject was history, geography or her favorite – English – not a syllable could be wasted.

She extracted meaning from passages I hadn't even noticed. To her the contents of books sang, especially those of the classics. "Carta Canta" – she said. "A good author takes the words and makes them do something." Words were eloquent messengers, not flat shapes lying on a page, and they had to be honored and absorbed. Her edict of "Let them keep you company until they stay with you," necessitated yet more studying. Familiar with Shakespeare's volumes, Catherine was fond of quoting gems like "the lady dost protest too much, methinks," when I had only opened my mouth to take a breath.

She had her opinions. I had my doubts, but I dutifully reported to her every day. My mind filled with her tutorials, I had arrived a few minutes early for my lesson when I heard the meditative sounds of a Chopin nocturne.

I looked through the window and was surprised to see Catherine at the piano. Though the sureness of her fingers defined each measure, notes dropped through the air with gentle poignancy. Complex and profound, it was all there – in full range of color and emotion. I recognized that no matter how often I listened to this rendition in the future, it would never affect me quite the same way again.

"Music has the ability to move and change people. Occasionally it says things that words alone cannot express," Catherine had once told me.

Yet after all this time, and everything I knew about her or thought I knew, I had been unaware of the importance of music in her life and how well she played. Not wanting to interrupt I stayed by the door, although it was not the sound that held my attention; it was Catherine.

She seemed to be lost in another world as she wove the melody to its conclusion. After the notes faded away into silence her hands remained on the keyboard a little longer before she removed them and placed them in her lap. For a moment she said nothing; then her eyes closed, and she bowed her head in prayer.

I dared not move an inch. If I could have stopped breathing I would have done that also, anything to avoid making the slightest noise. What was I to do? I had already stood there longer than I should have. Surely she would become aware of me.

I had never before been present at the intimate prayer of a person feeling herself unobserved. It was only words, faint at first, and then they became something more. The halting, broken sentences expressed sorrow for a place that had been lost and would not be hers again.

But in the anguish and wistful awareness of the impermanence of things, there was also thanksgiving and even a sense of peace.

Was this what Catherine had referred to when she said that no one needed to go through life alone? Was this the reserve from which she drew her courage?

Afraid to leave, I waited for what seemed like a long time. Then, I carefully inched back and quietly walked away, preferring to be scolded for being late, rather than letting her know I had been there at such a private moment.

When I returned and we began the day's lesson, I made a conscious effort to be light-hearted. I had been glad for the extra time to gather my emotions but even now I found it difficult to focus. My friend's heart-wrenching appeal for strength to better deal with her fate stayed with me. Hearing her pray had been like witnessing something pure and not meant for someone else, and I couldn't so easily set it aside. I had believed her to be invincible, without doubts or insecurities, able to manage anything. Seeing her vulnerable had been disconcerting.

"Let's not follow the manual," Catherine suggested. "On such a beautiful day we should be outdoors."

My unintentional intrusion still had me feeling awkward. If she had sensed me standing there she made no mention of it, and I took my cue from her, letting her set the tone. "I didn't know we had a manual," I answered casually. "But that's fine. I like people who subscribe to the one-day-at-a-time philosophy."

A shadow crossed Catherine's face and she gave a brief, sad laugh. "There are those who think I have that attitude and they may be right," she said quietly. "For a while after the accident I wouldn't have survived any other way. Even now, in my darker moments, I sometimes pray to God that there is a God. Otherwise everything would be senseless.

"I'm really not as good as you think I am, you know. The way you see me is the way I'd like to be. It has taken me a long time to absorb some very vital lessons. And I'm now convinced that there is seldom only one reason for anything – that no pain needs to be meaningless. Something positive can come out of it – if you give it a chance. Often there is a deeper purpose."

I bristled. A deeper purpose? That's where our thinking parted company. Catherine's comment had been so unshakably certain; I was not even sure how to interpret her declaration. She was more alive than anyone I'd ever met and I had always thought her resilience remarkable. She knew the blunt burden, the texture of things I had no idea about, yet she persisted in being strong and positive.

That was what I had thought... until today. I now wondered for how long she could maintain that level, however much she knew herself to be loved; and regardless of how brave she tried to be when fear whispered its message of discouragement in the sleepless hours of the night. Had I not already observed her in one unguarded vulnerable moment? Could it be that she made people see what she wanted them to see? Hiding behind a mask, never revealing too much?

And that was not the only matter troubling me. In a forest of question marks, the largest was why? Why the war? Why so much sorrow and pain? Her pain. Perhaps she had already asked all of these. I had not. I had lots of them. Questions. Too many questions! With too few answers! And it made me angry.

I had clearly not kept my thoughts private enough. Something must have shown. "As bad as that, is it?" Catherine asked, looking at me. "You'll get it sorted. Don't worry. It just takes patience."

"I'll never be able to do it then," I muttered. "I have thought about things and it hasn't made a difference. There is nothing shaped like hope on my horizon."

"I'm sorry to hear it. There will always be things we won't know. I'm telling you this because you're old enough to understand that sometimes there are no answers and you have to let the 'whys' go. Having a belief helps. It's there if one looks."

Again her tone left no doubt as to how she felt. I knew that the words were meant to be encouraging, yet their suggestion troubled me and my anger rose, strong and bitter.

"That's what the nuns kept telling us," I said, irritated. "They called it an unseen source of certainty. It may be all right for you. It doesn't sound particularly comforting to me."

Catherine either missed the cynicism or chose to ignore it.

"Why would you think that?"

"Because I've relied on myself for as long as I can remember," I answered abruptly.

"Ah," she said, as though it explained everything. "Then I hope that will change. You don't need to believe in what I believe, but you do have to believe in something. There was a time when I thought I could handle things by myself but I was wrong. It's too scary to go through life without some kind of scaffolding, without support. We find God or God finds us. Sometimes at the piano, I feel that I ever so slightly touch the unexplained."

She laughed a little pensively and left the rest of whatever else she may have wanted to say unspoken.

CHAPTER 39

LINE OF SIGHT

D ays chased each other across the calendar. My mother was in Germany, settling some last details of my father's estate. Afterwards she would visit friends and members of her family in Heidelberg.

Heidelberg brought back pleasant memories of my own. I remembered staying with these relatives on their farm. Despite some difficulties there was always laughter. One of my uncles had a lame leg. In his youth, a keg of wine had fallen from a cart onto his foot and the weight had crushed his bones, making it hard for him to bend down. So at the end of the day my task was to undo the laces and take off his boots.

Uncle Georg or Schorsch, as he was called, liked to tell stories. Interspersing history with fanciful imagination he shared intriguing details about the life of Johann Jakob Astor from the neighboring town of Walldorf.

He had also told me about the Schlüssel Blume (Primula elatior) and tried to convince me that this yellow flower was responsible for unlocking the season of spring. The stalk really did look like a ring with a number of keys attached. He had even shown me a picture of a medieval woman carrying something like them on her belt.

His wife, Aunt Luzie, was a good cook and an excellent baker. I remembered one occasion when Uncle Schorsch and I had each eaten one half of a gooseberry pie. Intended for their daughter Marie's engagement party, the pies had been cooling on the windowsill. Aunt Luzie, noticing that one had disappeared, asked if we knew anything about it.

Uncle Schorsch had assumed a guiltless expression and acted as if it were a mystery to him.

"Ich net, wehr noch?" He had asked with a smile. "Not I. Who else?"

These were good memories to reflect on but I had to deal with my present situation, and once again it concerned my relationship with Henry.

I had given this some serious thought. Both he and my father had a certainty about right and wrong, yet they had fought on opposite sides. If Henry was a good person I would have to adjust my perception of him. I had to be grown-up about it and realize it was a mistake to judge people too quickly. During the war, lives had depended on him. Soldiers formerly under his command frequently dropped by, often unannounced. I had seen their respect, so there had to be something worthwhile under the face he presented to me.

Perhaps I really had been going about this all wrong. Perhaps Catherine was right and I hadn't looked hard enough because my objectivity concerning him was shaded incorrectly. Maybe one effort on my part was not enough. But how to begin? How could I phrase a request without actually making it sound like a request? An opportunity presented itself when I saw Henry heading for the barn. A heifer was about to give birth and he always made sure everything proceeded smoothly. "Would you …would you mind if I went with you?" I asked nervously, waiting for Henry to laugh or dismiss my idea as ridiculous. He did neither.

"It's her first go at this," Henry motioned towards the soon-to-be mother. "And it usually takes some time. Are you sure you want to wait?"

"Yes! Please…"

"Jolly good. Then I'd be happy for your company."

I let go of a breath I didn't know I had been holding.

The large barn stood open to a gentle breeze. Henry set up two deck chairs on the barn's wide cement walkway while absentmindedly humming a Gilbert and Sullivan song. The fresh scent of the hay and the contented rhythmic chewing of the animals reminded me of Malix. Closing my eyes, I breathed in the memories and wondered if they would ever stop hurting.

The cows swiveled their heads and directed their unblinking stare at me. Anything different immediately caught their attention. And there was nothing fleeting about their awareness when it came to food. Out in the pastures it usually didn't take long for one of them to find a weak spot in the fence and squeeze through. Equally single-minded the others followed and defiantly grazed in places off limits to them. In persistent disregard for boundaries, the bovines repeated the act at the next possible opportunity.

But right now, here in the enclosed maternity ward, all was quiet. Henry and I sat with our thoughts, not at all uncomfortable. A mosquito whined through the air; insects clustered around the light fixtures. The heifer stood patiently waiting for things to take their course.

Anticipating the new arrival, Henry grew pensive. Leaning back in his chair, his long, booted legs stretched out in front of him, he shared how he had grown up in Norfolk, attended Oxford University, and had been a Colonel in the Regiment of Grenadier Guards.

I had seen a photograph of him looking very distinguished in his regimentals; a tall bearskin hat accentuated his height.

"Did you know that 'Scipio', the regimental march of the Grenadier Guards, was composed by Georg Friedrich Händel, and that he gave it to my regiment?" Henry asked.

I hadn't known, but I could understand his pride. Symbolism and ritual played a significant role. No one I had ever seen, and probably no one on earth, was able to put on the pomp and circumstance the way the English did. The precision of so many men moving as one to the slow cadence of the emotionally rich music was stirring.

Henry, warming to his subject, told me that he enjoyed reading old histories because they taught how him how other people had managed their problems. This reminded me of my daily learning sessions with Papa, and how I missed them. Had Henry somehow learned about them and was using that knowledge? People tended to serve their own interest or purposes.

What were his?

Talking about history and horses seemed safe subjects. Henry liked both and shared with me some facts. Whether walking or driving, I had never given any statue more than a passing glance. To me, they were just some historic figures standing proudly on a pedestal. Henry saw meaning in the details.

"In statues of a horse and rider, if the horse has both front legs in the air, the rider was killed in battle; four legs on the ground, the rider died of natural causes; one leg raised, the rider died as a result of wounds received in battle. Horses are intelligent creatures. If you want to reach your destination, talk to the horse. In other words, retain your line of sight. And that applies to life as well," he told me.

I liked his deep, hearty laugh and the way his forehead smoothed out when he smiled

Having told me more about himself in the last hour than he had since we first met, he no longer seemed so formal. I could feel a slow reluctant admiration growing. Well, maybe not admiration. Perhaps it was more something like respect. And even that seemed safer from a distance. Anything else would only complicate an already tangled situation. It was best not to get too attached. Something could be lost more quickly than it was found.

When a strong clap of thunder shuddered the barn, Henry stood up and walked to the heifer. "If she has a girl we'll name her after you," he told me, "but for right now, I need you to come in here and talk to the soon-to-be mom. She knows you. Hearing your voice will help settle her down."

His request was something I had not expected. Pleased by

his confidence, I took a deep breath and tried to act as competent as my nervousness let me be.

"Will you look at that," Henry said, when half an hour later he skillfully helped the calf make its appearance. "Glad to have you with us, Andrea."

I wasn't sure that I wanted to smile but a smile formed on my lips anyway.

CHAPTER 40

PULLS FERRY

O n most days, returning to Hill Farm after school, the usual menagerie of animals, a rooster, a calf, and the dog Shep, awaited me inside the gate. I fed, watered and took care of each one of them, and with a kind of eager hopefulness, they sometimes vied for my attention. I always made sure to treat the lot of them equally. "Just in case they know the difference," I told David. Thinking the welcoming committee amusing, he laughed and even better, never teased me about it.

One of the nice things about dating him was the courteous, attentive way he treated me. He had a gift for being comfortable with people and never withheld his compliments. Waiters and cooks in restaurants, sales people – everyone benefited and responded to him.

It was such gestures that had made him so appealing. And his parents had been very welcoming. When I expressed my appreciation, David's father said, "We like Germans…now!"

I liked David's smile and the way he said my name. He and I had become good friends. But along the way something subtle had shifted. What had been a teasing, affectionate, slightly flirtatious relationship had evolved into something deeper: a relationship that meant more than was apparent on the surface. How and when it happened I don't remember. I'd accepted it and knew that he felt it too. Both of us thought it. Neither one of us expressed it.

To love David would be easy. To marry him would be more difficult. I had tried to imagine myself as his wife and found it impossible. In a few months I would be eighteen years old – still trying to find out who I was – let alone thinking of getting married. David was almost twenty-three. He would make a wonderful husband – just not for me – not right now.

I wondered what he would say if I announced my intention about leaving England. Should I tell him now? Tell him everything? Nothing? Perhaps I should at least mention it. So far I had postponed that moment, but David deserved to know. I was only making things worse by waiting, yet each time I wanted to share, something had held me back. Talking about my plans should have been simple, but I knew what he was going to say. He would want to talk about my staying, and that didn't leave much room for a meaningful discussion about anything else.

Wanting to show me more of Norwich, David had come to pick me up for a date. He had been born in that city and liked to draw my attention to its charms as we walked along.

"The stone for Norwich Cathedral was cut and shaped in

France and brought by boat all the way from the continent," he said. "Once it arrived in England, it was transferred to barges. Imagine the work involved! To bring the stone close to the building site, men even dug a small canal, because roads were often impassable. This started somewhere around 1096. And Pulls Ferry became the watergate for craft carrying building material to the Cathedral."

As history was one of my favorite subjects I listened attentively.

"How do you know all this?"

David smiled. "I ask questions."

Pulls Ferry was a popular place with college students. And David and I enjoyed strolling there. A light breeze had scattered red and gold leaves on the water. Nature was preparing itself for a season that had not quite arrived.

For a moment we stopped to enjoy the surroundings.

"How still everything is at this time of evening. I really like it. Funny that, especially as I'm afraid of the dark," I said.

"That's why I'm here." David traced the contours of my face with his finger. And then he wrapped his arms around me and drew me close. Very close. He lowered his head until his lips were against mine and everything troubling receded. We were in our own universe. What mattered was the moment – this moment.

His kiss was gentle, light as the touch of a butterfly wing, and then it increased in passion, enough to leave me breathless. Time was suspended, passing slowly – then stopping altogether. I opened my eyes and waited for the world to steady itself. Silence and soft shadows stretched around us, deeper and more intimate than any words could have been.

"You're shivering." David's touch on my hand was warm and strong. He removed his jacket and put it around my shoulders. There was something gallant about his thoughtfulness; the reason why I took historic license and facetiously referred to him as Sir Walter Raleigh.

The jacket still carried the clean scent of his after-shave. David adjusted the collar and snugged it tight. "Is this all right?" He pulled me close, his breath feathering my cheek.

I nodded. 'Oh, yes,' I thought, 'it's very much all right'. The air was already tinged with night, muting everything in shades of black and pewter. Stars filled the sky and the light of a cratered moon flickered through the leaves.

"We call this a hunter's moon," David said in a hushed voice, as if he too was holding his breath, afraid that the slightest sound might dispel the magic. "What do you think? Will it help me catch you?"

He reached into his pocket, pulled out a small box and opened it.

The light was dim but bright enough for me to see a small hinged crystal ball on a slender gold chain. I took it and let it nestle in my palm.

Taking it back, David fastened it around my neck. "Our pictures are magnified inside. It's something I would like you to have. So you won't forget me."

He sounded so serious. Was he alluding to something different, more complicated? Forget him? I didn't see how I could. "But why would I do that?" I asked. On the surface his words could have been his usual banter but I sensed a more serious undercurrent. What was it he wanted me to understand? He said he loved me, and perhaps he did. He certainly seemed very sure of it. I was still grappling with the significance of his comment. Was there a deeper meaning in his gift? He and I always had a lot of fun. Barely a day went by without a call or visit from him. Why couldn't everything stay the way it was?

"You've changed," David reached for my hand, lacing his fingers with mine. "You're not angry anymore. But it's gone beyond that."

He smiled faintly and the moment passed. Yet he was right. I had changed… was changing. I had become more confident, though not sure enough to abandon plans I'd had for years.

David looked at me for a long moment. "You are leaving, aren't you?"

"I actually haven't said so."

"You don't have to. I can feel it," he said gently. "It's not as if I just met you. Sorry. I shouldn't have brought it up. It doesn't matter."

Of course it mattered, but at this very minute I could not summon the courage to tell him what was on my mind. I didn't feel like explaining, and I definitely didn't feel like defending. And so it hung in the air, unsaid between us. We left it there, but I didn't see how I could pretend that everything was the same as before.

CHAPTER 41

THE HUNT

"The important thing about time is not wasting it." David waved an impressive envelope. "You'll never guess what it is, so I'll tell you. It's an invitation to a hunt."

"A hunt?" I parroted.

He laughed at my reaction. "Yes, with an entire party, Master of the Hunt, hounds and everything." There was a boyish excitement about him. "It's the first one of the year." David paused. "You're not enthused."

"Sorry if it's that noticeable. Truthfully, I don't like to be present when an animal is killed. And on a more mundane level, I don't have anything to wear for such an event. I've never been on a hunt."

"Then you've missed one of the highlights of life. There's nothing to be concerned about. Animals don't get killed anymore. And as for having something to wear, that also shouldn't be a problem. I'm sure one of Catherine's outfits would suit you," he said, as if this were a perfectly acceptable way to deal with the situation.

Despite David's assurances I was hesitant in asking Catherine for assistance, yet when I finally did, she could not have been more helpful.

The hunt took place on a perfect day. Bird song colored the air but not with the urgency of Spring. I liked these seasonal markers. They gave everything a wonderful richness. Participants to the event arrived appropriately attired and thanks to Catherine's generosity I also fit in. David let out a long whistle when he came to pick me up, admiration in his eyes.

He sat his horse with easy poise and I was proud to be seen in his company. One young woman, exuding wealth and privilege, didn't appear all that pleased by my presence and the repeated glares she shot in my direction let me know it. But I refused to let her message spoil my enjoyment.

The hounds barked their eagerness; the horn sounded the beginning of the hunt, the fox was let out of his kennel and everyone took off in hot pursuit. My competitive side surged forth and I forgot all about the scents, the colors, the atmosphere.

We cantered and galloped over a quilted stretch of fields, through woods, jumped fences and hedges. After a while it seemed that there was some cooperation between the animals. Was I the only one getting that impression? To me it looked as if first the fox slowed down, and soon thereafter so did the hounds. And then they all circled back at a more leisurely pace, almost as if they were saying to each other, "All right boys, we've earned our keep. Those humans have been entertained enough."

The animals had learned their role, were familiar with each other's habits. Why should they exert themselves now when the whole contest would be repeated within a few weeks? We humans were the ones enthusiastically shouting, "Tally-ho." But when I tried to share these thoughts with David, he was not amused.

CHAPTER 42

A DISTANT PLANET

D avid and I had spent the afternoon in the country. Conversation had dripped slowly and when it eventually dwindled to nothing we cut the outing short.

I'd seen David like this before, quiet, deliberately not talking, especially not about a subject that might bring an uncomfortable issue to the surface.

In a way that was true of me as well. Both of us had a good many things to think about, and we had tacitly agreed to postpone a specific discussion, keeping the focus on safe, impersonal topics. But soon one of us would have to broach the matter.

By the time we reached Hill Farm a dark cloud bank had built up close by. Already a few errant spatters of rain marked the cement. Wind-tossed leaves looked as if they fought about who would leave and who would stay, in contrast to my own decision that had been made long ago. The symbolism was not lost on me.

When the breeze blew a strand of hair across my eyes, David gently tucked it back into place. "The storm shouldn't last long, but let's get out of the rain," he suggested, opening the door. We stepped inside and stood there awkwardly, neither of us knowing what to say next. A sudden bright flash of lightning illuminated the room. We were alone and I was very aware of the empty space.

David drew me close to him. It should have been comforting, though now it wasn't. "I wish," he said after another moment of quiet, "that you'd reconsider because truthfully, I can't help wondering if you are ready for this."

I felt a surge of irritation, but I bit my tongue. I knew what he was trying to tell me, even if I didn't like the way he said it. And it wasn't enough for me to change my mind.

"I'm not certain I'm ready," I said, "but I feel it's time…"

When it became evident that I was not going to say any more, David stopped waiting.

"And you're sure enough to go?" he challenged.

"Yes. Yes, I am," I repeated with conviction. "You can't go – and I can't stay. We both know it. Sometimes there are things you have to do even without understanding all the reasons. Right now it's the best explanation I can give."

I had tried to make it sound optimistic, but it was a struggle I lost.

"How do you expect me to respond to that? Because I'm confused. I just don't see how you can walk away. Walk away from us, from our relationship. You know! The one we have!" David reminded me. "I haven't stopped thinking about you leaving, but I'd tried to convince myself that you had forgotten."

His words were sharp and I felt their intent. It was almost the same conversation we'd had months earlier. Going over it again would not ease this moment. We were using language to cover our emotions and we needed to stop before anything we said became too painful to remove, like splinters.

Until recently I had tried not to think about the realities that lay between us. Now they demanded my full attention. I buried my face against the curve of his neck, my eyes stinging with tears I would not let fall.

I wanted to say yes – to agree with David – and stay in England, but Malix was like a thread that tugged at my mind, tugged at my heart.

Dreams were what happened when you slept. But memory murmured its details and I dreamt of Malix even when I was awake. I longed to go back, never questioning whether it was a good thing to wish for. Malix was where I wanted to be – where I would be. Without that assurance I could not have stayed away for so long.

In the quiet richness of those childhood days I had experienced – however briefly – a sense of belonging. And though I'd not been back since I was twelve, no other place had ever made me feel the same way.

David took a deep breath and let it out again. There was anger in the set of his shoulders. "I care about you. And I don't want you to go," he said bluntly. "From the moment we met I knew there was something special about you. Call me selfish, but I'm not willing to have you disappear from my life. I'd be lonely without you."

His admission reeled through me. "You haven't said this before. Not this way."

"I'm saying it now. I want you here… doesn't that count for anything…?" His words were infused with something between a demand and a hope.

"Malix is not that far. We could visit each other. I'll be staying with Papa. I'm sure he would like to meet you. I could show you places meaningful to me, places from my childhood. Perhaps…"

David was not about to let me cling to my illusion. "Perhaps," he said, without conviction. "Going there would be somewhat inconvenient. I suppose I could if it became necessary, but I don't believe that's likely."

"What do you actually know about this village?"

"Malix? Nothing at all." From the way he pronounced the name, it might as well have been something on a distant uninhabited planet – at least Siberia.

The room felt smaller than it had moments before. It was as if even the air we were breathing had changed. I walked to the window and looked out, not really seeing anything. The pane of glass felt cool and soothing against my forehead.

"Why do I think I have already lost you?" David whispered.

"You haven't lost me. I care for you, deeply…"

"So you say, for all the good its doing." David's laugh was short. "But anyway, right now that's not helping. Your decision just doesn't make sense! No one I know would agree with you. I've tried to see it your way, but I can't," he admitted. "You're not running away from something, are you?"

I shook my head.

"Then give me a reason, Andrea. A real reason. Even a logical excuse would do."

My heart beat uncomfortably. According to David, I was highly susceptible to loyalty and old promises were interfering with my judgment.

How could I explain to him a longing as powerful as hunger when I was sure he had never experienced anything remotely like it, had not taken that particular journey? I searched for the right words, but there weren't any, and those I said didn't seem to count. We have forgotten how to talk to each other, I thought sadly. Perhaps I should have tried harder, earlier, when our views had been less separate.

"I don't have a reason, other than what I've said before. I'm not sure it's the whole answer, but it's all I know. I had hoped you'd understand."

It was a foolish thing to say, especially at this moment. David had stepped towards me and I turned to face him. He held me at arm's length, his eyes searching mine. "This isn't a joke, is it? So let me make sure I have this right. Because taking second place to a mountain village is a little hard for me to swallow. How could being there hold any appeal?"

"I like living on the edge."

David dismissed my attempt at humor with an irritated wave of his hand. "That's not even funny. There really isn't anyone I should be concerned about?" he asked, sounding less sarcastic now.

"It's nothing like that! I've told you how much Malix means to me; all of it, not because of anyone in particular… not the way you're implying. And you shouldn't be worried! I can take care of myself."

"Can you? What if something goes wrong and I won't be there to protect you? Fight your battles! Slay your dragons! … I always thought I was your champion."

There was an attempt at a smile, but it was a sad smile; his anger not gone but tempered by something softer.

My throat ached from the effort of not crying. I could tell that I had hurt him.

David nodded, his expression still.

"I see…," he said after a while, more to himself than to me. "We're not going to agree on this, are we? But if this is your choice… what is there left to discuss?"

"Nothing needs to change between us…"

"Everything already has."

His eyes held a regretful acknowledgement that swiftly came and went. With just the merest brush of his lips over mine, he hugged me tightly before stepping back.

"I never said I'd be gone forever," I whispered, but the words fell hollow into an empty room. For the space of a breath I wanted to call him back – the temptation was strong – but then I didn't. I didn't say his name, but for a long time I stood without moving.

CHAPTER 43

SOMETHING ELSE

D avid did not call the next day, or the one after that. Had I wrongly assumed that the doors of communication had been left open? Autumn reluctantly doled out its last glorious days. With the arrival of cooler weather, it frequently rained all day and night. Foliage collected in wilting heaps.

Before long, the pewter light that comes ahead of winter moved over the land. The days grew shorter and grayer and the weeks edged towards the holidays.

In November, we had celebrated Guy Fawkes Day. Children especially looked forward to the annual bonfires and the fireworks; each display more dazzling than the last. Christmas came and went without communication from David. And I didn't know if there would be an opportunity to repair what so recently had been wounded.

Normally, I looked forward to the holidays, but this year I was homesick. I pondered the word and wondered how that could be when I didn't have a home anymore.

Even so, the day had been enjoyable as Sarah and her family had joined us for a festive dinner.

And then it was January. Last year David and I had attended a Burn's Supper, the formal annual tribute to the life of the Scottish poet, Robert Burns. David had some Scottish ancestry on his mother's side, and dressed in a kilt he looked elegant in a very masculine way.

"There is no man equal to a man wearing a kilt," Mrs. Gray told me. "Someday you'll have to attend the Tattoo in Edinburgh. But for now this will do."

Having always appreciated the sound of bagpipes, I gladly accepted the invitation. I was introduced to people whose names I knew I wouldn't remember for very long. But it had been an enjoyable evening.

~ ~ ~

"Let's go to my study," Henry told me. "You'll understand in a few moments what this is about. You have a decision to make."

My heart sank. Surely we were not going to have another chat? I knew that lightning could strike twice – I just hadn't heard of it happening three times. If I had felt comfortable enough to say anything, I would have asked him to just get on with it.

And then Henry said, "How would you feel about living in

Malix?"

I looked at him, gauging his sincerity. Was he offering me a chance at what had seemed impossible only moments ago? I thought I had heard correctly, but I needed to be absolutely sure. And the disappointment would not be so great if what he said didn't match what I longed to hear.

Gathering my courage I asked, "Could you please repeat that?"

There were not many ways to finish that particular sentence. So maybe if I acted disinterested he would give up his obvious attempt to break my heart. I wished I could believe him. Oh, how much I did. My own mother – the one person who should have understood my need for that tranquil mountain village – never had.

After a pause that seemed like a thousand years, but lasted only a few seconds, Henry said, "I want to know how long it will take you to pack."

Months ago, he and I had agreed, wordlessly, to a truce with a minimum of rules. I had stopped viewing him as my adversary. Because of it I'd had a faint hope that he would help me in my quest, but it had only ever been that. And for this to finally happen? Just like that? I didn't even try to hide my surprise. "Really? You mean it...?"

"So it would seem...but it's your decision," Henry answered, as if that was all there was to it. "Do you want to argue, or do you want to go and get ready?"

Malix. I suddenly could breathe again. I was allowed to go to Malix. At last. And the joy of it was so intense that it just about stole my breath. Close to tears with gratitude I threw my arms around Henry. "Thank you. Oh, thank you."

For a moment Henry was startled. "I hope this will make you happy," he said gently and gave me a nod of understanding. It told me that things were all right. He sounded sincere and I wasn't about to put his words under a magnifying glass. Something between us had changed – for the better. Not having been given a map to go by, we had created our own directions and somehow found our way.

I had wanted to celebrate since absorbing Henry's offer. But my excitement was subdued by my sense of loss. It was not cutting ties, not exactly, but I knew I would miss my friends, especially Catherine with her witty observations and warm smile. For the rest of my life, she would be my standard of bravery.

And then there was Major. The only way I could bear to think of leaving him was to know that he would be in her capable hands.

~~~

Angry-fisted clouds rode the horizon on the morning Catherine and Anton took me to the train station. The ritual of parting in a public place was uncomfortable and the three of us were silent and reflective. "A part of me will remain here," I thought, "but Malix is where I belong."

Catherine cleared her throat. "I want you to know that we'll save a place for you in our home," she said, and handed me a small wrapped package. "Open it later."

"For me?" I asked, surprised. She and Anton already had been incredibly generous. I didn't like to think where I'd be if I had not met them.

"But I don't have anything for you. How do I express my appreciation?" I said the words that were not only on my mind, but in my heart, trying to gather everything into one farewell. Yet there was nothing to make the moment less bleak.

"I haven't done enough. Not nearly enough. With time, I might have done more," Catherine assured me. Given that she had been such an intense taskmaster I didn't doubt her statement. I started to laugh but suppressed it, fearing that it might turn into something else.

I raised my hand in hesitant farewell and took the train to Harwich, reaching the port by late afternoon.

The process of boarding and the ship's motion beneath my feet were familiar. After I was settled in my cabin I opened Catherine's gift. Made of brass, it was a stylized Lion head holding a man's head in his mouth, and underneath, the lettering *Norwich Sanctuary*. It fit comfortably into the palm of my hand.

Catherine had told me a little about the meaning of a sanctuary knocker (a metal ring attached to the door of a church). A fugitive from the law had only to touch the knocker in order to claim the ancient privilege of sanctuary. It allowed a person to stay in the church, free from prosecution, for a period of time (usually 40 days). Then the accused was escorted to a port and forced to leave the country. Because of misuse, the right of sanctuary was abolished by law in the early 17th century.

I wasn't a fugitive, and for me, Catherine's gift held tender meaning. In the morning, after carefully placing her present into my suitcase, I made my way to the train depot for the last segment of the journey.

Belching a cloud of steam into the air the engine clanked

and hissed, waiting for last minute travelers to board. A whistle blew, doors slammed and the train began its slow crawl out of the station, gathering speed as it headed south. To Malix. Tracks and outlines of buildings began to blur before shrinking into the distance.

The countryside rolled by; fields, forests, and land folded like fabric against mountain ranges. Here and there villages dotted like islands in a sea of green, the steep tower of a church straining against the sky. Cattle stood motionless, patiently enduring the spatter of rain on their backs. Others stood bunched together under the umbrella of a single tree.

Tired, with no desire for company I leaned back in my seat, closed my eyes and tried to tune out the conversations going on around me.

I awakened as the train slowly pulled into the Chur station. The brakes gave a high-pitched squeal and screeched to a stop. Quickly, I lifted down my suitcase. I was the first passenger in the corridor; the first one to step onto the platform.

CHAPTER 44

AN URGENT LOGIC

I t had felt strange to arrive in Chur and not continue directly to Malix. I didn't have the freedom to go there until my eighteenth birthday even though that was only a few hours from now. But not wanting to get Henry into trouble, I would obey my mother's request – just in case. One did not take chances with her reaction to something she would see as flagrant disobedience.

I really had intended to wait but my resolve faltered. Feeling that with a phone call I did not technically disobey my mother's unreasonable demand made six years ago, I called Papa as soon as I had checked into my hotel in the late afternoon.

Guessing that his number had not changed I didn't take the time to look it up. I was not surprised when the phone just rang and rang. To discourage frequent use, only a single outlet had been installed. Papa insisted on a relatively quiet, uninterrupted home life. In his opinion a phone was something to run away from, not towards, and his study on the second floor seemed the perfect place to put it. It would take him or Uschi some moments to get there.

When Uschi instead of Papa picked up the receiver I was disappointed. Hers was not the voice I had hoped for, but I made the best of it.

"Hallo Uschi," I said.

"Andrea, it can't be." Disbelief marked the voice at the other end of the line. "After all this time is it really you?"

"The very one. I can hardly wait to see all of you again. Is Papa there?"

Uschi experienced another surprise when I easily switched to the well-remembered dialect of the region.

There was a slight pause. "I'm afraid you couldn't see Papa even if you came to Malix right now," she said. "He went to get the cattle at the lower alp. They were still up there because the weather has been very mild. Then two days ago we had a sudden storm, with snow and everything. The phone lines are down and I haven't heard from him since then. Men from the village tried to reach him but gave up for now. They'll start again tomorrow. The weather is supposed to clear up around noon. Come to the house whenever you're ready and wait for him here."

Papa would have to stay on the mountain to feed and water the cattle. Uschi assured me that the cupboards were always stocked with dry goods. So there was no concern for him in that regard.

I listened to her explanation and my head accepted her reasons. My heart did not. Impetuous as ever my thoughts gave birth to action. I would go and get Papa! The nuns had tried to correct in me, or more accurately extinguish anything that stood in the way of common sense and clear thinking. Yet here I was – not really changed that much.

In only a few minutes the idea took on an urgent logic of its own. There was more than one reason why I wanted Papa off that mountain. Days ago I had written a letter addressed to the Swiss people expressing my gratitude for their kindness shown towards the many destitute children, myself included, following WW II. And then I had sent it to the area newspaper.

An editor had assured me my contribution would be published and I wanted to be with Papa when he read that entry with its specific acknowledgement to him.

The evening was an exhausting test of patience, a trait which still did not come easily to me. Emotionally too keyed up for sleep I had tossed and turned throughout the night.

In the morning, now truly eighteen years old, I took the first bus for the twenty-minute ride to Malix. The last segment of any journey always seemed longest to me, but the two-lane road had to follow the shape of the mountain. After navigating a series of steep, winding s-curves we topped a ridge and the plateau widened, spread out like a palm opened in greeting.

The bus drove past a restaurant, a grocery store, the post office, and then, at last, the village of Malix came into view.

The route was not well traveled, no rush-hour traffic here, so no other passenger walked to the exit. Suitcase in hand I waited until the doors swung open and stepped down, not uncertain but filled with excitement and anticipation. I wanted to shout at the top of my lungs, to let whoever cared enough to listen know that I had returned. Restraining myself, I breathed in deep sighs of relief until they reached every last nerve end.

Dark clouds bumped and twisted against the mountains, obscuring the weak winter sun, yet it didn't matter. Nothing mattered except that I was here – back in a familiar place where I was welcome, where I belonged. I had kept my commitment. A bell in the church tower – still standing like a sentinel – rang the hour. The crisp air carried the scent of wood smoke and pine, a powerfully suggestive, transportive aroma. Everything had its own special fragrance, and added together, these meant Malix.

A few snowflakes swirled around as if scouting out the territory. No scouting was necessary for me. Just standing here I felt gathered in and I knew exactly where to go. Past Papa's white and gray barn, then up the well-worn path to the house. To Papa's house. And the welcome sight of it brought tears to my eyes.

Coming closer I saw laundry fluttering on the line. It made me smile. Nothing would stop Uschi from accomplishing her domestic duties. Everything familiar was as I remembered it, which is what I needed it to be.

Tall wooden panels enclosed the porch and shielded the front door from heavy snowfall. I noticed Papa's boot scraper embedded in the concrete and had not yet finished wiping my boots on the mat when Uschi opened the door, aproned and open-armed. Her smile was bright and she looked genuinely pleased to see me.

She had aged visibly; her hair was almost white and the lines in her face were more pronounced. And she was different in other ways – no longer curt and gruff. For whatever reason she seemed friendlier, as if I had passed some kind of test. And I noticed the change even in those first few moments.

It was embarrassing, but in the past I had only seen her as someone who cooked and cleaned, not as a person. On my part, a thoughtless dismissal. Despite our uneasy relationship she had taken care of me in her own brusque way. Efficient and accurate, but for a child's hungry heart, not adequate.

Instinctively drawn to Papa's warmth I had not accepted her. Yet I had never really considered what she expected from life, what she had wanted to be. Over the years my opinion of her had changed; parts of her personality had become easier to understand. Especially after I learned that after the death of Papa's first wife (leaving behind a seven and a nine year old daughter), Uschi married Papa and had raised the two girls but never had a child of her own. Would she have felt that lack?

Slowly I walked from room to room before I followed her upstairs to my old bedroom. Passing the Stube, I noticed the sideboard with its familiar collection of pewter plates and mugs. Hanging on the wall, also in the same place, was the framed gold-leafed print of a hazelnut bush. The word Hassler was written above the heraldic description of the family's name.

In my bedroom, I went to the balcony overlooking the valley. There was a momentary break in the cloud cover and I again acknowledged that I would never tire of the view even if I stood there for the rest of my life. I could still feel it, the same magic this place had had for me when I came here as a confused child. And the memory of it had held me with invisible strings.

After I rejoined Uschi in the kitchen there were some questions about my trip and school. In that regard she had not changed. But I was glad that she didn't ask me anything about my mother or about my plans and the real reason for my visit. Uschi had always taken things the way they came. "It makes life easier," she had once told me.

If she noticed that my mind was somewhere else, she didn't mention it. As soon as I saw her fully immersed in domestic duties, I left the house on the pretext of taking a walk through the village.

CHAPTER 45

A THIN SCARF OF SMOKE

I had not offered to help Uschi with getting lunch ready nor did I give a moment's consideration to the danger of avalanches as I furtively made my way up the mountainside. All I could think of was that I needed to see Papa! Today! And no one would stop me!

Getting to the lower alp was not a climb requiring ropes, just a steady, muscle burning step by step trudge in snow that was deep and soft and silencing. For the first little while I would be hidden from view by outlying houses and barns, but I needed to get far enough and high enough before I became visible in the open, sufficiently far enough to stop Uschi from marshaling her forces and spoiling my plans. Anyone watching would have a good idea where I was going. Distance was as important as direction now.

Once I was beyond the village it took me a moment to orient myself. I remembered the general route to Papa's chalet but the way there was hidden under feet of snow. Even boulders, which had always seemed to me like balls thrown by giants, were now covered. The terrain was getting steeper and more heavily wooded. Shrubbery encroached on the road, and trees had grown wider and taller. Some were bent beneath the powdery weight; others stood strong.

The frozen snow crackled and crunched under my boots. The only other sound disturbing the stillness was the harsh cry of a crow scolding me for invading his territory.

Winter had erased most colors from the countryside. Much of it was shrouded in white and soft gray, making everything appear hazy and indistinct. It was beautiful yet also unfamiliar, and I found my way, guided by memory. The road wound up the mountain, in and out of forested stretches. Walking in winter-twisted ruts was slower than I had expected. When I set out, the air had been cool and invigorating. Now it was getting thinner, making it harder to breathe and my lungs burned with the effort.

An owl – gliding on soft graceful wings – swept down from the trees and disappeared again, ghost-like. Tiny snow crystals made it look as if the earth were being salted. The next moment flakes fell in thick layers, swirling as if shaken in a globe. There was nothing timid about the wind. It moved even the large branches of the trees and a sudden gust almost toppled me over. In Chur, I had bought a parka, boots and gloves. I was dressed warmly enough to endure Antarctica, but the chill bite of the mountain air found a route to the back of my neck and the tips of my toes, and I felt it more deeply than I remembered it.

The weather was deteriorating rapidly. Snowflakes were falling in earnest – no longer gentle feathers but white slants that meant business – changing the landscape without making a sound. In some places they collected in uneven, waist-deep drifts. Perhaps they were the reason why the men of the village had decided to come to Papa's aid on another day. But there was no point wondering about that now. I needed to concentrate on keeping my feet moving.

I trudged on, my eyes on the ground to keep my balance. A drop of perspiration trickled down my face. Eager to see Papa, I had not paced myself. My mind frequently made plans without informing the rest of me. Now my muscles protested, letting me know that they were there but not too anxious to do what they were told. And their loyalties were blurred; some seemed willing to pledge allegiance to a different country. I just needed to remind them of their responsibilities and convince them to be trustworthy a little longer.

Determination, a familiar ally, kept me going. By the time I reached the chalet I was shaking with fatigue. Beyond tired, hungry and exhausted, yet also filled with accomplishment, I knocked at the door, grateful that Papa would be at this chalet, and not at his second one even higher up the mountain.

There was no answer! After listening for a moment I knocked again, but no one replied. How could this be? Other than the sharp smell of burning wood and a thin scarf of smoke wafting up from the chimney, there was no sign of activity, nothing to say that he had been here.

And then I noticed a single set of footprints leading away from the chalet. Guessing them to be Papa's, and not knowing what else I could do, I decided to follow them. Years ago I had tried to place my footprints into his, and even now I could not match the length of his stride.

On my last visit I had been twelve; now I was eighteen. During my absence I had often visualized the moment of meeting him again, wondering what his first words would be. I had counted the months, weeks and days. And then, at last, time finally narrowed to hours, even minutes. I had missed Papa. He was a tie to my past; he had been my protection, a cushion between me and whatever happened in my life. I so wanted to tell him that his efforts had not been wasted. I also wanted to share the things I had accomplished.

No matter how big or small a problem might be, my first thoughts always went to Papa. What would he want me to do? What would make him proud of me? Absolutely certain that someday we would meet again, I wanted to look into his eyes without shame.

But where was he? And then I saw him, retracing his steps; everything about him so achingly familiar. I couldn't yet see his face, but the way he walked was distinguishable even from a distance. And in a span of time too small for a heartbeat to measure I sensed that he would not recognize me.

I did not run to him. Stunned, I stepped into the deep snow and moved aside to let him pass. He acknowledged me with a nod, and smiling politely, as if at a stranger, he said, "Terrible weather we're having."

Had I heard right? Terrible weather we are having? His casual remark almost took the remaining breath out of my lungs. I could tell he was not joking, but did he really think that on a day like this anyone would just be out on a leisurely stroll? I struggled to find even one word, but my throat had closed tight. Sometimes words just couldn't make the climb and this was one of those occasions. Tears, thankfully hidden behind sunglasses, blinded my vision. How could he not know me? True, I was no longer an awkward teenager, but not to recognize me at all?

Surely I had not changed that much. The only difference was in size, and my hair had turned brown with reddish highlights instead of the blond color it used to be. My face was more oval now but my eyes with their flecks of amber were the same.

Unwilling to believe Papa's reaction, and for my own sake needing to give him another opportunity to recognize me, I called after him. "What time is it, please?"

He stopped. "About four, I should say," he answered and once again walked away.

Was this it then? Was an impersonal comment going to be the bridge spanning years of separation? Years in which I had wept, hoped, and finally dared to plan?

My memories did not always travel in a straight line, yet when it came to Papa they had never lost their crispness. I easily recalled his favorite expression of "So, so", said after he emerged from deep thoughts. It didn't mean anything; nor did he expect an answer; it was just one more of his endearing habits.

As a child everything about him had fascinated me. I remembered the way his horn-rimmed glasses were permanently perched at the end of his nose but somehow never fell off, and the way he clamped his teeth on the stem of his unlit pipe, keeping it there for hours.

These were not borrowed memories gathered from conversations with Ilse or Uschi. They were mine. Had always been mine.

I remembered the way he carefully tested his scythe with his thumb before cutting the grass on steep alpine meadows; how he used his hands to emphasize a point when he spoke with the other villagers discussing planting or harvest, success or failure of the crops, and the state of the world. I saw how Papa resolved issues, as when one neighbor allowed her chickens to run free after a village ordinance said she had to keep them fenced in. Or the way he settled disputes over shared tools and farm equipment.

I had absorbed lessons he didn't even know he was teaching me. On unimportant things I might only have fragmented recollections, but where he was concerned all of them agreed. Yet here I stood, unable to reply because I did not trust my voice. The only answer I could come up with was a thin, "Yes," and watch, as he walked away from me.

I waited until he was out of sight before I followed him. Right foot – left foot – right foot – left foot. It had been that way years ago. Some things never changed. Then, for the second time in the last half hour I knocked at the chalet's door.

It was opened by Urban, the husband of Uschi's sister Gretel.

"So you didn't lose your way," he smiled. "That's quite a chase you led me on. I'm glad you made it safely."

"Thank you. The feeling is mutual. It's good to see you again, Urban. I'm sorry you had to come all this way because of me."

"Ah, think nothing of it. He'll be glad for some additional help."

Papa, at the far end of the room, was in the process of changing his sweater when I entered and had evidently not heard our exchange. He moved into the circle of light created by a single kerosene lamp, looked at me and clearly puzzled asked, "Can I help you?"

Tongued-tied I just stood there until once again Urban came to my rescue.

"Surely you recognize her. It's our Andrea. If it weren't for this young lady you'd still be up here alone. Uschi saw her leave and made sure I followed her, but she went too fast. I couldn't catch up with her. By now your wife will have mobilized the whole village."

Since neither Papa nor I knew what to say, it was good that Urban's laughter broke the ice. I wanted to put my arms around Papa in a tight hug, but no longer a child I felt self-conscious and awkward.

Although he had not arrived at the chalet much ahead of me, his pipe was lit and clamped between his teeth. I thought of making a comment about his tobacco being the same as the one he smoked during my childhood but decided against it. Instead we talked about politics and the weather, again. Urban, uncomplicated and full of jokes as ever, did more than his share to enliven the conversation. I endured a gentle teasing about my headstrong nature which would not be deterred once a plan was made. As that fact was not a secret, least of all to me, I laughed at their comments. After a while I excused myself and went to bed up in the loft, leaving the two men to discuss plans for the next day when goats, chickens, and ducks were to be crated and readied for the trip to the valley. In the deep snow that would be no small undertaking.

CHAPTER 46

POTENTIAL CONSEQUENCES

E arly the next day the snow seemed even deeper. Papa and Urban tied the last crate to the heavily laden sleigh. Norma, anxious to be off, stomped her feet.

After checking to make sure that nothing had been forgotten and doors and windows were locked and shuttered, a miniature migration made its way down the mountain. Only the tips of the cattle's horns were visible as they plunged along, driven by Papa's voice and a strong desire to reach a warm stall. I walked in front of horse and sleigh, guiding it, and trusting Papa's ability to keep me safe.

At the house, not pleased with what I had done, Uschi only looked at me but I certainly received her pointed message, and it made me feel like a six year old again.

In the morning, when I awakened in my old bedroom, I

wondered why I felt happy and then I remembered. But of course – I was in Malix. Being here was like a dream, but the sounds and scents of my surroundings soon convinced me of its reality. I smiled, because this was home with its reliable daily routine. Encouraged by the aromas wafting up from the kitchen I dressed and went downstairs. There was food I hadn't tasted in a long time. I savored the texture and the memories and it seemed as if only days had passed, not years.

I was back among people who knew me from the past. They had come into my life and stayed there. In the evening I found myself in the middle of a family gathering. I felt their closeness, but it was their closeness, not mine. They were united by experiences I could not share, yet even so there was enough for me to be included.

It was good hearing a familiar language. Conversation wove back and forth across the table. Before long someone told a favorite story and soon everyone else began reminiscing, each adding their own brushstrokes and giving it more life.

They teased my about latest exploit and didn't let me forget the time I nearly gave Papa a heart attack.

That story also involved a fully loaded wagon and Norma, Papa's horse. And once again it took place on the alp. I had overheard Papa wondering how he could accomplish everything in one day. It was a question of herding his cattle or driving the wagon to the village. Being short-handed meant that he would have to go down and return within hours.

I didn't understand all the details, I only knew that I was available. My desire to be of help, and common sense, briefly met and then moved off in different directions. I had been with Papa numerous times when he guided Norma and a wagon up and down the mountain. It hadn't looked that diffi-cult and I felt confident that I could do the same.

Papa did not need to know about my plan. I spoke encour-aging words to the patient horse and we set out; with the best of intentions, and disregard for any potential consequences.

It was a slow, steady journey, but the novelty soon wore off as the thirteen-foot wagon shook and rattled over the unpaved road and wheels skittered on washboard turns. Norma's large hoofs sounded hollow on the wooden planks of a small bridge. I could have been afraid but I was not. Sensible creature that she was, Norma plodded along at her usual pace; compensating for my inexperience by carefully negotiating each of the nu-merous turns, somehow making adjustments for the length and weight of the wagon until she stopped at the first fountain at the outskirts of the village.

Here Papa caught up with us. He must have run the whole way. When I saw his flushed face, my idea, which had been filled with a lofty purpose and had seemed so noble earlier, didn't appear all that clever anymore.

The memory of it brought a smile to my lips. "You knew about that?" I asked, slightly embarrassed.

"Of course we did," Uschi answered. "In a small village not much takes place without everyone hearing about things eventually. Rumors have been known to climb over backyard fences."

That was the thing about friends. They didn't let you forget anything. They all laughed, but it was more truth than a joke.

The next day Uschi sent me to the store with a long shop-ping list. On the way there I looked at the buildings around me. A few barns had been repaired; otherwise everything was exactly like the last time I was here, the few streets just as winding. People smiled at me, as if I were a long-lost friend returning home.

"Hello," one woman asked. "I didn't know you had come back. Are you here to stay?"

"I don't know yet." That was not a real answer to her question. I had better prepare one, in case I was asked again.

Although by now I had met quite a few of the villagers, I had not yet seen my friend Ilse. She was engaged to Andres, a ski instructor, and busy with last minute wedding plans. But when we finally met we recognized each other simultaneously and it was as if we had never been apart. We spent hours talking about the many things friends discuss who haven't seen each other for a number of years.

When I asked about her life, she answered "I haven't done anything very exciting. Not compared to you."

She had remained in Malix and I wondered what it must be like to have lived in only one place feeling safe and loved. Was it wonderful to have such a knowledge of belonging? I wouldn't know. Certainty was not a world in which I dwelled.

~~~

Before long, the air had the taste of spring at its edges. And Papa bought another set of little goats, the same as those before, brown with a dark stripe on their back. Unhappily, the previous pair had left us, although not by their own choice.

Waiting for them was the butcher, a big, husky man. I didn't like the idea of the little animals being in rough hands longer than necessary during their last moments. So I had carried them in my arms, one at a time, up the hill to where he stood sharpening his knives. All the while I whispered to them; reminding them of the good life they'd had running around in fragrant meadows. And then I left.

I would not allow myself to get attached to these latest additions.

CHAPTER 47

THAT SCEPTERED ISLE'

I had received one short letter from David, written in his precise penmanship, and I had answered. After that – silence. But the distance between us had nothing to do with miles. A newspaper clipping announcing his engagement and forthcoming marriage had been mailed to me by his fiancée.

It certainly hadn't taken him long to find someone else. I even knew his future wife. She was the young woman who had been so annoyed to see me in David's company at the fox hunt, but I had learned to like her. She was someone from his circle of friends, a member of the sporting gentry with common concerns and backgrounds.

I told myself that I wanted to see David happy, even if I had nothing to do with it, and that it would be foolish to be jealous now. Yet I hadn't expected the news to hurt, and my sudden resentment came as a surprise. Perhaps it was more a blow to my ego than a deep hurt, but it was definitely more than just a slight twinge.

It seemed that everyone's life had gone on without me. But I also thought about making changes, such as returning to England.

"Would you ever do something like that?" I asked Ilse.

My common sense friend seemed surprised by my question. "I? Oh no, never. I wouldn't want to go so far or be gone for too long. You are stronger than I am."

I liked her illusion too much to dispel it. From what I could tell, she'd never had a real problem. Ilse's ambitions were practical. Her daily routine consisted of activities that would never be changed, nor would she want them to be different. She had not known anything but love and security, so she expected nothing else. All of it was very distant from the life familiar to me and it emphasized that possibly I could not stay here.

Sometimes things were supposed to be one way, and then they went in another direction. Perhaps I was longing to be part of something that was already gone. I felt separate from my friends, but I couldn't have explained it if someone had asked me.

I loved this home, the beauty of the valley, yet I felt disconnected. I didn't want to admit it, not to myself and certainly not to anyone else, but for some time nagging doubts had crept into my thoughts. Faint at the beginning, then increasingly the doubts had started to win.

Though I had a seat at the table, I did not feel fed. Where were the large luminous moments of my childhood? In the past it had all seemed so idyllic. Everything was familiar, but nothing brought the comfort it had in the past. I had been so certain, now I was confused and conflicted. For years all I had dreamed of was a return to Malix. I had waited for this, longed for this, and now I wanted to leave again? What was the matter with me?

After days of analyzing my feelings, I finally understood what was bothering me. Malix was a right place – just not *my* right place. Not anymore. I knew what I wanted and what I needed and I would not find it here. I acknowledged that fact to myself in a moment of certainty when everything fit together. And once you knew something, you could not 'unknow' it. I understood the real meaning now. Understood it well enough to embrace it. 'Late, but not too late', as Catherine liked to quote.

Before routine and any semblance of comfort set in I would return to England – the country of my healing and unexpected gifts, feathered and otherwise. I would go and accept that I was accepted there. It was foolish to ignore that realization. If I didn't follow through I would always wonder, possibly even have regrets.

Starting from a narrow place, I had held onto my cautions as a kind of protection. Obstinate, with anxiety obscuring my view, I had not allowed myself to see 'that sceptered isle' as a country offering new beginnings. To belong someplace takes time. Deep down I had been afraid – had always been afraid – of retaliation brought on by the war. Thankfully, that fear no longer existed. Anton had said that home could be where you felt welcome. And now, living in England would be my choice.

That also made a difference.

In many ways – in most ways – Papa was proud of me. He was interested in my life and concerned for my happiness, and I would forever be grateful for his care. But I had never told him that even at the best of times I had sensed a barrier, a barrier based on nationality. He would always see me as a German, however indirectly or unintentionally.

I had known – perhaps not in so many words – but I had known. Even if not everyone in Switzerland felt that way, this gulf between us would not be bridged. I had felt safe enough, yet deep down never truly at ease. Much as I wished it to be otherwise, this was my reality – and Papa's. And telling him this now would accomplish nothing. In some ways I belonged – and in other ways I did not. And despite his assurances that I was welcome, I knew that it was time to move on.

"If you really want to go to England then that is what you must do," Papa commented when I cautiously explained my reasons.

"Thank you. Yes. I think it would be a good idea to finish my schooling there. In Cambridge. My friend Catherine attended that University."

He nodded and I sensed his approval. "You've learned to be quite the diplomat. Clearly your time with the nuns has not been a total loss. Uschi told me you were leaving. She understood before I did."

His words came as a surprise. Had others known as well? And was Catherine one of them? I still remembered her parting words, "When you get back I'll be out of this wheelchair!"

Catherine, Anton, and I were infrequent correspondents. Since my arrival in Malix we had not been in touch other than sending an occasional card. On my part it was because I didn't know what to write. Some feelings were too big to put on paper. Perhaps my friends were being thoughtful, thinking it would give me time to adjust to my new life.

She and Anton had been sorry to see me go and I missed their company. Freely shared – and gratefully accepted – their example of courage and kindness had inspired me to be better, be more. By setting me on a path to find answers without fear of being judged, they had enabled me to put problems into perspective and turn mountains into manageable hills. I considered our meeting to be one of the most significant events of my life. The words 'Thank you' could never express the full measure of my gratitude.

EPILOGUE

After talking with Papa I had lingered for a few moments in the hallway; a weight off my shoulders and my thoughts far away. When I heard the phone ring I ran upstairs to his office, taking the stairs two at a time, somehow sure that the call would be for me. I didn't know how I knew...I just did.

"Hello. Andrea?" A familiar voice asked when I picked up the receiver. "Listen, I have a question. When are you coming home?"

Simple words. Yet they were not.

"Funny you should put it that way, Catherine," I answered, past the lump in my throat. "I've missed you too. How does next week sound?"

"If you can't make it any sooner," she said, and I sensed the smile in her words.

My heartfelt appreciation
for the visual artistry
of my friends Lynnea Washburn and Bob Hills.

Cover Illustration & Design by © Lynnea Washburn
Washburn Art & Design
www.lynneawashburn.com

Page Design & Production by Bob Hills
Hills Studio
www.bobhills.com
hillsphoto@gmail.com

CPSIA information can be obtained
at www.ICGtesting.com
Printed in the USA
FSOW02n0830281116
27891FS